AMERICAN ANTHEM
BOOK ONE

PRELUDE

B. J. HOFF

W PUBLISHING GROUP™

www.wpublishinggroup.com

A Division of Thomas Nelson, Inc.
www.ThomasNelson.com

CONTENTS

ANTHEM

Give my heart a voice
to tell the world about my Savior—
Give my soul a song that will ring
        out across the years,
A song that sings your boundless love
in sunshine or in shadow,
A psalm of praise for all my days,
through happiness or tears.
Make my life a melody
in tune with all creation—
Help me live in harmony
with every living thing.
Let my whole existence
be an anthem of rejoicing,
A prelude to eternal life
with you, my Lord and King.

—B. J. HOFF

CATCH THE DISTANT MUSIC

BLESSED DAY WHEN PURE DEVOTIONS
RISE TO GOD ON WINGS OF LOVE;
WHEN WE CATCH THE DISTANT MUSIC
OF THE ANGEL CHOIRS ABOVE.

FANNY CROSBY

New York Harbor, 1846

Michael Emmanuel was eight years old when first he heard the Music.

It was an overcast day in mid-September. He was standing at the railing of the ship that would soon be taking him and his family home from their visit to America. Any moment now, the *Star Horizon* would cast off, leaving New York and the United States behind, and Michael wanted to store up all the memories he possibly could.

His parents stood a short distance away, talking with an elderly Italian gentleman they had met in the harbor. Michael turned back to watch the crush of people on the docks. Everyone

1

seemed to be weeping or praying or shouting, all at the same time. Some stood with tears streaming down their cheeks, arms outstretched and hands extended, as if pleading to come along with those on board. Farther up the docks, a small band was playing, while just across the deck a priest led a small group of nuns in prayer.

The odor of tobacco smoke and ladies' lavender water mingled with the stench of floating garbage and the brackish smell of salt water. A hot, bitter taste filled Michael's mouth. As he stood on deck beneath a sky heavy with darkening clouds, he felt none of the same excitement that had rippled through him upon their arrival six weeks ago. Instead, a hollow ache wrung his heart at the thought of leaving this busy, boisterous land, where almost everything seemed big and noisy and new.

He had taken to America right from the beginning. Just this morning, before leaving their hotel, he had declared to his parents that one day he would return to live here. He already had *two* homes, after all, so why not three?

For as long as he could remember, they had spent most of the year in Italy, his father's land, staying in Ireland, his mother's country, for brief stints during the summer months. Michael liked both places, although Italy was his favorite "home." He liked the way the Tuscan sky glistened as the burning ball of the sun disappeared behind the mountains every evening. In Italy, there was always music playing and dogs barking in the streets and mothers leaning out of windows to call their children inside. In Ireland, everything—the towns, the people, the music—seemed overshadowed by a cloud. Even the wind seemed sad.

Suddenly, Michael realized that the ship had begun moving. They were putting out to sea, leaving America. As he watched, the harbor began to recede. Gradually, the people on the docks grew smaller, less distinct.

At that moment, something very strange occurred: there came to him the sound of music, a music unlike anything he had ever heard before. At first it was so quiet, so unexpected, that it might have been merely a sigh of the breeze or the lapping of the water beneath the ship. Or was the band in the harbor still playing?

Then, without warning, it began to hum and swell, growing louder, then louder still, until it seemed to leap across the water, heading directly toward him. Michael couldn't see where it was coming from. At some point, the wind had risen, and now it swept the deck, whistling through the rigging, whipping through the ropes and sails, diving in and out among the passengers at the rail.

The Music was everywhere now, falling out of the sky and marching across the water, like a vast army on the move or a great and majestic orchestra rising up from the ocean floor. Even the wind itself seemed to be singing!

As the sound built and surged, Michael could almost imagine that the doors to eternity had opened to let a band of angels come streaming through, singing and making thunderous music on a thousand instruments. And yet this music wasn't made of instruments or voices. It was neither—yet it was both. Just as it was both sweet and sad, brave and bold.

And beautiful. So beautiful.

It was everything Michael had ever imagined or felt or yearned for, but it was impossibly beyond his reach. It filled his ears, his head, his heart—filled him with such elation that he almost cried out in sheer delight.

One last mighty explosion of sound shook him from head to foot.

And then it was gone.

In a moment—even less, in a *heartbeat*—the Music died. And with it went the unutterable joy, leaving in its wake the most awful, sorrowful silence Michael had ever known.

At that instant, the sky really *did* open, not to release a chorus of angels, but instead to pour out a sudden, drenching rain. But Michael scarcely noticed. He was too intent on recapturing the Music that only seconds before had filled him to overflowing.

He turned and stumbled toward his parents, the rain pelting his face and stinging his skin. The other passengers also had begun to move in an effort to escape the downpour, and Michael found himself squeezed and pushed out of the way.

He was crying now, weeping as if he had lost his dearest treasure, and he could taste the salt from the spray of the ocean as it mingled with his tears. He shuddered, clutching his head with his hands as he tried to make his way through the crowd to his parents.

They saw him then and hurried to meet him, his father's arms encircling him protectively. "What is this, *mio figlio?* What has happened? Are you hurt?"

His mother stooped down and removed Michael's cap. She smoothed his hair and examined him as if searching for possible injuries.

The ship's whistle blasted, sending a white-hot knife of pain shooting through Michael's head. He cried aloud, tugging at his mother's sleeve. "Did you hear it, Mama? Papa? Did you hear the Music?" But he could tell by the way they were both staring at him that they had heard nothing.

His mother searched his face, then turned to look up at Papa.

"What music, Michael?" asked his father. "What music are you talking about?"

With the rain driving into his eyes and mouth, he tried to explain, to tell his parents what he had heard. He sobbed and stammered in his frustration. "I tried to catch it, don't you see, to keep it! I didn't want it to stop, not ever, but now it's gone!"

But he couldn't make them understand, and finally, exhausted, he let them lead him along the deck to their stateroom.

Much later, after his mother had brought him a light supper, Michael feigned sleep while his parents stood talking softly outside the door.

"What happened to him, Riccardo?" he heard his mama say. "What does it mean, this talk of *'catching the music'*?"

Michael rubbed his eyes, fighting the sleep crowding in on him.

"Who can say?" His father's voice was very soft. "Perhaps God has given the boy a gift. A vision."

"A *vision?* But he is only a child, Riccardo!"

His father said nothing for a moment. When he finally answered, he seemed to be speaking more to himself than to Mama. "In God's eyes, we are all children, are we not? And Michael—ah, Saraid, it seems to me that our son already soars closer to heaven than many grown men. Is it so unlikely that God would gift him in ways we cannot understand, allow him to hear something we cannot hear?"

"I don't understand this, Riccardo."

Mama sounded frightened, and Michael almost called out to her not to be afraid. The Music had been a wonderful thing, not something to fear. His pain had come from the glory of it, the inexpressible beauty and majesty of it.

And the *loss* of it.

"Music is the thing he loves best," Papa went on. "If God has indeed allowed Michael to hear a special music—perhaps even a *heavenly* music—"

He broke off, but Michael's mother prompted him. "What, Riccardo?"

"Then perhaps—" His voice faltered, then gained strength. "Perhaps our Michael has been chosen to be God's *trovatore*."

For the first time in hours, Michael felt the sadness lift and the ache in his head begin to drain away. His eyes were grainy from weeping and heavy with the need for sleep, but he heard his father's words, words he resolved to always remember:

"*Perhaps our Michael has been chosen to be God's* trovatore."

He felt as if he were floating, lulled into a distant world by the rhythmic rocking of the ship. His parents went on talking, their voices growing faint and far away. But the echo of that one truth continued to ring in his head and in his heart as he drifted off to sleep.

God's troubadour.

God's minstrel.

ONE

SUSANNA:
BEGINNINGS AND ENDINGS

HOME'S NOT MERELY ROOF AND ROOM—
IT NEEDS SOMETHING TO ENDEAR IT.

CHARLES SWAIN

Aboard the steamship Spain
New York Harbor, August 14, 1875

Was this an ending or a beginning?

Susanna Fallon had asked herself that question countless times since leaving Ireland, and now she was asking it again.

At first light, she had gathered on deck with the other passengers aboard the *Spain,* all of them eager for the sight of New York. Susanna wished she could believe that the sun rising over the sprawling American city heralded the dawn of an exciting future, a new life with new opportunities. But as the harbor came into view, any hopes she might have held for tomorrow threatened to sink. A flood of doubts rolled over her, vast and unfathomable as the ocean itself.

Susanna pulled her wrap tighter, watching as the ship slowly eased its way toward the pier. Floating garbage and debris littered the water, and she covered her nose and mouth against the stench. At the same time, a small barge angled up alongside them, and she could see an assembly of people thronging the smaller vessel, some waving at the passengers on the deck of the *Spain.*

"Why, look there, Mother—I believe some of our friends have come to meet us!"

Susanna recognized Mr. Moody's voice and turned to find him and Mrs. Moody, along with their children and the Sankeys, grouped just behind her. Nearby stood Dr. Carmichael, who had traveled to the States with the Moodys as a part of their entourage. Apparently, the Scottish physician had played some role or other in the British Isles crusades, although Susanna had never quite determined exactly what that role was.

"Ah, Miss Fallon, here we are at last!" boomed Mr. Moody. "How does it feel to be in America?"

The burly, bearded D. L. Moody and his wife were beaming at her, and Susanna attempted a smile in return. "In truth, Mr. Moody, the only thing I'm feeling at the moment is panic."

It struck Susanna that the American evangelist looked nearly as tired as he had when she'd first encountered him upon leaving Liverpool. And small wonder, given the fact that even aboard ship he had been continually attending to the needs of others.

His wife, who seemed to draw from a limitless supply of kindness, patted Susanna on the arm with a gloved hand. "You'll be just fine, dear," she murmured. "You're going to love America, you know. This is a splendid opportunity for you."

"Of course, it is!" Mr. Moody added, his tone enthusiastic. "Now, you did say there will be someone to meet you?"

Susanna nodded uncertainly. "That's what I was told, yes."

Mrs. Moody surprised her by pulling her into a quick embrace.

"We're so very glad we met you, Susanna. We'll be praying that everything goes well for you, dear. You're very brave, to come so far on behalf of your niece and brother-in-law. I know the Lord will look afer you."

To her dismay, Susanna felt hot tears sting her eyes. Her chance meeting with the Moodys and the Sankeys had done much to ease her dread of the ocean voyage. Upon learning that she was a young Christian woman traveling alone, both couples had gone out of their way to look after her, inviting her to sit with them at mealtimes, answering her endless questions about the United States, and engaging her in frequent discussions about her own country of Ireland, as well as their common interest in music.

Even before the crossing, Susanna had learned a great deal about Mr. Moody and his "campaigns," as he referred to them. It seemed that the whole of the British Isles had been taken by surprise at the success of the Moody/Sankey meetings, not only in England and Scotland, but also in the heavily Protestant north of Ireland—and in the mostly Catholic south as well.

Susanna had been only one of thousands who had flocked to the early crusades. She could scarcely believe her good fortune a few months later when she found herself aboard the same ship as the American evangelists, who were returning to the States. To have the privilege of spending time with these esteemed spiritual leaders and their families had not only made the voyage less harrowing for her, but had actually given her a number of pleasurable hours.

Only now did the finality of their parting strike her. She was going to miss them greatly.

"I don't know how to thank you," she choked out, "all of you—for your kindness to me. I can't think what the crossing would have been like without you."

"Well, dear, it was awfully good of your brother-in-law to arrange first-class passage for you," said Mrs. Moody. "Otherwise, we might not have encountered one another at all. And how fortunate for you, to be spared the ordeal of traveling in steerage."

At the thought of the brother-in-law she had never met, Susanna tensed. Mrs. Moody, however, seemed not to notice. "I'm sure we'll see each other again, Susanna. There are plans for Mr. Moody to hold meetings in New York this fall."

"And if that works out," Mr. Moody put in, "we'll expect to see you in the very front row. Until then, you take special care, Miss Fallon, and just remember that your friends the Moodys and the Sankeys will be praying for you."

He paused, then drew a strong, encompassing arm around his wife and motioned that the Sankeys and Dr. Carmichael should move in closer. "In fact, we would like to pray for you right now, before we leave the ship."

And so they did, standing there on deck. Susanna had heard Mr. Moody pray before, of course: at their table before meals, at a shipboard worship service, and during the revival meetings she and her friend, Anna Kearns, had attended at the Exhibition Palace in Dublin. It seemed that when D. L. Moody prayed, he spoke directly with God, whom he obviously knew very well and approached boldly and eagerly, with an almost unheard-of confidence.

But to have this amazing man praying solely for *her* was an overwhelming experience entirely. By the final *Amen,* much of the strain that had been weighing on her for weeks seemed to melt away.

—

Once they disembarked and the Moodys and Sankeys had joined their welcoming party, Susanna's earlier apprehension returned in force.

The harbor was a different world. She found herself unable to move more than a few feet in any direction because of the throngs of people milling about. The noise was almost deafening—a harsh, unintelligible din of a dozen different languages, all flooding the docks at once. The shouts and laughter of sailors and passengers, the cries of greeting and wails of farewell, the pounding of feet on the planks as children ran and shoved their way among the grownups, the occasional blast from a ship's horn—all converged and hammered against Susanna's ears until she thought her head would split.

She stood there in the midst of this bedlam, not quite knowing what to do, fighting off a rising surge of panic. In that moment, she realized with a stark new clarity how utterly alone she was.

A man's voice sounded behind her. "*Signorina* Fallon?"

Startled, she whipped around as if she'd been struck, ready to defend herself.

"You are Susanna Fallon?" he said.

He was young, with a fairly long, pleasant face and lively eyes behind his spectacles. And he was smiling at her, a wide, good-natured smile. He was also holding a bouquet of flowers and appeared not in the least threatening.

Susanna stared at him. The dark features, the Italian accent—it could be no one else.

But so young! According to Deirdre, Michael Emmanuel ought to be in his mid to late thirties by now. Yet he had called her by name.

"Mr. Emmanuel?" she ventured.

He gave his head a vigorous shake. "No, no! I am not Michael. I am Paul Santi, Michael's cousin. I have come to take you home."

"Home?"

He nodded. "*Sì.*"

Whether it was fatigue or anxiety, Susanna's mind seemed to have gone suddenly dull. "I don't—how did you recognize me? How did you find me?"

"Your hat," he said, gesturing toward Susanna's bonnet. "Did you not write that you would be wearing a hat with blue ribbons?" His smile brightened even more. "These are for you," he said, "with Michael's compliments."

He thrust the lavish bouquet into Susanna's hands. "If you will come with me, *signorina*, we must first go there, to the depot." He pointed to a granite, fortresslike circular building. "Castle Garden," he added. "I will help you with the registration and the paperwork. Michael has already made arrangements for you to be passed through quickly. Do not worry about your luggage—I will take care of it. I have been through this myself, you see. I know exactly what to do."

Susanna glanced across the dock and saw the tall, kindly featured Dr. Carmichael standing there, watching them. For an instant, she was seized by an irrational desire to run toward the man, to flee the solicitude of this dark-eyed foreigner for the pleasant-natured physician and his link to the Moodys.

But she hardly knew Dr. Carmichael any better than she knew this Paul Santi. She must be mad entirely to think of throwing herself at the mercy of a man who was known to her only by his association with the Moodys—themselves strangers until a few days past.

Regaining her wits, she turned back to Paul Santi and, bearing her bouquet and a hard-won sense of determination, managed a careful smile and a civil word as he led her across the docks.

TWO

HARBOR OF HOPE

HOPE OF THE WORLD,

AFOOT ON DUSTY HIGHWAYS,

SHOWING TO WANDERING SOULS

THE PATH OF LIGHT . . .

GEORGIA HARKNESS
FROM HYMN "HOPE OF THE WORLD"

Andrew Carmichael stood for a moment, taking in the sights and sounds around him.

No matter how many times he entered the harbor, it seemed new to him. Perhaps because of the ever-increasing flow of immigrants arriving each day, bringing with them their different languages and customs, their private struggles, their secret dreams. And their hopes that, in this land where others before them had found a future free of tyranny and despair, they, too, might build a new and better life for themselves and those they loved.

Andrew was convinced that no matter what brought them

here by the thousands, what kept them here was hope. America offered a new kind of hope, one without boundaries. A hope that here, just beyond the walls of Castle Garden, waited opportunities that in their old land would have always remained just out of reach. Opportunities for success and happiness, and for the priceless gift of freedom.

And what kept *him* here? What had motivated him to leave his native Scotland with surprisingly few regrets, holding fast only to his memories of people who loved him and still prayed for him so faithfully? Why had America molded itself to his heart, to his very being, so tenaciously that he no longer thought of anywhere else but New York as *home?*

He smiled a little. Only the Lord knew the answer to such questions. And so far God had revealed little to Andrew about any divine plan for his life, other than the fact that it included trust. Trust and obedience.

It required a monumental amount of the former, Andrew thought, to generate the latter. At least in his case.

He sighed. It had been a fine trip. In the words of Andrew's father, D. L. had "reeled them in" by the thousands, and Andrew himself had benefited greatly from every service, every Bible study, every prayer meeting.

His decision to delay his return home and join D. L. and Ira Sankey midway through the crusade had been a sound one after all. He had been able to assist with the new converts, as well as seeing to the health of the workers. But as always, *he* had been ministered to as much as any of the seekers who had come to the altar. His soul had been nourished, his spirit renewed, his faith strengthened. He had also been reminded once more of the depth of God's grace in his own journey of forgiveness and restoration. And he was thankful.

But now he was home again, back on the shores of New

York, preparing to return to his solitary flat and his cramped, dimly lighted office where too many patients crowded the waiting room, and too few possessed the means to pay their bills. Back to his own work.

He really had to get serious—immediately—about taking on an assistant, or perhaps even a partner, in his practice. He simply couldn't continue the exhausting routine to which he'd subjected himself over the past few years. But what manner of partner would be willing to share the kind of practice to which Andrew had committed himself? The search itself would be time-consuming and depleting. And in addition, a new partner would mean a new office—a larger space than the shoebox in which he now worked. When he considered the time and the effort it would require to locate both a partner and another office, the entire prospect seemed overwhelming.

Later. He would think about that later.

He flexed his neck and shoulders to ease the pain and stiffness that had settled into them, then glanced across the docks and saw Susanna Fallon, the young Irish woman the Moodys had befriended during the crossing. She was holding a bouquet and seemed to be deep in conversation with a slender, dark-haired fellow who smiled broadly and used his hands a great deal as he spoke.

When Miss Fallon happened to turn his way, Andrew touched his fingers to his cap and nodded. The young man looked to be a decent sort, and Miss Fallon was smiling, so after another moment Andrew gave a farewell nod and started off to hail a hack.

It was time to go home.

Paul Santi seemed a veritable tempest of energy and efficiency. Susanna found herself increasingly grateful for his assistance, for inside the enormous building all was confusion. Immigrants milled about everywhere, in the aisles or crowded together on benches, some sitting on boxes. The heat and humidity were stifling, and the odor of fear and unwashed bodies permeated the place. In the center of the building, a staff of a dozen important looking gentlemen engaged in what Paul Santi called the "registration process."

To her great relief, with the help of Paul Santi and an official who took over her arrangements, Susanna was whisked through the lines. It seemed no time at all before they had completed the questions and paperwork, then boarded the steamer that Paul Santi said would take them home.

Home. Susanna tried to ignore the twist in her stomach induced by the very mention of the word. Home was what she had left behind. Home was Ireland, her childhood, the family farm.

Whatever else might be waiting for her at the end of this reluctant journey, she could not bring herself to hope it would ever take the place of home.

THREE

Up the Hudson

I am trusting Thee, Lord Jesus,

Trusting only Thee . . .

Frances R. Havergal

Susanna Fallon endured the steamer ride up the Hudson River much as she might have suffered a trip to the gallows.

Her initial sense of relief that she'd been met by the pleasant-natured Paul Santi instead of her formidable brother-in-law had already given way to an escalating sense of dread. She was finally about to meet the man her sister had married in what Deirdre herself once called "a moment of madness." More than once she had questioned the wisdom of this new venture. Only the conviction that God's hand was in the entire experience—that and the thought of the motherless niece she had never seen—had brought her this far.

Deirdre's child, Caterina, was only three years old, still little more than a baby, and young enough to need the care and affection Susanna was eager to give. Even so, she harbored no illusions about her role in her niece's life, nor did she have any intention of trying to supplant Caterina's real mother.

Deirdre had been dead for over a year now, but surely the child would have retained some memory of her. Susanna had no desire to erase that memory. She meant only to assume her rightful role as the girl's aunt and, by doing so, offer her the love and guidance Deirdre would have provided had she lived.

Even Michael Emmanuel had insisted in his posts that his daughter needed Susanna. And the bitter reality was that Susanna needed a home. With her parents gone and the family's small dairy farm sold for debts, her choices had been few: stay in Ireland and hire on as a governess, make an undesirable, an *unthinkable,* marriage to Egan Dunn, or accept Michael Emmanuel's offer to come to America and make her home with him and Caterina.

And so here she was, installed on a ponderous steamboat, churning up a river that gouged its way through the wildest piece of countryside she had ever seen. Towering, rugged cliffs rose up on either side, and the low-hanging clouds of an August afternoon sky hovered overhead. She was about to commence an arrangement with a stranger she already distrusted, in spite of the fact that she didn't even know what the man looked like.

Perhaps, Susanna thought grimly, this was her own "moment of madness."

A sudden blast from the steamer's whistle jarred her out of her doleful thoughts. She looked toward the gorge stretching north, then raised her eyes to the massive rock cliffs and climbing woods that rose above them, on the east side of the river.

Beside her, Paul Santi gave a quick smile. "It is just beyond there," he said cheerfully, the words thick with his Italian accent as he pointed upward, to their right. "Bantry Hill."

Bantry Hill. Susanna swallowed against the hot taste of acid rising in her throat. Deirdre had named the place after their Ireland home, but her sister's letters had made it only too clear that she had never found the sort of happiness here she had known as a child on the farm back in Bantry.

When Susanna had first read Deirdre's glowing recollections of life on the farm, she had thought it a bit odd. Hadn't her sister been dead set on getting away from the farm and traveling all over the world? And now here she was reminiscing about a life she had been only too eager to leave.

Still, Susanna reasoned, she, too, had often daydreamed about exploring other places, in spite of her love for home. But she was different. She had never shared Deirdre's hunger for adventure, nor her boldness. Had it not been for the series of devastating events over the past year, she seriously doubted that she would ever have left Ireland.

Certainly not for so harsh a place as this appeared to be.

Again she strained to look but could see only a huge, jagged cliff, dense with enormous old trees, their heavy-laden branches waving in the wind like green banners.

"The house cannot be seen from here," said Paul Santi. "Soon, though."

He really seemed quite kind. He had made numerous rather transparent attempts to put Susanna at ease during the journey up the river, talking animatedly about his life, his work, and his own experience of coming to a new land. Apparently, Santi was not only Michael Emmanuel's cousin, but functioned as his assistant as well. He had immigrated to the States only a few years ago, he explained, "at Michael's wish—and his expense."

Susanna turned away for a moment, closing her eyes to shut out the strange, austere landscape. A cooling mist from the river flowed over her. When she opened her eyes again, Paul Santi was watching her closely.

"This is . . . most difficult for you, no?" he said. "Such a big change. But it will be all right, you will see. Michael is so happy you are coming, and Caterina—she is fairly dancing with excitement! In no time at all you will be right at home with us."

Susanna managed a smile. "You live at Bantry Hill, too, Mr. Santi?"

"*Paul,*" he corrected with a nod. "*Sì,* Michael, he brought me across, and I have stayed with him and Cati ever since. I help him with the music, you see. I am his eyes, Michael says."

Susanna winced. In her anxiety over meeting her brother-in-law, she had temporarily forgotten his blindness. "I understand that he's quite a fine musician, in spite of . . . everything," she offered.

Again, Santi nodded, more eagerly this time. "Oh, yes, Michael is most gifted! He has built an orchestra"—he lifted a hand as if to grasp just the right word—"*superba.* He conducts. He composes also, *wonderful* music such as you have never heard! Even Bechtold says he is brilliant. Ah—but you must know all this from your sister."

Susanna bit back a caustic reply. Deirdre's letters had told her a great deal about Michael Emmanuel, indeed—but certainly nothing that would incline her to agree with Paul Santi's euphoric rhapsodizing about the man. She took a deep breath and forced a benign expression. "Is it true that he no longer sings?"

She knew the answer to the question but deliberately tried to keep Paul Santi talking. She intended to learn all she could about the man her sister had married, the man who only a few years past had been hailed as the "Voice of the Century."

Once extolled as the premier tenor of Europe, Michael Emmanuel had been well on his way to the same phenomenal success in America when a riding injury claimed his sight. So far as Susanna knew, he had never returned to the operatic stage.

Paul Santi's reply was slow in coming. "Michael sings mostly for Cati these days. And in the church, of course. But the opera—no."

Susanna studied Santi. He was a young man, probably in his midtwenties. He seemed a perpetually cheerful sort, alert and animated. It struck her as somewhat peculiar that, as best she could recall, Deirdre had never once mentioned him in her letters.

Now, for the first time since meeting him at the harbor, Susanna saw his features turn solemn.

"He left the opera because of his accident?" she prompted.

Santi glanced at her, then looked away, straightening his eyeglasses a little with his index finger. "It is very difficult, singing and acting on a stage one cannot see."

"Yes, I'm sure it must be," Susanna replied, still watching him. "I can't imagine how he's managed to accomplish as much as he has, being at such a disadvantage."

Santi turned back to her. "Michael does not know . . . *disadvantage*. You will see. Ah, here we are." He gestured toward the shore as the steamer began to maneuver toward the dock. "A short carriage ride, and we will be home."

Susanna looked around at the wilderness closing in on them, the fierce-looking cliffs and menacing sky. And once again she closed her eyes to ward off the sight of the wild, threatening landscape Paul Santi referred to as "home."

FOUR

BANTRY HILL

IT SEEMED LIFE HELD

NO FUTURE AND NO PAST BUT THIS.

LOLA RIDGE

Apparently, the carriage driver, Dempsey, was also a part of Michael Emmanuel's household.

Paul Santi's explanation seemed to indicate that Liam Dempsey was Michael's "man"—a combination of household manager and caretaker.

"Dempsey," Santi elaborated, "takes care of"—he paused and gave a light shrug—"everything. Whatever is needed, that is what Dempsey does."

Susanna might have been relieved to see another Irish face in this strange new world she had entered, had that face been more congenial. But Liam Dempsey could have soured new milk with his bushy-browed scowl and gruff, taciturn manner.

The road itself was no less forbidding. Narrow and rutted, it seemed all twists and sharp angles as the carriage wound upward, then upward still more.

The difficult road notwithstanding, Susanna had to concede that the late summer foliage on either side was glorious. Despite the heavy clouds and afternoon gloom, the trees blocked out almost all other views, and the farther uphill they went, the more spectacular the scenery became. Yet it was a fierce, savage kind of beauty, one that she suspected might turn utterly bleak with the onset of winter.

As if to confirm her thoughts, a gust of wind shook the carriage. "We will have a storm soon, I think," offered Paul Santi.

In spite of the sultry heat, Susanna shivered but didn't move away from the window. A moment later, she caught a glimpse of a lighthouse tower and its cupola, but it was quickly gone, lost behind the dense trees.

They drove on, for the most part in silence, jostling over the pits in the road as Dempsey urged the horses at a much faster clip than Susanna felt necessary, or even safe. Startled when they hit a particularly hard bump, she cried out.

Paul Santi gave her a quick smile. At that same instant, they went into a sharp turn. The carriage pitched, forcing Susanna to hug the door.

"The road is deplorable, I know," Santi said. "But we are almost there now."

Still shaken, Susanna caught her breath and tried to anchor her hat more securely. Her hand froze in its movement. This was quite possibly the very road on which Deirdre had met her death.

Chilled despite the August heat, she glanced out the window of the coach. Her nails dug through her thin gloves, into the palms of her hands as she turned to Paul Santi. "This road . . . is it—" She stopped, her voice faltering.

He looked at her, and Susanna saw understanding, then sympathy, dawn in his eyes. "Yes," he said softly. "But we have already passed . . . the site of the accident." He paused. "I'm so very sorry, *Signorina* Fallon. It didn't occur to me that you might want to stop—"

Susanna shook her head. "No, not today. Perhaps another time."

Eventually, she would want to see where Deirdre had died. But not just yet. For now, it was enough that she was finally about to meet her niece.

But she was also about to meet the man who had made her sister so unhappy—so altogether miserable, in fact, that she had fled her home, even her child, in the middle of a raging, late-night thunderstorm.

Susanna took in a deep breath, steadying herself for whatever was to come.

At last the carriage slowed. They were passing over an ancient, ivy-covered bridge, its stone walls crumbling in places.

Paul Santi gestured toward the window on his side. "You will see the house in a moment."

Susanna watched, but even after they left the bridge, she could see nothing other than a stand of towering pine trees. They approached a high stone wall, its gate supported by two monolithic stone pillars, and then, without warning, an immense manorial house rose dramatically into view.

Not a house—a *fortress*. Susanna caught a quick breath. No wonder Deirdre had found the place oppressive. Conspicuous in its austerity, Bantry Hill was more than a mansion, but stopped just short of being a castle. It looked to have been quarried from river rock that would withstand the passing of centuries. Given the elevation of the grounds, the steeply pitched roofs, and a tower of several stories that rose off the far end of the main dwelling, the place almost seemed to touch the low-hanging clouds that hovered over it.

As they drew closer, Susanna allowed that her initial impression might have been too severe. It still appeared to be quite a grand house, but not necessarily such a forbidding one. Elms and stately old beech trees, as well as maples and oaks surrounded the structure. And evergreens: she could never have imagined so many evergreen trees on a single property.

A wide, high-ceilinged portico with massive pillars and carved balustrades rimmed the front and as much as could be seen of the south side of the building. Large pieces of wicker with chintz cushions graced the rambling porch, along with baskets and urns of greenery and late summer flowers. A glassed-in conservatory flanked the south side of the house, opening onto terraced gardens and small glades.

Although Susanna couldn't see them from here, she knew from Deirdre's letters there would also be extensive fruit orchards in back of the grounds, and stables. For in spite of— or perhaps, as her sister had suggested, in *defiance* of—the riding accident that had blinded him, Michael Emmanuel had refused to give up his stable of fine horses.

They advanced toward the front of the house, and Susanna caught sight of a marble wishing well, then a child's white shingled playhouse. Her heart quickened at this reminder of her niece, and she found herself feeling a rush of anticipation. Then the coach finally came to a halt in front of the imposing stone stronghold, and her throat tightened with apprehension once again.

As if sensing her trepidation, Paul Santi lightly touched her gloved hand and gave her a reassuring smile. "Here we are at last," he said with convincing warmth. "Welcome home, Susanna. Welcome to Bantry Hill."

FIVE

WELCOME HOME, DR. CARMICHAEL

BUT STILL OUR PLACE IS KEPT

AND IT WILL WAIT . . .

ADELAIDE A. PROCTER

A weary Andrew Carmichael surveyed his office with a practiced eye. Clearly his receptionist, Myrna Glover, had not been in for quite some time.

It took two trips to carry in the deliveries and newspapers that had been piled up in the small entryway. Inside, dust appeared to have bonded to the furniture, while various leaflets and advertisements lay tossed at random on the reception counter and across the waiting room. There was no sign that human hands had wielded a duster or a broom for several weeks.

Only the examining room appeared to be in order. That

stood to reason, since Silas Webster and Phin Carey had seen to Andrew's patients at their own offices in his absence.

Andrew sighed. All Myrna had to do while he was gone was to bring in and sort the mail, tidy the reception area, and keep an eye on things. Little enough work for the pay.

He should have expected this. At her best, Myrna was lazy and indifferent; on her bad days, she was downright useless.

It would seem she had undergone an entire season of bad days.

Perhaps she had decided to seek other employment. If she hadn't, Andrew decided that he would suggest she do exactly that. Without delay.

He checked the small pharmacy, where for the most part he processed his own remedies and, finding things as he had left them, crossed to his office and sank down on the chair behind his massive oak desk—the one extravagance he had permitted himself last year.

If he hadn't been so tired, he would have got up and begun clearing things away. But he had been without food for several hours, and the dull throb that had been prodding at the base of his neck from early morning had sharpened to an ice pick, chipping away at the back of his skull, one piece at a time. He needed to go upstairs and rest before lifting a hand to anything else.

At the moment, however, the act of climbing the steps seemed more effort than he could manage. An ocean voyage might invigorate others, but not him. The sea air, followed by the onslaught of the city's heat, had set his joints to aching with a vengeance.

So with a deep sigh, he shrugged out of his suit coat, loosened his tie a little, and leaned back in the chair. The office was silent and muggy, and it was all too tempting to give into the fatigue and malaise that had settled over him. He could easily fall asleep right here at his desk, if only he didn't have so much to do. . . .

—

"Doc! Wake up, Doc!"

Somebody was tugging at his arm as if it were a bell rope.

Andrew jerked awake, his heart pounding. Dazed, he struggled to focus. For a moment he couldn't think where he was, only that the ship wasn't rocking.

"Please, Doc, you gotta come! Sergeant Donovan said for you to come *now!*"

Andrew's eyes felt as if someone had tossed sand in them. He stared at the little Negro boy with the dirty shirt, shook his head, and came fully alert. The child was Georgie Pride, a round-faced, wide-eyed youth who lived on the street and earned his keep by shining shoes or running errands for the merchants.

The clanging of fire bells and shouting in the street outside pierced the air, and he sat up. "Georgie? What is it?"

"Fire over to Mrs. Bedford's boardinghouse, Doc! Sergeant Donovan said you were back. Said you need to come!"

Andrew scrambled out of his chair. A glance at his pocket watch showed him it was close on three o'clock. He had slept for over two hours!

He looked around for his case, but Georgie already had it in hand. "C'mon, Doc!"

Not bothering with his suit coat, Andrew followed the boy out of the office. Outside, the acrid smell of smoke clung to the damp August heat like a singed veil. As they took off at a clip, a fire wagon passed them, bells clanging furiously, the horses snorting and pounding the cobbles. A frenzied mob of people surged down Fourth Avenue—men, women, and children, shouting to one another as they went.

Two dozen or more young working women resided at Gladys Bedford's boardinghouse. Andrew thought of them and picked up his pace even more, ignoring the hot shafts of pain that shot up his legs as he ran. By the time they reached Third Avenue, his throat and mouth felt charred with the taste of smoke, and his eyes burned from the ash raining over the street.

The scene was a nightmare unleashed. The modest, three-story brick structure was surrounded by onlookers, with still more gathering nearby. In an instant, Andrew took in the dense black smoke spiraling above the building, the exploding bricks, the white, panicked faces at the windows on the third floor.

Most of the windows were open, and the screams of the women could be heard over the din in the street. Glass shattered, and Andrew looked to the side of the building just in time to see another window exploding.

The commotion spooked a horse standing in front of the building, and the animal went bolting down the street, dragging its empty buggy behind. Some of the bystanders were screaming, many weeping, while others merely stood gaping at the building as if transfixed.

Two fire wagons were on the scene by now, with men passing buckets and hoisting ladders. Frank Donovan was at the front of the boardinghouse, with two other policemen at the side, trying to push the crowd back.

Andrew sent the excited Georgie across the street. The boy protested, but Andrew jerked his head toward Seitzman's Bakery. "If you must watch, you do it from there," he ordered. "No closer. You're not to come back here, no matter what! Understand?"

He turned then and wedged his way through the crowd,

heading for Frank Donovan. Flames were shooting up toward the roof. Women crowded at the upper windows, screaming and crying for help. Sparks and cinders rained down, and Andrew beat at the scorching ash with his hands as he made his way through the mob.

The policemen were shouting at the bystanders to get back, and although a few in the crowd began to retreat, most ignored the warnings and simply continued to stay where they were, gawking at the fire. At the front, Andrew saw Frank Donovan jump astride a dun-colored police mount. Hauling hard on the reins, the tall, powerful figure drove the horse down the edge of the crowd, shouting as only Frank could shout when enraged.

"Get back! Get back now, you bloodthirsty fools, or you'll be burnin' right along with the building! Move, I said!"

The big Irish police sergeant pulled a pistol and shot into the air. The horse reared and shook his head in an obvious attempt to lose the wild man on his back. But Frank Donovan rode on, pounding down the row of bystanders, shouting and shooting well over the heads of the crowd as he went.

Within seconds, the crowd had dispersed, most of them withdrawing to a safer distance, some even leaving the scene entirely, though grumbling and cursing as they went. A few, however, merely crossed the street and stood watching.

Frank reined his mount to a halt in front of Andrew. His mouth below the dark red mustache was set in a hard scowl as he holstered his gun. "Vultures!" He spat the word out, swung down from the saddle, then turned on Andrew. "And what took *you* so long?"

"How did you know I was back?"

"Had one of the boyos watchin' your building now and then," the policeman replied. He grabbed Andrew's arm and yanked him back. "Watch yourself!"

His dark-eyed gaze swept Andrew head to toe, and he suddenly grinned, a flash of white in the smoke-blackened face. "Well, welcome home, Doc," he cracked, tipping his hat back on his head. "And about time, I'm thinkin'."

Andrew ignored the jibe, noticing for the first time the group of women huddled off to the side of the boardinghouse. Many looked disheveled, their faces sooty and streaked from weeping. Some stood holding each other, while others appeared to be dazed, perhaps even in shock.

He turned to Frank Donovan. "Lodgers?"

The policeman nodded. "Aye. None seem in a bad way. Just rattled some, as you'd expect."

"How bad is it, Frank?"

The other's mouth turned hard again. "Worst of the damage is to the building. Some of the lasses weren't home from work yet. Those who were, we got out in good time. But there's still a few upstairs. They'll have to jump, if the smoke don't get 'em first. The stairway is burning, and there's no steps down the back."

Andrew saw two firemen hurriedly stretching a safety net. Another, his face blackened, came vaulting out the door, shouting, "Hurry it up with that net! Everyone's out but the top floor, and they don't have long! We're losing it!"

"I should see to those women," Andrew said, starting off.

But Frank caught his arm. "No, you stay here. We'll need you for the jumpers. Dr. Cole has things in hand over there."

Andrew frowned. "Dr. Cole?"

The policeman was eyeing the crowd, but turned back to Andrew. "Ah, that's right. You haven't met our lady doc as yet, have you?"

"Dr. Cole is a *woman?*"

"Last time I looked," Frank said dryly. He motioned to one

of his men to go around to the side of the building. "You'll have to wait for an introduction, I'm afraid."

Andrew turned and saw a small, fair-haired woman intent on examining a young girl's hands.

"Aye, that's herself," Frank said. "Dr. Cole—Dr. *Bethany* Cole. Right bonny for a lady doc, wouldn't you say?" Frank was watching him closely, his dark eyes glinting with a trace of amusement. "It's said that she—"

Abruptly, he broke off, his words swallowed up by the cries and shouts behind him as the women trapped inside the building began to jump.

SIX

MICHAEL EMMANUEL

THERE WAS A MAN WHOM
SORROW NAMED HIS FRIEND . . .

W. B. YEATS

Susanna had rehearsed her first meeting with Michael Emmanuel dozens of times, but now that the moment was here she felt suddenly panicked and wanted nothing more than to flee from it.

Paul Santi flung open the massive oak doors and stood back, waiting for her to step inside. Immediately she heard the laughter of children and what sounded like the barking of a very large dog. An instant later, an enormous wolfhound came barreling down the hallway, two shrieking little girls hot on his tail. Spying Susanna and Paul Santi, the dog came to an abrupt halt directly in front of them. The children, however, merely giggled and reversed directions, quickly disappearing down the hallway.

The wolfhound, a light fawn-colored giant with a deep

chest, sat staring at Susanna. His tail whipped about in circles, his large head cocked to one side as he took her measure.

"*Signorina*, meet Gus," said Paul Santi, laughing as he reached to rub the big hound's ears. "He makes himself out to be the bully of Bantry Hill, but don't let him fool you. He is nothing more than an overgrown, overindulged *bambino*."

The wolfhound shot Santi an indignant look at this uncommon lack of respect.

Susanna was no stranger to the great hounds of Ireland. Indeed, she fancied them and was thoroughly pleased to find one on the premises. Gus was by far the largest of the breed she had ever encountered. With only the slightest hesitation, she extended her hand to the dog, allowing him to examine her scent. He wasted no time in nuzzling the palm of her hand, his tail wagging with almost comic excitement.

Paul Santi clapped his hands together. "Ah! He likes you! He will give you no peace from now on, I fear."

"He's grand," Susanna said, smiling, grateful that, at least for the moment, the wolfhound had eased her nervousness.

"Those children—," she said, remembering the little girls.

"Caterina's playmates." Santi shrugged. "Cati will be in the music room with the others. There's a small birthday party for her today. That's why Michael did not come to the harbor with me."

"Oh, no!" Susanna brought a hand to her forehead. "I can't believe I forgot!"

But she had. In all the confusion and flurry of the past few weeks, she had completely overlooked the fact that her niece would turn four years old today.

"You mustn't trouble yourself," Paul Santi assured her. "Cati will understand, I assure you. Here, let's have your wrap, and I'll take you to her."

Susanna loosened her shawl and handed it to him, hoping he wouldn't notice its shabby condition. She took in the lofty vestibule that rose to a skylight three stories above and a magnificent staircase, its second-floor landing emphasized by a broad, stained-glass window with jewel-colored panes.

She was surprised at the lack of any visible ostentation. The house was cool—a welcome respite from the August heat. The walls were paneled in light mahogany, and the tall windows were draped only in sheer fabric, as if to allow as much light as possible. To the left, French doors stood open on a large drawing room, tastefully furnished. She caught a glimpse of a fireplace, framed by a wide mantel and colorful tiles.

Lush flowers, arranged carefully in porcelain vases, splashed the vestibule with bright hues, and a lovely Oriental carpet in delicate shades adorned its center. A restrained collection of oils and fine prints enhanced the overall air of gracious, but comfortable, living.

For a moment Susanna felt a vague sense of confusion. Deirdre had written of the house's "gloom" and "depressing atmosphere." But what she had seen so far shattered her preconceptions. She had been expecting the garish trappings of extreme wealth and luxury: ponderous furniture, perhaps, and tasteless accessories. Instead, her first glimpse of the house was actually inviting—and anything but dismal.

With the wolfhound loping along in front of them, Paul Santi led her down a long hallway, off which several rooms opened. Although some were only dimly lit, none were completely dark. They passed what was obviously the library, a thoroughly masculine-looking room, high-ceilinged and spacious, with walls of shelved books and an immense, octagonal desk.

The hallway was wide and well-lighted, and Paul Santi, lean and not much taller than Susanna, set a brisk pace for them.

Next to the library, they passed a room which looked to be an office, with a large, cluttered desk and more bookshelves lining the walls. Adjoining it—or more accurately, an extension of it—was another small study, crowded with storage cabinets and a variety of musical instrument cases.

It was obvious where the party was taking place. The hallway ended abruptly, converging on a large, open room from which poured a considerable commotion. Someone was playing a piano with great energy, accompanied by the uninhibited laughter of children.

They stopped just inside the doorway, and Susanna stood staring at the unlikely scene within. Only in the vaguest sense was she aware of the distinct Florentine flavor of the spacious room: the black-and-white marble floor, a variety of sculpted busts resting on pedestals, a few well-worn damask chairs, and several pieces of colorful Italian pottery.

Several musical instruments were scattered about the room, but her gaze quickly went to the splendid rosewood grand piano, at which a handsome, middle-aged woman was seated, pounding the keys with enthusiasm. At the end of the room, a circle of small children squealed and bobbed up and down around a dark-haired man who towered over them. Blindfolded, he was holding up a strip of paper and laughing as a little girl turned him round and round, then gave him a sound push toward the wall.

"Careful, Papa!" the child cried, then promptly covered her mouth with both hands, consumed with laughter.

At that instant, the wolfhound broke free and went charging into their midst, clearly intent on joining the fun.

Susanna realized at once that the little girl was her niece, Caterina. The tall, blindfolded man had to be her brother-in-law, Michael Emmanuel.

Yet for the very life of her, she could not comprehend why a man unable to see should be wearing a blindfold.

—

Suddenly the child turned toward the doorway, her eyes locking on Susanna.

She squealed and tugged at her father's hand, pulling him away from the wall. *"Papa! She's here! Aunt Susanna is here!"*

Smiling—and still blindfolded—Michael Emmanuel allowed himself to be hauled along by his daughter as she and the wolfhound came leaping across the room.

The little girl came to a breathless halt directly in front of Susanna, her dark, piquant features pinched with excitement. Finally, as if she could bear it no longer, she clasped her hands together in front of her face and gave a cry of pure delight. "Aunt Susanna! You *did* come! You are finally here!"

She was a wisp of a child with a wild mane of jet-black curls, a sprite dressed in yellow-and-white ruffled muslin and shiny black slippers laced with ribbons. Even if this had not been her niece, Susanna would have found it impossible to resist the dancing eyes and sharply defined features. She opened her arms, and without the slightest display of shyness, the little girl swooped into her embrace.

As she held her small niece snugly against her, Susanna was aware of Michael Emmanuel, who stood quietly waiting, the blindfold still in place.

Caterina pulled free just enough to look up at Susanna. "I knew you'd arrive in time for my birthday party, Aunt Susanna! I told Papa you would, didn't I, Papa? Did you know I am four years old today, Aunt Susanna?"

Susanna tried to apologize and explain why she hadn't brought a gift, but Caterina seemed not in the least disappointed. "*You* are my gift, Aunt Susanna! The best gift of all!"

Paul Santi moved to intervene. "Here, Cati, let your Aunt Susanna catch her breath. Your papa might also like to say hello, you know."

He went on then to offer a quick introduction, upon which Michael Emmanuel extended both hands to Susanna as if he could see exactly where she stood. Susanna hesitated an instant, then gave him her hand, which he clasped between his much larger ones.

"*Benvenuto alla nostra sede,* Susanna."

Welcome to our home.

"Papa," Caterina said sternly, "you said we must speak English to Aunt Susanna, remember?"

Susanna smiled down at her niece. "It's all right, Caterina. I understand Italian—at least a little."

"Ah, of course, you would, with your music," said Michael Emmanuel. "But Caterina is right. We should speak the English most. We are Americans now."

He pressed Susanna's fingers lightly before releasing her hand. "We are delighted to have you with us, Susanna. I hope you will consider this your home."

Caterina broke in with a giggle. "Papa, you are still wearing the blindfold!"

He laughed and reached to remove the cloth from his eyes. Susanna was puzzled when his eyes remained closed even after he dropped the blindfold away. Puzzled, but oddly relieved.

She tried to study him without being too obvious, then remembered that his blindness would prevent his being aware of her scrutiny. Just as Deirdre had said, he was large enough to be intimidating. Yet he was not quite as Susanna had envisioned him. His voice was unexpectedly gentle, even mild, and his smile hinted of uncertainty. In truth, his overall demeanor seemed surprisingly void of the arrogance and flourish she had expected.

It came to her that there was also an air of something akin to sadness about the man, and again she felt an unsettling flicker of confusion.

"This child shows her papa no mercy," he said, ruffling his daughter's hair with one hand and dangling the blindfold from the other. "She insists I must follow the rules of the game like everyone else, even though I hardly have need of the blindfold." He dipped his head a little, adding, "And now, Caterina, you should go back to your guests, I think."

"But, Papa, I want to stay with Aunt Susanna!"

He shook his head. "Your aunt has only just now arrived. You will have all the time you wish to spend with her later. Besides, you must be polite to your guests. Go along now."

He turned to Paul Santi. "Would you mind keeping an eye on them, please, Pauli? Only for another half-hour or so."

The younger man rolled his eyes good-naturedly and smiled at Susanna. "If I must. Come along, Cati," he said, reaching for the girl's hand. "Let us see if I can find this donkey in need of a tail."

Still, Caterina hesitated. "Papa, you won't forget that I'm allowed to have supper with Aunt Susanna? My *birthday* supper."

Michael Emmanuel lifted his hands in a gesture of hopelessness. "How can you possibly think of supper? You and your friends have been eating all the afternoon!"

"*Papa*—"

He laughed. "*Sì*, of course, you will have supper with us. Go now. Your friends will be leaving soon."

He waited while Caterina scampered off with the wolfhound and Paul Santi firmly in tow, then turned back to Susanna. "If you are not too tired, Susanna, why don't we find a quiet place and talk a little before you go upstairs?"

Susanna looked at him. The last thing she wanted at the moment was a private conversation with this man, but he was already offering his arm.

Before she could respond, however, he turned, saying, "Ah, I almost forgot. There is someone else who is eager to meet you." He called to the woman seated at the piano. "Rosa, come meet Susanna."

Susanna studied the pianist as she approached, a strikingly attractive woman who appeared to be in her late forties. Her glossy dark hair was streaked with silver and brushed smoothly away from her face into a thick chignon, revealing strong features and dark, keen eyes that Susanna sensed would miss nothing. Not tall, she nevertheless conveyed a sense of utter confidence and authority.

The moment Michael Emmanuel introduced them, Susanna recognized the woman's name. Deirdre's letters had mentioned Rosa Navaro, the renowned opera diva who was both a neighbor and a close friend of the family.

"Welcome, Susanna," she said in a low, well-modulated voice, reaching for Susanna's hands. "How good it is that you have come. Caterina has been wild with impatience."

Susanna felt an instant of discomfort as she recalled that Deirdre had never trusted "the Navaro woman," had in fact thought her "meddlesome" and "presumptuous."

She battled for a moment with those conflicting feelings. Deirdre had often been unmercifully ruthless in her character assessments. Rare indeed was the person who won her sister's unqualified respect or admiration. Hadn't Susanna herself suffered more than her share of her sister's barbed criticisms?

Still, it seemed disloyal, somehow, to disregard entirely Deirdre's assessment of Rosa Navaro. And yet Susanna could not help responding to the warmth of the woman's greeting and the faint glint of humor in her dark eyes.

Looking into those eyes, Susanna decided that, for the moment at least, she would put her sister's remarks out of her mind. She smiled, meeting the other woman's welcome with a cordial greeting of her own.

The wolfhound skidded up just then, falling in beside Michael Emmanuel, who gave a quick flick of his hand. "Everything is under control, Gus," he said dryly. "You may stay with Caterina."

The dog apparently deemed Susanna a reliable companion for his master, for after only the slightest delay, he turned and trotted back to the party.

"If Rosa doesn't mind," said Michael Emmanuel, "we will leave her at the mercy of the children for now. The two of you can get better acquainted this evening. I took the liberty of planning a small supper," he explained. "Just a few friends, including Rosa."

Susanna had all she could do not to groan aloud. She felt almost limp with fatigue, wilted from the heat, and increasingly anxious to get away from her towering brother-in-law. She would have liked nothing better than to spend a quiet hour or so with Caterina and then retire early. Even so, she managed what she hoped was a polite, if not exactly enthusiastic, response.

Rosa Navaro gave her a quick look of understanding. "I'm sure Susanna is exhausted from the trip, Michael. You must allow her enough time for a good rest before evening."

"Oh . . . *sì*. Of course! If you would rather go upstairs right away, Susanna, we can talk later."

Susanna was sorely tempted to accept his suggestion. But she would have to face him sooner or later. Perhaps it would be best to simply have it over with. He would undoubtedly want to question her to some extent before allowing her to supervise Caterina, and she conceded, albeit grudgingly, that he was well within his rights to do so.

For that matter, she had her own questions to ask. So this time when he offered his arm, she took it.

A Soul Alone

So goes the lone of soul
amid the world . . .

Dora Shorter Sigerson

T he drawing room was large but inviting and seemed to lend itself more to comfort than to formality. The windows were tall and narrow, the draperies a rich, golden hue, the sturdy but finely molded tables uncluttered with ornaments. Soft-toned Persian carpets were laid here and there over gleaming floors, while tapestry and damask chairs in cream and varying shades of brown added a feeling of warmth and coziness.

Michael Emmanuel waited until Susanna took a plump, comfortable chair in front of the fireplace before seating himself in a massive armchair opposite her. "What would you like, Susanna?" he said, ringing a small bell. "Tea or coffee? Or a cold drink, perhaps?"

Susanna clasped her hands in her lap, trying to still their trembling. "Tea would be fine, thank you."

They sat in silence until a small, middle-aged woman with a piercing stare arrived to serve their beverages and a tray of pastries. Michael Emmanuel introduced the woman as Mrs. Dempsey. The wife, no doubt, of the sour-faced driver who had brought them upriver.

The woman's demeanor toward her employer seemed surprisingly casual, more maternal than subservient, and after she left the room, Michael Emmanuel confirmed that she was no ordinary employee. "At one time, the Dempseys were neighbors and good friends to my grandparents in Ireland. Some years ago, I brought them here to work for me. They are like family, you see."

At some point he had slipped on a pair of dark glasses, and Susanna wondered why. It occurred to her that the glasses made him appear even more distant, less approachable. She found it almost impossible to think of this man as related to her in even the most obscure way. He was a forbidding, foreign stranger. And from what Deirdre had told her, his marriage to her sister had been a thoroughly unhappy, if not actually an *unholy*, alliance.

She caught herself resisting the urge to study him, in part because his very presence disturbed her. In addition, she feared that by observing him too closely, she might be guilty of taking advantage of his blindness.

Instead, she let her gaze wander aimlessly around the room, curious as to whether anything of Deirdre's influence might remain. Given her sister's fondness for the flamboyant, however, she saw nothing in the quiet charm of her surroundings that hinted of Deirdre's taste.

When she finally turned her attention back to Michael Emmanuel, she was again struck by the sense of *separateness* that seemed to hover about him. With his dark head bent low, a stoneware mug of steaming coffee cradled in both hands, he seemed almost removed from his surroundings, as though a kind of invisible barrier set him apart.

Susanna knew little about the man, only what Deirdre had written of him. His earlier mention of his Irish grandparents reminded her that he was indeed of mixed parentage: his mother had been Irish; his father, Italian. But in his appearance, as in his speech, the Mediterranean had clearly vanquished the Celt. There was no visible trace of the Irish in the arrogant Roman nose, the generous mouth, the darkly bearded face and dusky complexion.

Like his accent, and despite his claim of being "American now," the man was clearly Tuscan through and through.

He was, as Susanna had already observed, a very large man. She had been prepared for this, of course. In the first wild throes of her infatuation, Deirdre had spared no detail when she wrote of her new swain's "great stature," the "magnificent sweep of his shoulders," his "powerful and manly bearing."

In truth, Susanna, then still in her teens, had paid her sister's ravings little heed. Deirdre had always tended to be somewhat wild-eyed about her romances, of which there had been many. At the time, there had seemed no reason to believe that Michael Emmanuel's appeal would last any longer than that of his predecessors.

But Deirdre had surprised everyone by marrying her Italian suitor, supposedly at his insistence. Watching him now, Susanna found herself vaguely puzzled that this man had managed to capture her older sister's affection so completely, and in such a brief time.

Her confusion had little to do with his blindness, although the Deirdre she remembered surely would have found such an affliction disturbing, to say the least. Of course, he had not been blind when they married, and to be fair, Susanna had to concede that he did possess a certain dark handsomeness. Even now, in casual attire and with a somewhat rumpled appearance, he bore a kind of unstudied elegance that, combined with the dazzle and allure celebrity had always held for Deirdre, might easily have charmed her sister, especially in the beginning.

Still, he did not seem at all the type of man Deirdre would have ordinarily fallen for, certainly not the kind of man Susanna would have expected her to marry. Deirdre had always favored the slender, golden-haired, "aristocratic" types—the bloodless English squire sort of fellow. Indeed, most of her sister's beaus had been predictably alike: slim, fair-haired, pretentious—and, more often than not, drearily self-important.

Michael Emmanuel, however, was not only a startling physical contrast to the others, but had so far displayed none of the dash and debonair fussiness Deirdre had seemed to find so attractive. To the contrary, he appeared to be a solid, *earthy* type of man: quiet, self-contained, and without the "glitter" Susanna would have associated with a luminary of the music world.

Of course, she had met the man less than an hour ago. Appearances could be deceiving.

Deirdre had been deceived. And she had paid for it dearly.

For no apparent reason, Susanna found herself remembering the early weeks when Michael Emmanuel had been, in Deirdre's words, "pursuing" her. It seemed that during that same time, an aspiring concert pianist had also caught her sister's fancy. Soon, however, all mention of the pianist was forgotten, and no other name but that of Michael Emmanuel filled Deirdre's letters.

Unexpectedly came the image of a younger, laughing Deirdre, framed between two besotted suitors as they made their way

down a dusty road to a penny fair. The truth was that Deirdre—
at least in her adolescent years—had always loved being the
center of attention. By her own admission she had thrived on
the headiness, the feeling of power, that the pursuit by more
than one beau seemed to give her.

*And she had never hesitated to play one against the other as it
suited her purposes.*

Once again Susanna was assaulted by a sense of disloyalty,
the same sense she had felt upon meeting Rosa Navaro. She
forcibly shook off the unpleasant memory of her sister's youthful coquetry, reminding herself that she had never really known
Deirdre as a mature woman, after all. Surely she would have
changed a great deal since their final parting years before.

Still, Susanna couldn't completely dismiss the fact that
Deirdre had written of her attraction to another man in the early
days of her courtship with Michael Emmanuel. Perhaps, had her
sister chosen differently, she might have found happiness.

She might even still be alive.

⸺

Michael had heard the reserve, the edge, in her voice almost
from the beginning.

The girl resented him; that much was clear. Perhaps her
resentment shouldn't baffle him. He had no way of knowing,
after all, what Deirdre might have written to her younger sister over the years. Although she always insisted that she and
Susanna were too far apart in age and too different in nature
to be close, Michael knew many letters had been posted to
Ireland throughout the months preceding Deirdre's death.

He drew a long breath. She was here—that was all that
mattered for now. She had come, and he was convinced that
Caterina would benefit greatly from the presence of a younger

woman in her life, especially given the fact that Susanna was her aunt by blood.

There was no doubting Moira Dempsey's love for the child, but her advancing years and her household duties made it impossible for her to provide Caterina with the attention and understanding she would need in the years ahead.

Still, Susanna was very young. More than once Michael had wondered if at twenty-three she might not be *too* young for what would be required of her. She was little more than a girl herself. Yet he was asking her not only to become a member of their family, but to assume a highly responsible role as Caterina's companion and governess.

When he had first learned of Susanna's circumstances, it had seemed a perfect arrangement. Susanna was in need of a home, and Caterina, he believed, was in need of her aunt. He had prayed long and hard over the decision, and at the time he believed God's direction to be clearly given. Now that his plan had actually been set in motion, however, he was faced with the enormity of his decision. He could only hope he had not made a terrible mistake.

He took encouragement from the warmth he had heard in her tone toward Caterina—and in the firmness and steadiness he sensed, despite her youth and despite the fact that she must be overwhelmed and perhaps even a little frightened by her new circumstances. With that in mind, he determined he must be very careful in his behavior toward her. Still, there were things that needed to be discussed, matters to be explained and settled.

Before he had a chance to say anything, however, she took him off guard with a declaration of her own.

"I'm very anxious to hear about Deirdre," she said in a voice that made it clear she would not be denied. "I would like you to tell me how my sister died. And why."

Michael drew in a long breath. He had expected this, but not so soon, and not with such directness.

Very carefully, he set his coffee mug on the table. How much should he tell her? How much *could* he tell her, about the tragedy of her sister's death—and the travesty of his marriage?

EIGHT

QUESTIONS

THE HOPE OF TRUTH GROWS STRONGER,

DAY BY DAY . . .

JAMES RUSSELL LOWELL

Susanna could see him struggling for words. He set his cup down on the table, raked a hand through his unruly black hair—which was glazed with quite a lot of silver, she now noticed for the first time—and gripped his knees with both hands as he faced the cold fireplace.

"I did write to you of the accident—"

"You did," Susanna interrupted. "But—"

"The storm, the washed-out road—"

"Yes, but I need to know more than what you told me in your letters," she broke in again. "There must be more. You didn't actually—explain."

She clenched her hands even more tightly, ignoring the cup

of tea on the table beside her. "I've yet to understand what Deirdre was doing on the road in such a terrible storm—and in the middle of the night."

Other than a slight clenching of his jaw, he gave no visible sign that he'd heard her, much less any indication that he intended to elaborate further.

"Surely you knew I would have questions," Susanna pressed.

He turned his face slightly toward her. "Of course," he said quietly. "But I think this is not the time that I should answer those questions. After you are rested and have had an opportunity to become more settled with us, perhaps then, we will talk."

Suspicion reared in Susanna, but she managed to check the retort that sprang to her lips. Clearly, he meant to put her off if she allowed it.

But why?

"Mr. Emmanuel—"

"Michael," he said with a slight turn of his hand.

"Michael," Susanna said tightly. "I understand that it might be difficult for you to discuss this, but please try to imagine what it's been like for me. I had not seen my sister for years. When she died, I was an ocean removed. There was no chance to say good-bye. I couldn't even attend the burial." She caught a breath, then added, "I need to know how she died, what happened."

His features registered no change of emotion, except for a slight tightening about his mouth. "*Sì,* you are right that it is difficult for me to speak of this. And I know it must have been most painful for you, as well, to lose your sister when you are so far away. As for your questions, naturally I understand your need to know, but you must see that this is not the best time for us to discuss these things. I would prefer that we wait, please."

He would *prefer—*

Again, Susanna fought back an angry response. A confrontation was hardly the best way to begin her association with this man. Even though Deirdre had been gone for over a year now, and although he displayed no noticeable signs of grief, she had to allow for the possibility that he *might* still be in mourning.

But what about *her* grief? Ever since she'd made her decision to come to America, only her determination to finally learn the truth about Deirdre's death had eclipsed her eagerness to become a part of Caterina's life.

Now she was here. After one brief meeting with Caterina, she knew the child would easily win her heart. But it was blazingly evident that she would learn nothing more about the accident in which her sister had died until Michael Emmanuel was good and ready to tell her.

So, then—apparently he was just what Deirdre had made him out to be, an obstinate, difficult man. Bent on having his own way. Stubborn and unyielding.

Her earlier exhaustion suddenly renewed itself, and Susanna had to admit that even if she were so foolhardy as to instigate a skirmish with her daunting brother-in-law on her first day at Bantry Hill, she was far too depleted to carry it off. There would be time enough. He couldn't avoid her questions forever; she wouldn't allow it.

Sooner or later she would compel him to tell her everything. For the moment, however, perhaps he was right. Perhaps it would be best to have that discussion after she had rested and could think more clearly.

Besides, there was another subject waiting to be raised.

"Very well," she said as evenly as she could manage. "I can wait. For now, perhaps we should discuss my position here, exactly what will be expected of me."

She could actually see him relax a little as he lifted his hands from his knees and flexed his fingers, then turned toward her. "I would hope, Susanna, that you will not think of this as a *position*. It is as I told you: I want you to consider this your home, and be a part of our family. We want very much that you should be happy here."

"I appreciate that," Susanna said. "But in our correspondence, we agreed that I would assume certain responsibilities with Caterina. Which, of course, I'm only too happy to do," she added quickly.

He lifted one hand in a casual gesture. Not for the first time, Susanna noticed his hands. Large as they were, there was nothing clumsy or coarse in their appearance; to the contrary, they conveyed an unexpected grace, a quality of refinement that somehow caused one to follow every gesture, every movement, no matter how slight.

She glanced quickly away.

"What I am hoping," he went on, "is that you will give Cati your companionship, your affection," he said. "You indicated that you might be willing to instruct her as well, to act as her governess if I wanted."

Susanna nodded, then remembered his blindness. "I should be more than willing to teach Caterina, if you like. I served as governess to the Maher children for a time, after the death of our parents—"

"Your father died only a few weeks after your mother," he put in. "That must have been most difficult for you."

Susanna's throat tightened at the memory of her parents. "Difficult, yes, but not all that much of a shock," she said softly. "They were very close, my parents. Once my mother was gone, my father seemed to fade almost overnight. He had been ill with his heart for a long time as it was. Without her, he simply— gave up."

Michael Emmanuel leaned toward her a little more. "To lose a parent is a great grief. I still remember the pain of losing my mother."

Susanna thought it strange that he would refer to his pain at the loss of his mother but not his wife. Still, they had been speaking of her parents, so perhaps she was making something of nothing.

Watching him, she was caught by the contrasts in his face. He looked younger than she'd expected, and in spite of the strength and ruggedness of his features, she thought she could detect faint touches of humor about his mouth. True, the unyielding set of his jaw attested to the stubbornness she had glimpsed earlier, but at the same time, her long-held notion of him as a hard, unkind man wavered slightly under the unexpected air of courtesy and even gentleness in his demeanor.

She was still unnerved by the dark glasses, the barrier they seemed to erect, the way they distanced him, precluding so much as a glimpse into his thoughts or emotions. It would be extremely difficult to gauge this man's feelings, unless he chose to reveal them. Either his sightless, unopened eyes or else the dark glasses would serve as closed shutters to his soul.

She realized with a start that he had apparently asked her a question.

"I'm sorry," she said, embarrassed that he might have caught her studying him so intently.

"Your music," he repeated. "I understand you are an accomplished pianist and organist."

"Not all that accomplished. Competent, perhaps." The fact was, Susanna loved both instruments with a passion, but in the face of Michael Emmanuel's genius, she knew whatever talent she possessed would surely shrink and seem lackluster, at best.

He smiled a little. "Well, please know that you are most

welcome to use the piano in the music room. You will also find an adequate spinet in Caterina's playroom. She is trying to learn, so perhaps you will work with her a little?"

"Yes, I'd enjoy that." Susanna hesitated, feeling the need to reassure him as to her capability. "Just so you'll know, Mr.— *Michael*—I *am* a fairly experienced teacher. In both piano and organ, in addition to classroom curriculum. I would have tried to support myself with my teaching, but our community was poor, you see, and there was simply no interest or demand for an instructor. I could have gone to Dublin, of course, but when you wrote about Caterina—"

She suddenly realized she was rambling and broke off, leaving the rest unspoken.

"I'm sure it will be our good fortune that you chose to come here, Susanna." He paused. "You seem to have had the benefit of an excellent education. Yet Deirdre—" He stopped, as if the name of his deceased wife threatened to curb his tongue. "Deirdre admitted to little formal schooling, other than her music."

"That was her choice," Susanna said. Then, anxious that she not seem to speak ill of her sister, she hurried to explain. "We had sponsors—the Mahers—who were quite wealthy Anglo-Irish. They took an interest in us because of their fondness for our parents. Without them, any formal education would have been impossible. They offered Deirdre the same opportunities as they did me, but she chose to concentrate only on her singing."

"But you went further."

"Yes. I had a desire to teach. But even so, music was always very important to me."

Susanna cringed. She must sound like a mawkish schoolgirl. But Michael Emmanuel merely smiled and gave a slight nod. "I think you will find Caterina to be very much like you in that respect." He paused. "So, tell me, do you also share . . . your sister's love of singing?"

"I—no. Deirdre had all the vocal talent in the family."

Actually, Susanna found much joy in singing, as well as in playing the instruments. But she had always known her vocal talent to be smaller than Deirdre's, so she confined her singing to those times when she was completely alone and would not be compared to her sister.

In truth, it seemed that the balance scales had always tipped heavily to Deirdre's benefit, not only in terms of musical ability, but in appearance as well. Where Deirdre had been petite but buxom, Susanna was tall and too slender by far. Her sister had possessed the dramatic, attention-getting features and engaging personality most men could not resist. As for Susanna, boys her own age had usually treated her like a chum—or, worse still, like a sister—while older, more attractive men invariably seemed to shy away from her.

She had never measured up to her older sister in any capacity, nor did she delude herself that she ever would. And given her present situation, perhaps that wasn't such a bad thing. If Michael Emmanuel *was* still grieving for Deirdre, at least she would not serve as any sort of awkward or painful reminder of his loss.

"It would seem," said Michael Emmanuel, "that you are more than qualified to instruct Caterina. But let me emphasize that first of all I would like you to concentrate on feeling at home with us and learning to think of yourself as family. You are Caterina's aunt and, as such, will be accorded the respect of the entire household." He stopped, then added, "You will, however, be paid a fair wage for your responsibilities as her governess."

Susanna might have protested, had she not been so overcome with relief. She had feared being entirely dependent on her brother-in-law's largess, but now apparently she would actually be in a position to earn her keep. There was such a thing as being *too* proud, after all. She was a good teacher, and she knew it; she would accept whatever compensation he offered and be grateful for it. At some point, when Caterina was older, she could use any acquired savings to establish her own home and take responsibility for herself.

"Thank you," she said quietly. "That's very generous of you."

She tasted her tea, found it cold, and set the cup back on the table.

"It will be of great help to have you here for Caterina," he said, leaning back in the chair and steepling his fingers in front of his chin. "Of necessity, I must sometimes travel. And during rehearsal, I occasionally stay in the city at night. Even when I'm here, at home," he continued, "I must work a great deal. It has been very difficult, to balance all the work and make certain Caterina isn't neglected."

He took a long sip of coffee, then went on. "You will find Cati an easy child to be with, I think," he said. "At the risk of sounding prideful, I believe my daughter to be very sweet-spirited, with a genuine interest in others and a desire to please."

He turned toward her with a rueful smile. "She is also incessantly curious, somewhat precocious, and can be a bit of a minx. At times she may try your patience."

"The Maher children I cared for were twin boys of eight years with unlimited energy—and boundless mischief," Susanna said dryly. "I somehow expect that Caterina will be a welcome change."

"Let us hope you feel the same in a few days," he said, still smiling.

He got to this feet then, indicating that their discussion was at an end. Susanna also stood, waiting for her "dismissal."

"I've kept you longer than I should have," he said. "I'll have Mrs. Dempsey show you to your rooms and help you get settled."

Susanna turned to go, but his voice, low with an unmistakable note of kindness, stopped her. "Susanna, if there is anything you need, you have only to ask. Supper is at seven, by the way, and we are very informal. Tonight, as I said, will be only family and a few close friends."

He stepped closer to her, and for an instant Susanna had the irrational thought that he was about to touch her. She suppressed a shudder and stepped back.

As if he had sensed her withdrawal, he also moved away. Immediately, he rang for the housekeeper, who appeared so quickly Susanna wondered if she'd been standing right outside the door.

Upon leaving the room, Susanna glanced back to see him standing at the fireplace. As she watched, he removed the dark glasses and slipped them into his coat pocket, then passed his hand over his eyes in a gesture that hinted of extreme weariness.

She hesitated, struck by an inexplicable twinge of self-reproach at the coldness and utter lack of courtesy she had shown this man, in spite of the graciousness—and generosity—he had displayed toward her. Shaken, her mind swimming with confusion and fatigue, she had to fight the urge to break into a run in her haste to escape him—and the troubling tumult of emotions he'd managed to set off in her.

NINE

AFTER THE FIRE

SHE SMILED AND THAT TRANSFIGURED ME
AND LEFT ME BUT A LOUT.

W. B. YEATS

By late afternoon, the fire was out, and no lives had been lost. Most of the injuries ranged from smoke inhalation to a few minor burns. There were a number of sprained or broken limbs, but only one or two had suffered more serious injuries. Those who required further medical treatment had already been transported to the hospital by ambulance. The rest of the women, at least those who had nowhere else to go, were being packed into a police wagon and taken to one of the city jails for temporary shelter.

The building itself was still standing, but no one would be living there for a very long time. Andrew Carmichael and Frank Donovan both agreed, however, that, all things considered the situation could have been much worse.

As they stood talking and surveying the fallen bricks and

other debris, Frank broke into a grin. Andrew, who was quite certain he had never been so tired in his life, was at a loss to imagine what Donovan found so amusing.

"Well, now, it strikes me, your honor," said the policeman, his always thick Irish accent more pronounced than ever, "that this is the first time I've ever seen you with so much as a wrinkled shirt collar, much less a dirty gob, don't you know. I wouldn't have thought you could look so downright disreputable, and that's the truth."

Andrew grinned. Frank Donovan was known as quite a ladies' man, with his arrogant good looks and more than a splash and dash of charm, which he could lay on ever so thick when he had a mind to. At the moment, however, his face, including the rakish mustache, was gray with smoke and soot.

Frank doffed his hat and flicked some ash from it, then settled it back on his head. "Aye, no doubt I'm a sorry sight as well. So, then—you'd like to meet the lady doc, I expect."

"Yes, of course. Is Dr. Cole a resident of the boardinghouse?"

Frank shook his head. "No. She has a flat near the square. Seems she heard the commotion on her way home and came to help. Come along, then, and you can make her acquaintance. Of course, you'll keep in mind that I'm rather taken with the woman myself. Not that an Irish cop would stand a chance with her kind."

Andrew attempted to smooth his hair, then pulled his handkerchief from his pocket and swiped at his face. "Her kind?"

Donovan wiped his face on the sleeve of his uniform. "I don't know what she's doing in this part of town, but I'd wager Dr. Bethany Cole's blood runs as blue as her eyes."

Andrew studied him for a moment. "Ever the cynic, aren't you?"

The policeman merely laughed.

Andrew liked Frank Donovan as much as he had ever liked another man. They had become fast and solid friends, but Frank made no secret of the fact that he thought Andrew outrageously naive where his fellowman was concerned. Naive, and perhaps even a little foolish. The "Missionary Medicine Man," Frank was fond of calling him.

The big policeman gave no quarter when it came to what he labeled the "dregs of humanity"—which in Frank's estimation included just about everybody "except for you and me, Doc, and at times I tend to worry about you."

If asked, Andrew would have been hard pressed to say exactly what it was about the big Irishman that he liked so much. They could scarcely have been more different. Other than the fact that they were both immigrants, they held almost nothing in common.

Andrew knew little of his friend's past, for Frank wasn't given to personal confidences. What little he did know he'd learned from others, and he suspected that many of the tales told about Frank Donovan were nothing but rumor. One story had it that Frank had come across as a stowaway when he was still a tyke, only to become one of the innumerable homeless waifs who wandered the notorious Five Points slum on the lower east side, shifting for themselves by indulging in petty thievery or running errands for the gang bosses.

According to that particular tale, Donovan had gotten mixed up in a gang only to be arrested for knifing a youthful rival, though he protested his innocence right up to the doors of the jail. It was said that a good-natured policeman had believed the boy's story and, after taking it upon himself to find the real assailant, had eventually gained Frank's release.

This was only one of the many colorful accounts Andrew had heard about Frank, and he had no way of knowing if it—

or any of the other stories told about the man—contained a grain of truth. Nor did he care. What he did know was that Frank Donovan was the most thoroughly honest man he had ever come across. At times, that honesty could seem harsh, even brutal, but it was a trait that Andrew could not help but appreciate.

There was also a strength about the big Irishman that had nothing to do with his physical prowess. Donovan's brash courage and fortitude, combined with an uncommon sense of loyalty, made him a formidable foe and an incredible friend.

Andrew suspected that no matter what the big policeman might happen to come up against, he would prevail. Frank, no doubt, would describe himself far more simply with a single word: *hardheaded.*

And come to think of it, that probably summed him up about as well as anything.

—

It seemed to Andrew that Frank barely made it through the introductions without smirking.

Even with her hair and face dusted with ash, Dr. Bethany Cole was a pretty woman. No—she was more than pretty; she was *lovely.* Exceptionally lovely. Small with delicate features and hair the color of flax, she appeared too young to be a physician. Andrew saw in an instant why Frank had said what he did about her blood running blue. Everything about the woman bespoke *breeding.* She looked as if she would be far more at home serving tea in a Fifth Avenue drawing room than toting a doctor's bag around the squalid streets of Manhattan.

They exchanged somewhat awkward pleasantries, Frank taking it all in with that maddening grin of his.

"So, then, Dr. Cole—how long have you been in New York?" Andrew asked.

She had unusual eyes, he noted: startlingly large and remarkably blue, eyes that gave the impression of looking straight into one's soul. The thought disquieted Andrew, and he felt suddenly gawky and foolish, as if he had been transformed into a plowboy on the spot. Not to mention his "disreputable appearance," which Frank had so gleefully pointed out.

But Bethany Cole seemed not to notice. Perhaps he didn't look quite as disgraceful as Frank had intimated.

Or perhaps Dr. Cole was simply nearsighted. Come to think of it, she was peering up at him as if she might be just that.

"Actually, I haven't been here long at all," she said in a voice tinged with the well-modulated refinement of the upper class. "I arrived only a few weeks ago. From Philadelphia."

"So you're opening a practice here in New York?"

She lifted one delicate eyebrow. "Well—not just yet," she said, her tone dry. "I'm still—exploring the possibilities."

"I see. But you've applied for your hospital privileges, I expect?"

Andrew thought her smile might have wavered slightly. "I've applied, yes. So far, however, I haven't found a hospital interested in my particular skills."

Andrew knew only too well what she was insinuating. Most male physicians had no use whatsoever for women doctors—in fact considered the female "nature" itself unfit for the practice of medicine, aside from midwifery. Most of his contemporaries thought women should be barred from medicine altogether.

He did not share the popular opinion and, for some reason, found himself wanting to convey as much to Bethany Cole. "What about the Women's Infirmary? Have you spoken with them?"

She nodded. "As it happens, I'm already working at the Infirmary. But I'm still anxious to establish my own practice.

I'll have to wait for that, however. I haven't a place or the means as yet to set up an office. Besides, I don't know the city well enough to decide where to locate."

Something tugged at the fringes of Andrew's mind, and had Frank not been standing there, arms crossed over his chest as he took in the exchange with more than a casual interest, he might have been able to verbalize it. As it was, however, he felt increasingly awkward and unable to concentrate on anything other than Bethany Cole's unnerving blue eyes and Frank Donovan's annoyingly insolent grin. So he simply stood there like a post, saying nothing.

Abruptly, Frank uncrossed his arms and made a move to leave. "Well, now, I expect I should see to my men. I'll just be leaving the two of you to your medical talk." With that, he doffed his hat, then set it back on his head at a rakish angle and left them alone.

Under Bethany Cole's steady scrutiny, Andrew suddenly found that he, too, was eager to get away. They made small talk for only another moment before he offered a clumsy good-bye and turned to go.

He could almost feel her inquisitive gaze following him. On an impulse he stopped and turned back to her. "Dr. Cole?"

She tilted her head a little, her expression quizzical.

Andrew had never been given to acting impetuously. Yet something urged him on. He returned to offer her one of his calling cards, and as he did so, he studied her for a moment. "If you'd like," he said, "I might be able to help with those hospital privileges. If you're interested, that is."

She looked at the card he'd handed her, then at him. "Why—of course, I'd be interested."

Andrew swallowed against the slick of numbness creeping up his throat. "And about your practice—I might have an idea about that as well. If you'd like to . . . ah . . . stop by my office when it's convenient, we can discuss it."

He must sound like a dimwit—he *did* sound like a dimwit; he could hear it in his own voice. No doubt, she'd be too put off by him to venture anywhere *near* his office.

"Thank you," she said, still regarding him with a questioning look. "That's very kind of you, Dr. Carmichael. And, yes, I'll be sure to stop by your office." She paused. "Should I make an appointment?"

"An appointment? Oh . . . no, that's not necessary. Just . . . stop by anytime."

That said, Andrew again wished her a good day, turned quickly—nearly stumbling as he did—and made a hasty retreat to the front of the building.

TEN

Surprises, Small and Not So Small

Blessed day, so calm and restful,
Bringing joy and peace to all,
Linger yet in tranquil beauty
Ere the shades of evening fall.

Fanny Crosby

Her rooms far surpassed any expectations Susanna might have had. Mrs. Dempsey opened the door onto a high-ceilinged, spacious chamber with frilly yellow curtains, an enormous fourposter decked with yellow and white linens, a wall of neatly shelved books, and an upholstered rocking chair so large and inviting Susanna could scarcely wait to try it.

The room's sunny atmosphere fortified Susanna in a way she wouldn't have thought possible. She brightened even more when she realized she was to have her own private water closet and dressing room. She would be living in absolute luxury compared to the small farmhouse where she had grown up. But when she looked at her battered trunk resting on the bench at the foot of the bed—conspicuous evidence of her straitened circumstances—she felt a sudden, unexpected longing for the simplicity of her home back in Ireland.

Mrs. Dempsey seemed not to notice. She pointed out the lovely view of the gardens from the window, and then instructed Susanna to have a "proper rest" before supper. Susanna declined the housekeeper's offer to help her unpack; the idea of a total stranger sorting through her few frayed garments and thread-bare lingerie made her stomach clench.

She did try to express her appreciation for the room, but the housekeeper summarily dismissed her gratitude. "'Tis himself you'll want to be thanking. He was the one who saw to the fix-ings. He and the wee wane."

Taken aback, Susanna stared at her. "Mr. . . . *Michael*, do you mean?"

"Aye, the *Maestro*, as they call him in these parts. Didn't he plan the job and see to it himself, he and the darling girl?" The housekeeper preened as if this evidence of her employer's gen-erosity was a matter of personal pride.

Susanna waited until Mrs. Dempsey left the room to do a more thorough inspection. No detail seemed to have been spared in outfitting a room designed for the utmost in charm, coziness, and comfort. And it had been provided especially for her benefit—by Michael Emmanuel himself! The very idea left her feeling bewildered.

She forced herself to unpack her things before resting, hanging her few garments in a wardrobe twice the size she would need, then neatly stacking her personal items in the meticulously lined drawers of a highboy several inches taller than Susanna herself.

Finally spent, she sank down into the enormous rocking chair by the window. The late summer gardens below were splendid, but not formal. Instead of perfect designs, random quilts of color met her view. Like the gardens, those parts of the orchards that were visible appeared well-tended, but with no particular pattern or order.

For a time, Susanna closed her eyes, craving sleep. But she was too tense, too anxious about what might lie ahead, to thoroughly relax. Moreover, she was still trying to take in the fact that Michael Emmanuel had gone to so much trouble and expense on her account. A room decorated specifically with her in mind was the last thing she would have expected from what Deirdre had written of her "cold," "inconsiderate" husband.

All along she had expected to be treated like an impoverished relative—useful for looking after Caterina, but with no real place of her own in the household. She most certainly hadn't foreseen that anyone would have exerted even the slightest effort to make her feel *wanted* here.

Still, she couldn't help feeling suspicious of her brother-in-law's intentions and, consequently, hard-pressed to summon any real feelings of gratitude. The man Deirdre described in her letters had never acted unselfishly, but had been motivated solely by a desire to manipulate and control.

But why on earth would Michael Emmanuel attempt to manipulate *her*? She was already indebted to him, after all. He had paid her passage across, opened his home to her, even offered to pay her a wage. Certainly, there was no reason he should have gone to the additional expense of redecorating and furnishing a bedroom for her.

Susanna could make no sense of any of it, and finally her exhausted body had its way over her swimming thoughts. The next thing she knew Mrs. Dempsey was rapping at her door, informing her that supper would be served in twenty minutes.

—

To Susanna's relief, supper turned out to be just as Michael Emmanuel had promised: a small group, and a comfortably friendly one at that.

Paul Santi was there, of course, and Rosa Navaro, who was, Susanna learned during the course of the meal, a widow of several years. Also among those gathered about the enormous dining room table was a tall, intense Protestant pastor named Jeremy Holt and a Catholic priest whose thick head of silver hair made him appear, at first glance, to be older than closer inspection indicated. Everyone there called him Father Flynn, except for Michael Emmanuel and Pastor Holt, both of whom referred to him by his given name, Dermot. The pastor and the priest appeared to be great friends with each other, and with Michael Emmanuel as well.

What an uncommon thing such a friendship would be in Ireland!

The other member of the group was a petite, lively woman referred to as "Miss Fanny" by everyone there. Like Michael Emmanuel, she was also blind.

They were well into the meal before Susanna realized that "Miss Fanny" was none other than the acclaimed hymn writer, Fanny Crosby. She was a small woman, bedecked in an out-of-date suit and shiny, green-tinted eyeglasses, with a very large cross hanging around her neck. Miss Fanny looked to be middle-aged, but her chirpy voice and robust laugh made her seem much younger. Apparently, she had once been a teacher at the New York Institute for the Blind, the same institution where Michael had received instruction in Braille and other services for the blind after his accident. The two seemed to have become good friends, in addition to sharing a common passion for music.

It was obvious that all the dinner guests knew each other quite well, and yet Susanna felt no exclusion from their midst. To the contrary, they seemed to make a genuine effort to draw her in and put her at ease.

She was caught off guard entirely, however, when Michael Emmanuel stood, tapped lightly on his water glass, and said, "Although you met Susanna earlier as you arrived, now that we are all together, I would just like to say how pleased Caterina and I are that her aunt has come to make her home with us and be a part of our family."

Susanna, always uncomfortable with being the center of attention, felt the heat rise to her face. She was grateful when Miss Fanny spoke up. "I think we should ask the Lord's blessing on Susanna and your entire household, Michael. May I?"

With that, she bowed her head and offered a truly heartwarming prayer for Susanna, for Caterina, and for "our dear Michael." Susanna found herself deeply moved by the vivacious little woman's prayer on her behalf, by her obvious sincerity, and by what was clearly a close, very special relationship with her God.

"... May Susanna find this house to be more than a shelter, Lord. May she find here a new home, a true home, and may your love and peace abide with her and all who dwell within."

After a collective and enthusiastic "Amen," Caterina immediately leaned toward Susanna to plant a quick kiss on her cheek. On her other side, Miss Fanny squeezed her hand. "You will be blessed here, Susanna. Just you wait and see! You've come to live with a wonderful family, you know."

Among the other surprises of the evening was the discovery that her enigmatic brother-in-law seemed to be a deeply spiritual man. He talked naturally with the others at the table about matters of faith, the church, and spirituality. Indeed, he and the two clergymen seemed to toss remarks back and forth with an ease and enthusiasm Susanna would have expected to find only among family members. Apparently, this kind of evening was fairly commonplace for them.

If she had thought about it at all, she would never have expected Michael Emmanuel to be a man of faith. Of all the things Deirdre had written about her husband, she had never once touched on this particular aspect of his character.

But, now that she thought about it, Deirdre had never exhibited any interest in spiritual matters herself.

Susanna was grateful for her companions' attempts to include her, but she nevertheless found it difficult to take in much of the conversation—in large part because of the bright and irresistible little girl seated at her side.

Back home, it would have been highly unlikely for such a young child to be included in an adult gathering. Of course, this was Caterina's birthday, and she really did conduct herself very much like a young lady—though a highly animated one. Her table manners were impeccable, and although she chattered away throughout the meal, making no secret of the fact that she found Susanna altogether fascinating, she paid immediate heed to her father if he happened to clear his throat or lift an eyebrow, as if to gently remind her that perhaps she might be monopolizing her aunt a bit too much.

For her part, however, Susanna relished her niece's prattle and the way her blue eyes virtually danced with every word and gesture. Caterina—"Cati," as her father and Paul Santi frequently referred to her—was an absolute delight of a child. Her high spirits seemed to infect everyone present, and Susanna was no exception.

Suddenly she realized, with a touch of surprise, that she was actually enjoying herself. She had even begun to feel more at peace about her arrangement with Michael Emmanuel—if not about the man himself.

—

Sometime in the night, Susanna was awakened by the faint sound of music coming from downstairs. It took her a moment to recognize the soft strumming of a mandolin. She lay listening, strangely soothed by the plaintive melody, and within minutes she drifted back to sleep.

Later, she awakened again, this time roused by the clock in the downstairs hall striking one. Her head felt heavy, her eyes leaden, but the night had turned cool, and when the wind wailed outside her window, she stirred enough to pull the bedcovers up more snugly about her shoulders.

But just as she was about to doze off again, she heard something else, something that jarred her fully awake.

Footsteps.

She sat upright, instantly alert to the sounds in the hallway outside her room. She tensed as the footsteps grew nearer, then seemed to stop at the door to the room next to hers. Caterina's room.

The door creaked open, then closed again.

Chilled, Susanna held her breath, only to give a sigh of relief when she heard the soft chuffing of the big wolfhound. It was just Michael Emmanuel and the hound, she realized, checking on Caterina. Still, she didn't completely relax until the footsteps moved on and she heard a door close at the end of the hall.

The wind rattled her window, as if to remind her how secluded and removed from civilization this place called Bantry Hill really was.

She slumped back against the pillows, thinking about the music she had heard. Obviously, that, too, had been Michael. Apparently he was only now retiring, although he had appeared to be nearly as fatigued as she by the end of the evening.

Did he do this every night, she wondered? Stay up until all hours, wandering about the lonely halls with the wolfhound at his side?

Unexpectedly, the thought saddened her. Her emotions had been in turmoil ever since meeting her inscrutable brother-in-law. She had come here already distrustful of him, convinced that she would dislike him. Yet so far the man had exhibited none of the undesirable traits Deirdre had described, save for the possible display of stubbornness she had glimpsed earlier in the drawing room. In truth, he had been nothing but kindness itself since she'd arrived.

Susanna tried to will herself back to sleep, but the thought of that big, sightless man roaming about this cavernous mansion, alone except for his faithful wolfhound, kept her awake until long after the clock had chimed two.

ELEVEN

CONN MACGOVERN
AND THE BUSKER GIRL

WINDS AND RAIN HAVE *LIBERTY* TO ENTER FREELY

THROUGH THE WINDOWS OF HALF THE HOUSES—

THE PIGS HAVE *LIBERTY* TO RAMBLE ABOUT—

THE LANDLORD HAS *LIBERTY* TO TAKE POSSESSION

OF MOST OF HIS TENEMENTS—

THE SILK-WEAVER HAS *LIBERTY* TO STARVE OR BEG.

BY AN AMERICAN DOCTOR IN THE LIBERTIES OF DUBLIN, MID-1800S
QUOTED IN *DEAR, DIRTY DUBLIN, A CITY IN DISTRESS*
BY JOSEPH O'BRIEN

Dublin, Ireland, September

Conn MacGovern was in a hurry this cold, rainy morning. The good Lord willing, today would mark his last trek through the Liberties, his last look at the moldy, decaying buildings, where petticoats waved from the windows instead of curtains, and where the streets were strewn with vegetable and animal refuse, broken glass, and shattered dreams. Please, God, after today he would never again have to endure the rancid, foul stench that seemed to rise up like a poison fog from the streets, nor dodge the vermin-covered inhabitants and the starving, raggedy children come to beg.

Indeed, this was his last day in Dublin—his last day in *Ireland*—and though the thought stirred an entire tide of clashing emotions, his eagerness to put the slums behind him took precedence over the other feelings warring within. Had it not been for Baby Emma forgetting her rag dolly, he would be in the harbor with the rest of them now, waiting to board ship. But it would be a hardhearted man indeed who could resist the unconsolable wailing of his baby girl. So he had hurried back to the cellar flat to retrieve Dolly, now tucked safely inside his coat pocket.

Conn heard the shouts before he saw the small figure hunched down at the entrance to the alley. He stopped, struggling to take in the scene in front of him.

He recognized the girl almost immediately, though her face was partly concealed by her arms as if to ward off a blow. The shabby clothing that hung loosely on her and the crushed cap perched atop the tangled black hair gave her away at once: the young street busker called Patches—a name earned, most likely, from the multicolored pieces of material that decorated her baggy skirt.

But what was the girl doing here in the slums? She and her pack of vagabond musicians were usually to be found in the vicinity of Grafton or Henry Street, performing for whatever crowd and coin they could attract. There would be little chance of profits for them here in the Liberties, the most deplorable slum in Dublin.

Then Conn saw the cause of all the ruckus. Even though the alley was half hidden by shadows, there was no mistaking the other figure hulking over the girl—a woman grown, and quite a large woman at that. It took him only a second or two more to realize that the woman was beating on the scrawny little busker as if she meant to murder her entirely.

The sight of such unfair advantage fueled Conn's temper. He tore into a run, shouting as he went. "Hold off, there! Let up!"

He took the rain-slicked cobblestones in three wide leaps. Not until he was virtually on top of the woman did he recognize her. Nan Sweeney was an aging money lender—a sour old hag who lived like a pig in the heart of the Liberties and "employed" a number of the homeless ragamuffins from the streets to carry out her despicable deeds. It was said that Nan Sweeney would slice a throat as quick as a cheese and never give the act a second thought.

Conn took in the situation in a heartbeat. It was plain enough that the hatchet-faced old woman was in a rage with the young street musician. Her craggy face was distorted with fury, while the girl's sharply drawn features, though mottled with her own anger, could not quite mask the terror in her eyes.

Whatever the little monkey's crime, Conn reasoned, it could scarcely be license for such a thrashing.

He grabbed the woman's arm to haul her off the girl. "No more of that now!" he ordered. "Leave off."

The woman was as ugly as she was mean. She shook free of Conn, then turned on him with an upraised arm. For a moment, he thought she would go after him instead of the girl.

"You don't want to do that, old woman," he warned her.

The crone glared at him, but dropped her arm to her side. "This is none of your business, man!"

Conn shrugged and gave her a nasty smile. "A mad old woman beating on a slip of a girl? I'm thinking to *make* it my business. And while I'm about it, Nan Sweeney, perhaps you'd care to explain what the girl has done to warrant such shameful treatment from you?"

Her fierce scowl changed not a bit. "And who might you be, sticking your big nose in where it don't belong?"

For all the woman's bravado and her considerable size, Conn topped her by a head and outweighed her by far. He also suspected she might not be half so fierce as she obviously fancied herself if her opponent were a man grown, rather than an underfed street urchin.

He brought his face close to hers, forcing himself to ignore the disgusting stench of her breath as he knuckled a fist under her sagging chin. "Conn MacGovern is the name, you old dragon. And you don't want to be stirring up trouble with me, I promise you. Now get yourself out of here before I forget you're an old woman and give you the trouncing you deserve."

The woman narrowed her eyes as if to challenge Conn, but he saw her uncertainty, and sure enough, she backed off a bit. "She's naught but a filthy, thieving little guttersnipe, is what she is! That's what you'd be defending, man? She *stole* from me, she did, the little mongrel!"

Conn couldn't think why he should be putting himself out for this "Patches" creature. Because of her, he was already late in meeting Vangie and the children at the docks. Vangie would be worried and worn to tears with the little ones. But he had watched the young busker's antics on the streets so many times that he seemed to have taken on the idiotic notion that he *knew* the girl. He even felt a kind of protectiveness for her.

No matter what she had done, he simply could not bring himself to abandon her to the malice of this deranged old woman.

He turned to the girl, still huddled against the wall like a shivering alley cat as she eyed him and Nan Sweeney with a baleful glare. For the first time Conn saw the ugly bruises that splotched the side of her face.

"Is it true, then?" he said, his tone more gruff than he'd intended. "Did you steal from this woman?"

"Stole my moneybag, she did!" Nan Sweeney ranted on. "Dirty little thief!"

The busker gave the woman a nasty scowl, then shot Conn an equally fierce look. "I was only after taking what was mine! 'Tis *her* that's the thief, and that's the truth!"

Her voice held the familiar roughness of the street raga-muffin, the words hurled rather than spoken. She stumbled to her feet, and when Conn saw her wince with pain at the effort, he realized that she had been hurt more badly than he'd first thought.

But it wasn't entirely this evidence of the girl's ill-treatment that tugged at his heart and stirred the desire to protect. In the shadows of his mind lurked the awareness that were it not for his strong back and his capacity for hard work, any one of his own children could just as easily be reduced to this girl's state, sleeping in alleyways, living the slum child's life, and risking health and hide by consorting with riffraff like Nan Sweeney.

Besides, there was something else about the girl—some vague, intangible quality that seemed to set the spindly little busker apart from the other strays who wandered the Dublin streets all hours of the day and night. As unlikely as it was, and despite her outrageous rags and that ridiculous mop of hair, an unaccountable aura of dignity seemed to hover about the girl.

All the same, why would she resort to thievery? Although the buskers were often dismissed as common beggars, Conn knew that many of them were skilled and clever enough at their trade to manage a fair living for themselves.

Every now and then one would stand out from the crowd as genuinely gifted. And since no one appreciated musicians more than the Irish, especially the Irish of Dublin City, even the poorest among a busker's audiences were inclined to be generous with their meager coin.

The small figure known as Patches was a great favorite. Of all the itinerant musicians, she was said to draw the largest crowds wherever she happened to perform. The little guttersnipe might be a wretched sight entirely—and perhaps a thief to boot—but she was one of the brightest buskers in Dublin. More than likely, there wasn't a stepdancer in the county she couldn't shame with her flying feet, funny old-fashioned shoes and all.

She was a natural mimic and had a way with the instruments, too: a fiddle or a simple tin whistle took on a kind of magic in her hands. And when she sang one of the sad old tunes, her voice seemed to squeeze a body's soul, wringing out all the secrets and sorrows long hidden and thought forgotten.

But perhaps more than anything else, what evoked Conn's nagging urge to help the girl was something behind those enormous eyes, something the hard glare of defiance could not quite mask. In the end, it was that hint of energy and keen intelligence that prevented him from turning his back on the pair and leaving them to slug it out as they would.

"Give her the moneybag," he ordered the busker in a tone that brooked no argument.

The girl glowered at him.

"*Do* it!" Conn warned. "Or I'll call the peelers on the pair of you."

Her glare didn't waver, but one hand slid behind her back. When she continued to hesitate, Conn narrowed his eyes and jabbed a finger in the direction of Nan Sweeney.

With a murderous look, the girl thrust the moneybag at her attacker.

The old woman fumbled to examine its contents. "No doubt the little cheat has taken most of the money out by now."

Conn gave her a nasty smile. "You've got it wrong, Nan. 'Tis *you* who are taking some of the money out. Now give the girl what's due her."

The woman turned on him, and her expression would have cowered a mad bull. "There be *nothing* due her!"

The girl lunged forward. "You bargained with me for a job, and I did what you said!"

Nan Sweeney lifted a threatening arm, but Conn grabbed her. "Pay her," he ordered. "Pay her what you owe, I said. And don't be lifting a hand to the girl again, or I'll scrape the streets with you myself, old woman or not."

She stared at him as if to take his measure, and Conn braced himself in case she swooped in on him. But after a few more seconds and a muffled curse, the woman dug into the bag, withdrew a few coins, and tossed them at the girl's feet.

"You didn't earn a bit of it, and well you know it, you little thief!"

Conn took a step toward the woman, and she quickly added in a grudging tone, "But I'll not have it said that Nan Sweeney don't pay for a job done."

The girl grinned at her, revealing a slight gap between her two front teeth, then bent to scoop up the coins at her feet.

"Get out," Conn snarled at the old woman. "Now."

She went stumbling out of the alley, muttering to herself about "thieving blackguards."

After a moment, Conn turned to the busker, who stood watching him, poised as if to run. "Now then, satisfy my curiosity," he said. "What, exactly, was this job the old harridan paid you to do?"

She stood, jingling the coins in her right hand as she watched him with a speculative expression. "I was to collect overdue rents from two of her tenants. And so I did. But then she refused to give me my take."

Conn stared at her, then burst out laughing. "What, you're such a fierce creature the landlords send you around to inspire fear in their debtors?"

She curled her lip. "Don't matter if they fear me or not. 'Tis old Nan they don't want set against them." She paused, and then, with the same streak of impudence she displayed when performing, added, "And what is it to you anyhow?"

Conn sobered. "Why would you lower yourself to work for the likes of Nan Sweeney?"

"I do as I please," she said with a shrug. Then she pulled her face into a look of distaste. "Though I'll not be turning a hand for old Nan Sweeney again, I can tell you. Refusing to pay me what we agreed, and her as rich as the queen herself! That's why I made off with the moneybag. I was only going to take what was mine and leave her the rest. But then she started in on me like the demented old witch she is. Would have murdered me entirely, I'll warrant."

Conn studied her, but she wouldn't quite meet his gaze. "Is that the truth, then?"

When she looked at him, the pale blue eyes had turned to ice chips. "Didn't I say it was so?"

"Beggin' your pardon, m'lady," Conn said with exaggerated sarcasm. "Far be it from me to question the word of such an upstanding citizen."

Her face flamed, but she made no reply.

"Where do you live?" Conn said.

"Wherever I choose," she shot back, turning on her heel as if to go.

"*Thank you very much, sir, for saving my neck and sparing me a thorough pounding,*" Conn taunted. "*'Tis ever so grateful I am, sir.*"

Slowly, she turned back to him. "Thank you very much, sir,"

she mimicked, yanking the tired-looking cap off her head and giving him a sweeping bow.

Conn shook his head, but to save him he could feel no real pique toward her, only a bit of amusement—and perhaps even a faint respect—for the little hoyden's insolence.

"How badly are you hurt?" he said, for he figured she'd taken a fair bruising.

She waved off the question. "How much could she hurt me, a crazy old woman like that?"

The girl had pride. Perhaps too much of it, Conn speculated. "Crazy old woman or not, you'd do well to stay out of her sight for a time. She'll be after evening the score with you, I'll wager."

She sniffed and gave a toss of her head, then scrunched her cap back into place.

Still amused by the girl's bravado, Conn speculated as to her age. When seen up close for the first time, he realized she might not be as young as he had thought when watching her perform at a distance. Given her diminutive size, she might pass for ten or eleven years, but he thought it more likely that she was close on twelve or even thirteen. "What's your name, lass?"

Again she tossed her head. "I'm called Patches," she replied archly.

"I know what you're called. But don't you have a proper name?"

She frowned at him as if he'd insulted her. "'Tis *Renny*," she finally said. "I chose it myself. Renny Magee."

"What do you mean, you chose it yourself?"

She shrugged. "I got no folks. Never knew 'em. So I gave myself the name I fancied, and why shouldn't I?"

In spite of the roughness of her voice, she spoke with a certain flair Conn wouldn't have associated with one of the street orphans. In fact, he suspected the girl might have managed at least a token education for herself.

But here, what was he thinking? Standing about blathering with a busker girl when Vangie and the children were most likely wild for the sight of him by now.

"Well, Renny Magee," he said brusquely, "although it's been a grand experience, making your acquaintance, I must be away now. I've a boat to catch. But I don't mind telling you that I will miss your performances in America."

She gave him a questioning look and Conn nodded. "We are leaving today, my family and myself."

The thin, elfin face seemed suddenly transformed. "You're going to America?" she said, eyes shining with the kind of wonder ordinarily reserved for paying homage to royalty.

Again Conn gave a nod. "Aye, that I am. If the ship doesn't set sail and leave me behind, that is. My family is waiting for me at the docks, and late as I am, my wife will box my ears for certain."

The girl continued to look at Conn as if he were about to be knighted. "It must be a fine feeling entirely, leaving for America."

There was no mistaking the envy in her tone. Conn understood, though some of his own excitement had ebbed, now that the big day had arrived at last. Even Vangie, never one to back away from an adventure, had been showing her nerves this morning.

The thought of his wife roused him to action. She would be in a terrible state, Vangie would, thinking him murdered by robbers or run over in the street by a team of horses.

He stooped to retrieve his neckerchief and some papers the busker had apparently dropped during the altercation with

Nan Sweeney. When he straightened, the girl had moved even closer and stood watching him with that same expression of envy and fascination.

Conn handed her her things, saying, "Well, then, look after yourself, young Renny Magee. I must be on my way."

The wide, glistening eyes seemed locked on his face as Conn gave her a farewell wave and started off, but her voice stopped him.

"Mister?"

Conn turned, waiting.

"I—did I hear you tell Nan Sweeney your name is MacGovern?"

"You did, and it is."

"Well—" She broke off, looking away from Conn as she shifted her weight from one foot to another and screwed up a corner of her mouth. "Well, then, Mr. MacGovern, I expect I ought to thank you for your help. Not many would have stopped as you did, I'm thinking."

The words tumbled out quickly, like pellets shot from a gun. Her face was flushed with crimson, her gaze locked on her own feet. Clearly, this Renny Magee was not overly familiar with even a simple thank-you. But then, perhaps she'd had few occasions in her young life to express her appreciation to another.

"You are very welcome, I'm sure," Conn said, unable to suppress a smile.

"And safe home," he added, wondering even as he said it if indeed Renny Magee, the girl called Patches, had a place to call home.

TWELVE

VANGIE

HAD I THE WEALTH THAT PROPS THE SAXON'S REIGN,
OR THE DIAMOND CROWN THAT DECKS THE KING OF
    SPAIN,
I'D YIELD THEM ALL IF SHE KINDLY SMILED ON ME . . .
                    ANONYMOUS, FROM EIGHTEENTH-CENTURY IRISH

A punishing rain had set in by the time Conn reached the dock.

He was relieved to see that Vangie and the children had found shelter under a tarpaulin. Vangie held Baby Emma in her arms, while Nell Grace—who at seventeen looked more like her mother every day—had the twins well in tow, one on each side.

Aidan, the oldest, stood looking out over the docks with the same dark scowl he'd been wearing since the day Conn broke the news that they were leaving Ireland.

Aidan was a good lad, Vangie's joy and pride, her firstborn. But he was also a hothead. At nineteen, he was a man grown and seemed to believe himself called to challenge any and every decision his father made. He had kicked up a terrible fuss over the idea of going to America, so much so that he and Conn had scarcely spoken for weeks now.

Conn told himself that once the crossing was underway and Ireland behind them, the boy would surely come round and see the sense of things again.

For Vangie's sake, he hoped he was right.

The rain, uncommonly cold for this time of year, was falling harder now. Even so, Conn stood for a moment, drinking in the sight of his wife. The same rush of love that had made him a bumbling fool over her as a lad came rolling in on him again. It was always this way, even after more than twenty years of marriage and five children—seven, if he were to count the two gone to the angels in years past.

As he stood there, watching Vangie, her dark red hair blowing in the wind, her deep-set eyes searching the throng that lined the fence along the length of the dock—searching for *him*, Conn knew—he marveled, not for the first time, that the good Lord had blessed such a man as himself: a great, thick-necked oaf who had never been able to give the woman he loved anything more than hard times and shattered dreams.

With her vibrant beauty, still unfaded at thirty-seven years, her strength of spirit, and her good, true heart, his Vangie could have had any man she wanted—sure, a far better man than himself. But she had chosen him, Conn MacGovern, and, though he would always puzzle over his good fortune, he would never take it lightly.

Life had been hard for them right from the beginning. In the early years, they had merely scraped a living off the land, barely getting by, handing over almost all Conn's meager wages to the landlord. Yet they had somehow managed to be content with what they had, finding their fulfillment in each other, the children, their faith, and in the land itself.

But then had come the winter of the sickness. With never enough to pay for the medicines Vangie and the twins needed—not even enough to pay the rent—they had finally lost it all: the cabin, the land, the cow, and Vangie's hens. Indeed, they had lost everything but the clothes on their backs and their few poor pieces of furniture and pottery. And so they had moved to the city, to Dublin, where ever since they had lived like rabbits in a warren, boxed into two cramped rooms of a dreary hovel on the edge of the slums known as the Liberties.

Conn's reluctant decision that they must leave Ireland had nearly broken Vangie's heart and had all but destroyed his relationship with his son. More than once, Aidan had bitterly accused his father of betraying them all, of having no love for the land, no loyalty to their native country—and, worse still, no concern for his family's well-being.

In truth, it was Conn's concern for the family that had finally pushed him into the decision to emigrate, though of course the boy couldn't begin to imagine what that decision had cost his father. There were nights when, long after Vangie had fallen asleep, Conn lay wide awake, nearly frozen in his own anguish at the thought of leaving all he had ever known and taking his family across the formidable Atlantic.

The idea of starting over again, in a new country, among strangers—and he a man of forty years—filled him with almost as much dread as the possibility of watching his family starve to death on familiar soil. How many times had he been on the brink of throwing his resolve to the winds and announcing that they would not go to America, but would stay in Ireland after all?

Stay in Ireland and starve.

That was the reality that kept Conn from backing down

and giving in to his son's continual haranguing. That, and Vangie's strength.

A weaker woman would have given up on him long before now, would have lost all hope and heart and left him to his own folly. But not his Vangie. When things had been at their worst and the future appeared most bleak, she had kept the family going—had kept *Conn* going, encouraging him to keep his faith in his dreams and in his Maker.

His wife's strength and unflagging faith had been the wind that buoyed Conn's own spirit, kept him from crumbling into the half-man, half-beast to which the English, if they had their way, would reduce every male in Ireland. Somehow Vangie had convinced him that the Almighty had not abandoned them—or the rest of the Irish. How often had she committed to him that she loved him more than everything in spite of the latest "setback," and would continue to love him, no matter what the future held?

But when Conn first voiced his intention to leave Ireland, even Vangie's confidence had plainly faltered. It had taken him days to persuade her that it was their best hope—most likely their *only* hope—of survival.

At first, she tried everything to talk him out of the idea, had pleaded with him, shrieked at him, threatened to leave him— indeed, she had aimed every weapon in her feminine arsenal at him—in a desperate attempt to convince him that his idea was madness itself. And then, without warning—and at the very moment Conn thought he might just as well give up the idea altogether—hadn't she announced that, despite her prayers that the Almighty would "let this cup pass from them," the good Lord had instead confirmed Conn's decision to her. Indeed, it seemed they were to go to America after all.

And that had been the end of her resistance—though not her fears, Conn knew. The apprehension still pinched her features as they made their plans, and the tears still welled up at almost any mention of leaving. But her God had spoken, and she would obey.

For Vangie, it was that simple, and always had been.

So over the past several months, allowing themselves only the bare essentials needed to survive, they had managed to squeeze out enough from Conn's wages, Vangie's sewing money—and the sale of every item they could spare—to secure their passage. And now here they were, about to board the ship that would take them to their new life.

At that moment, he saw Vangie turn and catch sight of him. Her entire countenance brightened, and with a wave, Conn called out and started toward her.

Vangie saw him coming, and the worry that had been gnawing at her for the past hour immediately gave way to a flood of relief so powerful her legs very nearly buckled under her. She knew the Lord would have her entrust everything to him. And most of the time, she managed to do just that. But, God forgive her, the hardest thing she faced at the beginning of each new day was to surrender her *family*, even to the One she knew to be merciful, the One she trusted with all her being. And now that Conn had made this life-changing decision—a decision that struck terror into her heart every time she thought of it—she found it nearly impossible not to worry, not to allow the weight of fear to crush the pinions of her faith.

She stepped away from the children a little, watching him hurry toward her, her big, good-looking husband—a "fine doorful of a man," as old Widow Dolan was wont to say—with that smuggler's smile and those sea-green eyes that could make her forgive him almost anything.

Not that there was much to forgive Conn MacGovern, she thought, warming with love at the sight of him. A woman would be a fool to wish for more in a husband than what she had found with Conn. He was no saint, and that was the truth, but he was a good man with a back carved from granite and a heart so soft the sight of an injured lark could bring him to tears. He was a strong, brawny man who could work from dawn till dark and bear the weight of two other men if need be, yet so light on his feet he could dance a jig on a spider's web and never tear it.

He was her husband, her best friend, her lover. After all these years, Vangie had only to look upon him and suddenly it was as if time itself had melted away and she was a young, lovesick girl again, and not the mother of five—including a son who was a man grown and a daughter about to pass into womanhood.

That's how it was *most* of the time.

For now, however, she firmly set aside her girlish foolishness and reminded herself that until this very moment she had been near sick to death with worry over the great *amadan*. And would you look at him now, hoofing his way toward her, late as a tinker's rent, yet smiling like the deadly charmer he fancied himself to be, and all the while expecting her to never mind his lingering.

Well, they would see about that. She gave Baby Emma a hoist and met her husband's foolish smile with a well-deserved glare.

"Ah, and so you have decided to favor us with your presence at last, Conn MacGovern!" she snapped at him. "I expect we should be counting ourselves blessed entirely that you showed up at all."

He had the good sense to look sheepish. "I'm sorry, my beauty, but it couldn't be helped. There was this girl, you see—

well, you'll recall the one I mean, the little busker girl called Patches—she got herself into a stew of trouble, and so the only thing I could do was stop to help."

Vangie merely lifted an eyebrow.

"'Tis true," he said, reaching to give the baby's chin a tweak. "That miserable old witch Nan Sweeney was beating on the girl when I came along. Well, I couldn't simply pass on by and ignore the situation, now could I?"

Vangie pretended to scrutinize his broad, rakish features, but of course there was no question of his telling the truth. Conn couldn't lie to save his own hide, and wasn't she the better off for it?

She moved to shift the baby's weight to her other side, but Conn reached to take her to himself. Pleased, Emma chortled and grabbed at her daddy's nose. He pulled a face at her, which only made the tyke laugh that much more.

Vangie rubbed her back, which ached from standing in the damp so long with the weight of the baby upon her. She watched as Conn made a great show of producing the rag doll from his pocket, tickling Emma's nose with it. The baby squealed and buried her face in the doll's limp yarn hair.

He turned back to Vangie. "I am sorry, love," he said over the tyke's head. "I didn't mean to be so long."

Too weary to fuss at him, Vangie waved off his apology. "I was worried, is all. I want this over and done with."

She turned, a renewed wave of dread overtaking her as she stared at the steamer that would take them to America. Someone behind prodded them to move forward, and now they were in the thick of the passengers about to board.

Vangie looked to make certain the children were all accounted for, then again turned her gaze toward the ship. She felt Conn's large hand on her shoulder, steadying her. Unwilling to let him see the anguish and fear pressing in on her, she reached to cover his hand with her own.

"It will be well, love," he said softly, his breath warm against her hair. "'Tis the right thing we're doing."

Vangie didn't trust her voice to answer, instead merely nodded as they continued their march toward the vessel that waited to take them away from Ireland, from all that was known and familiar, to a place where only the Lord himself knew what awaited them.

THIRTEEN

THE PROMISE OF HIS PRESENCE

"FOR I KNOW THE PLANS I HAVE FOR YOU,"
SAYS THE LORD.
"THEY ARE PLANS FOR GOOD AND NOT FOR
DISASTER, TO GIVE YOU A FUTURE AND A HOPE."

JEREMIAH 29:11 (NLT)

They were in the thick of the passengers approaching the gangplank now, and there was no shelter from the bitter rain.

Vangie stopped long enough to turn around and make sure Conn had covered Baby Emma's face with her blanket. Immediately, she was shoved to the side by the driving crowd. Conn caught her arm, holding onto her as they continued toward the gangplank.

Now everything was confusion, a wild scramble as the steerage passengers rushed ahead. Children were screaming, women weeping, their men trying to shield them from those who would trample them outright in their haste to board and ensure themselves the best berths.

And all the while, the rain continued to batter the harbor with a vengeance.

Vangie saw a large, raw-boned woman and two strapping youths bearing down on the twins and Nell Grace, who had fallen behind.

"Nell Grace—behind you!" she called out to her daughter.

The girl looked at her, then turned, stumbling in her effort to keep the boys in tow. At the same time, Aidan left his place up ahead and came whipping through the mob, shoving his way to his sister and little brothers. He took James, the smaller of the twins, to himself, grabbing Nell Grace's arm with his free hand to buoy her and John along.

Vangie blinked against the tears burning her eyes. She tried to ignore the sick churning of her stomach as the reality of their departure slammed through her like a wrecking ball. By the time they neared the gangplank, her legs felt so brittle that it seemed the slightest movement would shatter her to pieces.

Sheer terror barreled down on her, and she bit her lip so fiercely she could taste her own blood. She felt Conn's hand tighten on her arm as if he had seen the surge of fear in her. Somehow she managed to force a smile for his benefit.

"Nothing matters so long as we're all together," she said, raising her voice above the pandemonium in an effort to reassure herself as well as her husband. "We have each other and the children. We will be all right."

He gave her a grateful smile and squeezed her arm. "We will, love," he said. "We will make out just fine. We are going to a better life, after all."

Vangie turned away so he couldn't see the panic struggling to overtake her. *Please let it be so!* She prayed silently. *Please let us be going to something better and not to our own destruction.*

She became gradually aware that the movement of the

crowd had slowed and now was stopping altogether. People muttered among themselves, shifting the weight of their burdens as they speculated as to the reason for the delay. Finally, someone farther ahead passed back the word that a crew member had halted their progress until their numbers were called. There was much grumbling and scattered cursing, especially from some of the rougher men, but there was nothing to do for it but stand and wait in the relentless rain.

With Baby Emma still cuddled against him, Conn moved forward a little to stand between Aidan and Nell Grace and the twins. Vangie saw the hard, unyielding look Aidan gave his father, which Conn ignored.

They were so alike, the two of them. Aidan, the very image of his father, had inherited both Conn's good looks and bullheadedness. And Vangie loved him so deeply it made her heart ache.

She still remembered, as though it were yesterday, the night he had been born. Perhaps there was always a special bond between a mother and her firstborn son, especially when that son was so much like his da. The first moment she held him, he had stolen her heart entirely, and now, nearly a man grown, Aidan still never failed to warm her with his teasing and boyish laugh.

A laugh she had heard all too seldom in past months. Vangie sighed, her eyes going from husband to son. Why couldn't the two of them find their way to an agreement—or at the very least, a truce?

She watched her family for a moment, then let her gaze wander over the others who, like herself, stood drenched and miserable as they waited to board ship. Vangie saw her own fear reflected in the eyes of most of the women and in some of the men as well. Bony, whimpering children, some wearing little more than rags, clung to their parents, while young people who looked to be near the age of Aidan and Nell Grace shuffled their feet, as if anxious to get on with the adventure.

So many leaving. Leaving home and family and all they had ever known. Most would probably never set eyes on Ireland again, herself included. They were leaving their past, not knowing if they even had a future.

Vangie shuddered, fighting back tears. Suddenly from behind her, she felt a gentle touch on her shoulder. She turned to look, but there was no one except a gnarled old grandmother staring out into the distance, moaning softly to herself.

But something happened as Vangie stood watching, something not so much seen as *sensed*. It was as if all movement had ceased. The restless, querulous crowd fell silent, frozen in the moment like a painting, with the great ocean in front of them and the isle of home at their backs. Everything seemed to fade and grow still, leaving Vangie as a solitary observer, removed from the press of bodies all around her.

Again she was struck by the sensation of being touched. Vangie stood, scarcely breathing, her heart hammering as she saw, as if from a great distance, a kindly featured figure, dressed in homespun, moving among the crowd, murmuring to them, ruffling the hair of the children, consoling the women, encouraging the men, reassuring the elderly.

He laid a hand to their heads as he quietly made his way through the masses, and his every touch was like a blessing. With each step he took, an encompassing warmth and light seemed to radiate from him, overshadowing the fear of the voyage ahead, the dread of the waiting unknown, even the sting of the cold, slicing rain. A strong but gentle presence, he walked among them with a touch and a word of kindness like a benediction for them all. And no one seemed to acknowledge that he was even in their midst.

Then he was gone, and the crowd began to move forward again. The shouts of the crew could be heard over the wailing of the children and the futile attempts of their mothers to hush and comfort. A blast from the ship sounded, and somewhere in the distance the sound of a mournful fiddle could be heard.

Vangie had fallen behind her family and had to hurry to catch up. But now as she threaded her way through the throng of other passengers, there was a new firmness to her step. Her feet no longer felt leaden, and her heart no longer hammered with dread. Instead, a sweet, inexplicable peace enfolded her like a cloak as she pressed on.

She could not explain what had happened, but she knew what she had seen . . . she knew in her heart of hearts that she had not imagined it. That comforting presence, that caring touch, had been real—wonderfully, incredibly real.

It was a promise, and she seized upon it as such. A promise to cling to, not only for today, but for all the days to come. A promise to carry with her across the fierce Atlantic and into the new land they would one day call home.

A promise that, wherever she and her loved ones might venture, no matter how long their journey or how far their final destination, they did not go alone.

FOURTEEN

THE WATCH

SHE HAD THE LOOK OF ONE WHO WOULD

HAVE GLADLY TRADED ANYTHING—

ANYTHING BUT HER PRIDE—

FOR THE SWEET TASTE OF FREEDOM . . .

FROM THE DIARY OF NELL GRACE MacGOVERN, 1875

Long after Conn MacGovern had disappeared from view, Renny Magee stood at the end of the alley staring at nothing in particular. Finally, she pulled her left hand free of her coat pocket and opened it to reveal the watch she had palmed from the street, where her rescuer had dropped it during his clash with Nan Sweeney.

Odd, he didn't look the sort to own such a fine piece. In truth, his attire had marked him as a man down on his luck, perhaps in circumstances not much better than Renny's own.

Not that her lot was all that bad. She got by, she did.

The timepiece's case was etched and carved all fancy-like, with strange, foreign-looking little houses and dragons and boats that made Renny think of some of the decorated knick-knacks and baubles in the Chinaman's shop over on Henry Street.

After examining the watch's gold casing—at least it *looked* to be gold—she opened it to study the numerals and dials. Were it not for the frayed clothing MacGovern had been wearing, she would have thought she'd captured herself a real treasure.

Perhaps she should not be too quick to discount the watch's value. It looked to be expensive, perhaps *very* expensive.

Old Nan Sweeney would not see this particular piece, she wouldn't. Renny would take it to Henchy's, above the chandler's place. Most likely, the moneylender would pay more by half than that awful old woman would offer anyway. Not that she'd be foolish enough to go near to Old Nan again anytime soon.

Renny closed the case and stood flipping the watch from one hand to another a few times. She was not entirely comfortable with the idea of keeping it. The thing was, when had anyone ever put himself out to help her before this day?

Aside from Thomas Lynch and one or two of the other buskers, she had no friends, not really. You couldn't trust anyone, and that was the truth. There was always someone on the prowl to pick your pocket or kick you about and take your money.

But Conn MacGovern had stood in for her, and him in a terrible rush on his way to the docks. Not only had the man put himself in harm's path for her, but he had treated her kindly enough, in a gruff sort of manner. Why, he had even said he'd miss her *performances.*

What if the watch was a family heirloom, something treasured and handed down now and again?

What if it was? That would make it all the more valuable.

Renny lifted the watch to look at it again, letting her fingers trace the engraving. The chafing at the back of her mind refused to go away. She looked down the street in the direction of the harbor, indecision sweeping through her.

Finally, propelled by an urgency that started her heart to thundering, she tore out of the alley and took off at a fierce run toward the docks.

———

The next few minutes were all confusion, with the crowd pressing forward like so many cattle prodded into movement, and members of the crew shouting commands and curses at them as if cattle they were indeed.

Conn saw Vangie weaving her way through a family with half a dozen children or more, trying to reach him. He was relieved to see that she was smiling. She no longer appeared quite so frightened and weary as she had only moments before. He flung out his arm above the heads of the little ones between them, grasping her hand and pulling her to him.

Immediately, the twins began hammering her with excited questions about the ship. Baby Emma squirmed in Conn's arms and reached for Vangie. Conn handed her over to her mother, then moved in front of them, using his large body as both shield and guide to propel his family through the crowd.

When a voice shrieked his name from behind, Conn whipped around to see who in this herd of strangers would be calling out to him. To his amazement, he saw the busker girl—Renny Magee—a fist stabbing the air as she snaked her way through the crowd, obviously intent on reaching him.

"Conn MacGovern! Ho! Conn MacGovern!"

Vangie looked at Conn, then turned to watch the girl.

Conn stood staring, ignoring the people nearest him who had begun to grumble at the MacGoverns for impeding their movement. Indeed, his entire family had stopped where they were, gaping in bewilderment as a red-faced Renny Magee slipped almost effortlessly through the crowd and practically threw herself directly in front of Conn.

"What in heaven do you think you're doing, girl?"

Her cap was askew, both it and the shaggy hair beneath streaming with the rain, but she seemed completely indifferent to her wretched condition. Instead, she stood there, grinning at him as if she were altogether witless.

"Move along, man," a skinny, whiskered fellow complained, shoving Conn in his impatience to board the ship. "You're blocking the way, you are."

Conn glared at him, stepped aside a bit, then turned back to Renny. "What's this about, girl?"

The busker girl looked from him to Vangie and the children, then thrust out her hand, in which she held a watch.

His watch!

Instinctively, Conn reached inside his coat, but of course the watch was not there. It was cupped in the none-too-clean palm of Renny Magee.

"What are you doing with my *watch?*"

He fairly shouted at her—an accusation, not a question. It seemed she wasn't about to meet his gaze, but instead locked her eyes on something just over his shoulder. "You dropped it," she said, the rough-edged voice grating like a file along Conn's backbone.

He stared at her for a long moment. "I think not," he bit out. "You *stole* it; isn't that so, you little hoaxer? You stole my watch, and after my saving your neck at that!"

Renny Magee curled her lip and shot back, "Think what you like, MacGovern! But if I stole it as you say, then why did I run all this way to return it?"

Conn reached for the watch. She slapped it into his hand,

and he stood eyeing her with disgust and no small measure of disappointment. "So Nan Sweeney was telling the truth after all. You *are* a thief! Have you no shame, girl?"

The pointed chin snapped up. "That old witch was *not* telling the truth!" Her face darkened. "Not . . . entirely, that is," she stammered. "It was as I said—I took from her only what was owed to me."

Conn lowered his head until he was in her face. "Well, my watch was not owing to you, you little guttersnipe! And you won't get by with it this time—I'll set the law on you for this."

He was surprised when Vangie put a hand to his arm to restrain him. "Conn—"

Still furious with the busker girl—and with himself for playing the fool to her chicanery—Conn ignored the note of caution in his wife's tone. "I'll handle this," he muttered.

But when he glanced around, he saw that his entire family was watching him and the girl: Aidan with his customary glare, Nell Grace and the twins with patent astonishment, and Vangie with a frown of disapproval. He also noticed that the other passengers had left them behind and were well on their way up the gangplank, while he stood listening to the lies of a sorry little trickster.

Still, he could not ignore the girl's flagrant thievery. The watch was the only thing of any value he had ever owned, and the Lord knew it would more than likely have to be sold when they reached America, to help them survive until he found work.

It was a fine piece, bestowed upon his Uncle Ryan for saving a landlord's daughter from certain death by drowning in an icy stream. Their uncle had left it to Conn's older brother, Taber, who had passed it on to Conn just before entering the priesthood.

Conn fancied the timepiece, had guarded it with his life.

The time might well come when it was the only thing that stood between his family and starvation. And now this scrawny, dirty-faced busker girl had pocketed it for herself.

"Conn—"

He turned, impatient with his wife's continued interference.

"She's only a girl," Vangie said quietly. "And isn't she returning the watch? There's no real harm done, after all. Besides," she added, "there's nothing to do for it now, except to thank her."

"*Thank* her—" Conn gaped at his wife, who lifted her chin a little and met his gaze straight on.

"She didn't *have* to bring it back," Vangie pointed out. "You probably wouldn't even have noticed it was gone until long after we set sail."

Speechless Conn continued to stare at her, ignoring the prickle of truth in her words.

"Conn, we have to go." Vangie inclined her head toward the ship. "'Tis not as if they'll wait for us."

He looked from his wife to Renny Magee. "Why would you do such a disgraceful thing, girl?"

For the first time, she seemed to show some sign of remorse. "I didn't *steal* it, MacGovern! I didn't!" she blurted out. "You dropped it, and that's the truth. I might have *thought* of keeping it—but only for a shake, I swear it!" The pale blue eyes met Conn's directly. "I brought it back, now didn't I?"

Conn studied her a few seconds more. "And am I supposed to reward your *honesty*, then?" he shot back.

The girl seemed to be deliberating as to whether she should say more. She shifted her weight from one foot to the other, lifted a hand to straighten her sodden cap a bit. She opened her mouth as if to speak, then seemed to think better of it.

Finally she found her voice. "I was thinking that if . . . if I did you a good turn, perhaps you'd allow me to go along with you and your family." She stopped, gulped in a deep breath, and added, "To America."

Conn reared back in astonishment. "Are you demented entirely, girl? Why on earth would you think such a thing?"

Her mouth tightened, but she didn't look away. "I'm wild to go, MacGovern. 'Tis all I've ever wanted to do, don't you see? But now there's more to it than that. If I stay in Dublin City, sooner or later Nan Sweeney will set her bullyboys on me, and they won't finish until they pound me to a puddle in the street! No one crosses old Nan without paying the piper."

She stopped and caught a breath, then went on. "I thought—if I returned your watch, I could convince you to take me with you. I'd work for you however long it took to pay my way, I would! I'm fit, and I'm as strong as any lad, I promise you."

"You are *daft*, is what you are!" Conn threw back at her. "As if I'd subject my family to the likes of you!"

Vangie gave his arm a hard yank, and when she spoke this time, her tone was much sharper than before. "Stop it, Conn! The girl says she's telling the truth, and you have your watch. Now let it be."

In truth, Conn had begun to feel a bit shamed by the way he had harangued the girl. But she *was* a thief, despite what was almost certainly an uncommon attack of conscience, not to mention her outrageous scheme to wangle her way aboard ship with his help.

Well, she could forget *that* idea. He might look the great *amadan*, but the little trickster would learn soon enough that he was not the dolt she apparently took him to be.

But what could have gotten into Vangie, to be rebuking him in front of the children so? It seemed for all the world that she was taking the little reprobate's side against him!

He shot the girl one more look of contempt, then swiped

his hands in a gesture of disgust. "I have no more to say to you. You know what you did, and that's the end of it."

He would have walked away, but Vangie restrained him with a firm hand on his arm.

—

In spite of the girl's disreputable appearance—and even taking into account her thievery—Vangie couldn't help but feel sorry for her. The child's ridiculous clothes were in tatters, her hair looked a fright, and she was soaked all through. She also appeared to be none too clean. And that terrible fierce look of pain in her eyes when Conn had lashed out at her—

But what caught at Vangie's heart more than anything else was the girl's seemingly feverish desperation to go to America. Was she alone altogether, then, that she would take up so casually with a family of strangers—with a man she had robbed, or at least thought of robbing—simply to get away?

For an instant, Vangie almost felt guilty at her own reluctance to leave when the girl in front of her would obviously have traded places in an instant.

It occurred to her that the busker girl might be in trouble with the law. Perhaps the reason she was so intent on getting out of Ireland was because a gaol cell was waiting for her if she stayed.

And yet, she didn't seem a bad sort. Sure, this was no hardened felon.

"Please, MacGovern," the girl pressed again. "You won't be sorry for taking me—"

"Now you listen to me, girl!"

Conn had gone red in the face, and he was jabbing a finger at the girl as he began to revile her again—a sure sign that he was about to lose control of that wicked temper of his.

"Even if I were mad enough to pay any heed to your fool-ishness," he said, his words cutting the air like a blade, "which I assure you I am not, I couldn't take you with us! It takes money to go to America, or are you so thick-skulled you didn't know that?"

The girl paled, and Vangie was sure she was close to tears, but she stood her ground, not quite looking at Conn but clearly not about to let him cower her either. Vangie couldn't help but admire the youngster's grit.

"What, are you thinking the captain will simply tip his hat to your highness and welcome you aboard out of the goodness of his heart?" Conn ranted on. "You have to *pay* for passage, don't you know? I've sold near everything but the shirt off my back as it is, just to take my family across! I haven't the means to secure passage for a lying little thief like yourself as well!"

—

Vangie gripped his arm, obviously hoping to silence him. But it was not her touch that shamed him. It was Renny Magee herself, lifting her thin face to reveal an utterly stricken look. Conn felt a rush of self-reproach over his harshness with the girl.

Even so, there was no chance to make amends. Aidan chose that moment to step up and insinuate himself between Conn and the busker girl.

Nothing could have prepared Conn for what followed.

"Give the girl my ticket, Da," his son said quietly.

Conn froze, staring at his son without comprehension. "What—"

The boy's lean face was that of a stranger, hard and cold and openly defiant. "Give her my ticket."

Conn clenched his fists, bracing himself against the pain

roaring up the back of his skull as disbelief clashed with the rage already boiling inside him.

"Aye," Aidan said, his tone quiet but edged with challenge, "I mean what I say, and you know I do. She can have my passage, for I will not be using it."

The Parting

WHAT BRINGS DEATH TO ONE
BRINGS LIFE TO ANOTHER.

IRISH PROVERB

Aidan's low, even voice startled Vangie into silence.

Conn, obviously as stunned as she, stood as rigid as a rock, watching Aidan as the boy stepped up to him.

Without so much as a glance at the busker girl, Aidan faced his father. "Didn't I tell you from the first I wasn't going, Da? I only came with you today to help with the little ones and say good-bye."

"I'll not be listening to this!" Conn exploded, his features contorted with anger and incredulity.

"And isn't that just like you?" Aidan said, his voice still chillingly quiet. "You *never* listen. But this time you need to hear me, Da. I am *not* going with you. So if this girl wants to go, then she might just as well use my passage."

A terrible heaviness lodged in Vangie's chest, a weight so crushing it stole her breath away. Her mind flashed through scenes from the past nineteen years: Her infant son snuggled against her breast. Conn lifting the laughing boy over his head, swinging him about as if the two of them could sprout wings and fly. Aidan's tenth birthday, in better days, with the family gathered around him.

No. For the love of God, no! He couldn't mean to leave them now, to stay behind in Ireland while they traveled to America. They would lose him forever, never see him again in this life.

She desperately wanted to deny it, to shut her eyes to the truth she saw in her eldest son's face, to open them again to find that it had all been a terrible misunderstanding. But she knew. With a sick certainty, she knew that Aidan had set his mind to this, and there would be no changing it.

He *had* told them he would not go, told them repeatedly. And just as repeatedly, Conn had refused to listen.

And what about herself? She had been desperate to believe Conn when he insisted that the boy was simply talking to the wind, that he would never stay behind and watch his entire family set out without him. Hadn't she turned a deaf ear to her son as well?

Now, however, as she stood watching the boy challenge his father, she admitted to herself that she had never been quite convinced. Unlike Conn, who simply could not believe that in the end Aidan would actually defy him, Vangie had merely suppressed her fear that he might do exactly that. Perhaps if she had faced the inevitable from the beginning, then she would be better able to bear the pain now ripping through her.

She looked at her son and, as was so often the case, saw a younger Conn.

Indeed, the boy could have *been* Conn twenty years ago.

They were almost the same height, and although Aidan was the more slender of the two, he was already showing signs that in a few years he would grow as sturdy and hard-muscled as his father. He had the same sun-burnished copper hair, the same stubborn chin. The same fire in his eyes. The same pride: the fierce, hardheaded, at times irrational pride that clearly marked him as the son of Conn MacGovern.

God in heaven, how can I bear this?

She would surely go mad. And Conn—

Merciful Lord, it might destroy Conn entirely!

Quickly, she handed the baby to Nell Grace, then laid a hand on her son's arm. "Aidan—"

He turned to look at her, his expression going soft and regretful. "I'm sorry, Mother. Truly, I am. But I told you. I told you and him both. I can't go. 'Tis not for me."

"You young *fool!*" Conn shouted at him. "Do you have any idea at all what you're throwing away? You would actually stay in Ireland to starve while your entire family goes off without you? *Think*, boy! Your passage is paid! Do you really mean to throw away the only ticket to freedom you may ever have?"

"I don't call it freedom for a man to desert his country!" Aidan returned. "And I won't be throwing away my ticket, unless you're too stubborn to make use of it." He gestured toward the busker girl. "She wants to go with you. I don't. Take her."

"Do you really expect me to hand over your passage to *her?*" Conn flung an arm out toward Renny Magee, nearly striking the girl as he did so. "What, I'm to take a common little thief to America in place of my own *son?*"

He took a step toward Aidan, his face murderous. "You are *going*, do you hear me, boy? You will go with us if I have to pound you senseless and *throw* you onto that ship!"

Aidan's eyes went hard, and Vangie saw him knot his fists,

but he never wavered. "I warn you, Da. Don't lay a hand on me! *Don't.*"

The ship's whistle pierced through the pouring rain. There was no time left to them now. No more time for talk, no time to beg or try to reason with them. If they didn't go aboard soon, none of them would be leaving Ireland this day.

But it mattered little how much time they had. Conn and Aidan would simply go on blasting each other with the pent-up fury and frustration that had been seething between them for weeks. And in the end nothing would change. There would only be more pain.

Conn lunged toward Aidan, who in turn gave his father a hard shove backward.

"No!" Vangie shouted, throwing herself between them. "No, Conn! You'll not do this. Aidan—stop it! Both of you, stop!"

They looked at her, then backed off—but only a little—as they stood glaring at each other.

"Conn," Vangie said, her voice trembling, "he *did* try to tell us. He said he wouldn't go. We didn't listen. We didn't *want* to listen!"

But even as she tried to defend her son, Vangie felt her heart begin to shatter.

She turned to Aidan. "I can't believe you mean to do this! Can you actually turn your back and walk away from us, son? From me? From your father, your sisters and brothers? The Lord knows when we'll see one another again, if ever! Aidan, *think!* Think what this will mean—to all of us!"

"I have thought about it, Mother." His voice gentled as he took Vangie's hand. "And, of course, I'll miss you. You know I will. But I'm not a boy anymore, can't you see? I'm a man grown, and I've a life of my own to live, without Da telling me how to live it—or where. And I don't choose to live my life in *America!*"

He fairly spat the word, as if the very taste of it would poison his mouth.

By now Aidan's face was a mask of barely controlled fury. "Either you give my passage to the busker girl or else toss it into the Atlantic," he grated out. "I don't *care* what you do with it, but I'll not be using it. If the day ever comes when I change my mind, I'll pay my own way across. But this is not that day."

Conn stood, shaking with scarcely restrained rage, as Aidan embraced the others, first Vangie, then Nell Grace, who by now was weeping openly. He kissed both her and Baby Emma on the tops of their heads before leaning down to the twins.

Vangie thought she would surely strangle on her grief as she watched him say good-bye to his little brothers.

"Be men for our mother, Seamus. Sean," he said, using their Irish names as he almost always did, "she will need you to be fine, good lads."

The two boys, similar in appearance though not quite identical, gazed up at their older brother with solemn, freckled faces. Johnny—Sean—whose hair was more golden than the copper fire of his father and two brothers—was clearly about to burst into tears, while James—Seamus—was already weeping. Even so, each of them managed to shake Aidan's hand.

And then the lad straightened and again faced his father.

Vangie thought she would not survive the pain that knifed through her as she watched her son and her husband stand there staring at each other in unforgiving silence. In their pride and hotheaded stubbornness, they were so much alike, though neither would ever admit to it.

"Conn—*do* something!" she cried.

But he merely turned away, his face a mask of stone.

A swell of despair overcame Vangie, and she closed her eyes, unwilling to watch this final, heartless farewell between her husband and her son. When she again opened her eyes, Aidan had turned and was walking away, without so much as another word or a backward glance.

In that moment, a ray of light died somewhere in Vangie: the light that had been born with her eldest child, her darling boy. In its place remained only a cold, suffocating darkness, and she wondered how long it would take before it swallowed her whole.

Then she looked at Conn and realized with dreadful clarity that a light had gone out in her husband as well. It struck her that Conn's suffering might actually be more grievous than her own, for the bond between a man and his son was a fierce tie, more than blood and birthright, more than name and honor. A man saw in his son his own hopes, his dreams—his future. When Aidan turned his back on them this day, he not only rejected his father's authority, but he renounced Conn's dreams and brightest hopes as well.

Her head thundered as she watched her son walk away, his back erect, his shoulders squared. The ship's whistle sounded again. Her glance went to the busker girl for an instant. Then, ignoring the shrieking agony inside her, she made a decision.

"Conn," she choked out, "there is nothing left to do about Aidan. We can only pray that in time he will come to his senses and join us. But there *is* something we can do for that frightened child." She motioned toward the busker girl. "I think we should take her with us."

"For the love of heaven, woman!" he began to rail at her. "That *frightened child* stole my watch. Have you forgotten that? She's a *thief,* and who knows what else!"

"You don't know but what you *did* drop the watch, just as she said, Conn. All you know is that the girl *returned* it." Vangie gripped his thickly muscled forearm even harder. "And she *is* frightened! Look at her! Oh, Conn, listen to me—please! It's *wrong* to waste Aidan's passage, I tell you, wrong not to help that girl when we have it in our means to do so. Let her come with us."

He stared at her in open disbelief.

"I don't mean to simply give her the ticket for nothing," Vangie pressed. "We will see that she earns her way. She will work for the price of her passage."

He went on studying her, his eyes still brimming with bewildered anger. "You'd actually do this? You'd let a gutter-snipe like her use our son's passage?"

Anger flared up in Vangie. "Our son doesn't *want* his passage! The girl does. She's begging to go. I say we take her. Let *something* worthwhile come of all this!"

"You mean it," he said, looking at her as if he scarcely knew her. "You actually mean to help the little thief."

"I do," Vangie said evenly. "What can be the harm?"

He let out an ugly laugh. "Oh, no harm, I'm sure, so long as she doesn't murder us all in our beds!"

"She's a child," Vangie shot back. "And perhaps a thief. But not a murderer, I think. She's just a poor girl looking for a future. Looking for some hope. We have it in our power to give her that hope, and I believe our Lord would have us do just that."

She pressed his arm, refusing to let him turn away from her. "I want to do this, Conn. We *need* to do this."

Conn's eyes brimmed with resentment as he glanced from Vangie to the girl. "What does it matter?" he said, giving a shrug. "Do as you like. Our son has gone mad, so why shouldn't the rest of us follow after?"

His tone was laced with bitterness as he went on. "But don't be expecting any thanks from the likes of her. And you would do well to forget any notion of her earning her way, I'll wager.

She will no more step foot on deck before she disappears to work her mischief elsewhere; you wait and see if she doesn't."

"You may be right," Vangie said, too heartsick and exhausted to argue any further with him. "But at least we will have done what we could to help her. 'Tis not for us to take responsibility for what she does with that help. That's for our Lord to deal with."

He pulled his mouth into a hard line. "'Tis not for me to take any responsibility for her at all. This is your idea, not mine, Vangie. I will have no part in it."

—

A chant played over and over in Renny Magee's mind as she watched the two of them, MacGovern and his woman. *Let him say yes . . . let him say yes . . .*

Renny had reached the point where she believed her entire future might very well hang on what the MacGoverns decided. Despite the fact that she would have preferred to put Nan Sweeney completely out of her mind, she had not exaggerated her present situation. In truth, no one crossed old Nan and got away free. Nan would never let up until she had her justice. And old Nan's kind of justice was an ugly thing, as everyone knew. She was a terrible woman entirely.

This Mrs. MacGovern, now, she was a different sort, that much was clear. A good woman, Renny could tell. A tall, fine-looking woman with skin of rich cream and a grand head of hair the color of the bay at sunset. She had kind eyes, she did, but the way she was squaring off with her thickheaded husband gave Renny high hopes that for all her kindness, she was more than a match for the man.

Even so, Renny cautioned herself not to be too hopeful. MacGovern had no reason to go easy on her, not with the bad business of the watch and all.

Just then, she saw them both glance in her direction. Renny held her breath as the woman turned and started toward her.

———

Vangie stood studying the thin-faced busker girl for a moment. "What's your name, child?"

"Renny Magee, missus."

"And how old are you, Renny?"

The girl shrugged. "Don't know, missus. I never knew my people, you see, so nobody ever told me how old I was."

Vangie looked at her more closely. "You're an orphan, then?"

"I am."

Vangie speculated that the girl was probably close on eleven or twelve, perhaps even older, though she was small and wretchedly thin for her age.

She drew a long breath, praying she was not making a terrible mistake. "Very well, then. My husband has agreed to allow you the use of our son's passage. But"—she lifted a hand to silence the girl's attempt to speak—"*but* you will not bring so much as a scrap of trouble or dishonor on yourself or upon this family for the duration of the crossing. My son's ticket is yours to use, but as of this moment you will conduct yourself with Christian decency, or my husband will have you put off the ship to your own destruction. Your hands will touch no other pockets except your own, and you will be obedient to what either my husband or I instruct you to do. Do you understand what I am saying, Renny Magee?"

The girl stared, her odd, pale blue eyes unnervingly steady, although Vangie sensed that she was restraining herself only with great effort. With one hand then, Renny Magee removed the sodden cap from her head and bowed slightly, as if in deference to a great lady. "I understand, missus," she said in a voice that was noticeably shaky. "And I'll not be a bit of trouble to you, my hand on it."

Vangie glanced at Conn and saw her own weary resignation reflected in his face. She would have no help from him; that much was plain.

She faced the girl again, injecting a note of sternness into her voice. "Since you will be traveling with us, you will take on your share of the work, is that understood? The children will have to be looked after. And there will be laundry—though I don't know as yet just how we will manage it. And mending. There is always mending with the children. Do you know how to sew, girl?" she asked abruptly, knowing the answer before she ever voiced the question.

Renny Magee glanced away. "I've never exactly tried my hand at it. But I can learn," she added hurriedly, looking back at Vangie. "I can learn most anything I set my mind to, and that's the truth."

"And learn you will. You will not be idle, miss."

Again the girl moved as if to speak—and again Vangie silenced her with a shake of her head. "When we reach America, you will continue to work for us no less than six months unless Mr. MacGovern says you may leave us sooner. Is that clear?"

"You've only to tell me what you want done, and I'll do it," said Renny Magee, now cracking a grin that revealed a pronounced space between her two front teeth. "For as long as you want."

Vangie was surprised to realize that the girl was almost fair when she smiled. Her piquant features took on a certain pertness that was somehow agreeable. She actually possessed a kind of impish charm in spite of her unkempt appearance.

But there was no more time for questions or a closer examination of Renny Magee. The ship gave a final warning blast, and a crew member shouted at them to get aboard or be left behind.

As they hurried up the gangplank, Conn in front, Renny Magee just behind him, Vangie turned to look back, irrationally hoping that perhaps Aidan might have lingered nearby to watch them go. But there was no glimpse of him. He was gone, and now they were leaving, too.

As the crew herded them belowdecks, Vangie struggled to regain the memory of what she had experienced in the harbor. They were not alone, she reminded herself. Nor was Aidan.

Perhaps not. But being alone wasn't the same as being lonely, and Vangie knew that without her son, her firstborn, she would always be lonely. Even in the midst of her family, she would be lonely.

She already was.

SIXTEEN

A Man and His Music

In his music, consecrated,
The Divine is celebrated,
As his seeking heart embraces
Heaven's high and holy places.

Anonymous

New York City

The theater shimmered with gaslight and candle glow, dimmed only by the reflection of the ladies' jewels and glistening gowns. A palpable sense of excitement hung over the concert hall, an anticipation so keen it could be felt above the shuffling and conversation of the audience.

"Papa will be coming out any minute now, Aunt Susanna! And he'll be so handsome! Wait and see!"

Seated between Caterina and Rosa Navaro in Michael's private box, Susanna smiled at her niece. She, too, was excited about the opening of tonight's concert. This would be her first time to attend a performance by Michael's orchestra, but that was not the sole reason for her anticipation.

In Dublin, she had often attended the symphony with the Mahers, her former employers. Her last outing with them had been over a year ago, but until tonight, she had had little time to reflect on the lack of music in her life, or the emptiness that lack engendered in her soul. Now, awaiting the concert, she realized how very much she had missed the experience.

Indeed, there had been precious little time to reflect on anything since she'd arrived in New York. The days had been filled with the effort of settling into her new home and acclimating herself to the routine of the household.

She had determined early on that considerable adaptability was expected from everyone at Bantry Hill, even from those who lived on the periphery of Michael Emmanuel's life. If she had once envisioned her brother-in-law as a brooding recluse, spending his days in self-imposed seclusion while he labored over his music and massaged his inflated ego, it hadn't taken long to send those preconceptions packing.

In truth, she had seen very little of Michael during the weeks since her arrival. He had been in rehearsal, staying in the city almost every night, some days coming home only long enough to spend a few hours with Caterina before rushing off again.

Other than what she'd learned from Deirdre's letters, Susanna had been forced to glean the little she knew about the man from Rosa Navaro and Caterina. Her own contact with him had been sporadic and at times frustrating. Although he was invariably gracious and never failed to show a concern for her comfort and well-being, he was most often preoccupied, even more remote than he'd been the day she'd first arrived at Bantry Hill.

More perturbing still, he had yet to offer a full explanation of Deirdre's death. By now, Susanna was almost convinced that he was deliberately avoiding the subject.

If that was his tactic—and she was increasingly suspicious that it was—he would soon realize that she wouldn't be put off indefinitely. He had promised her answers, and she had every intention of getting them.

She was determined to know what had happened to Deirdre. It was true that they had never been close; actually, there had been times when she wasn't even sure she *liked* her older sister. Nevertheless, they *had* been sisters, and there would be no peace for her until she learned the truth about Deirdre's death.

She had already decided that if Michael persisted in his evasion, she would take her questions elsewhere, perhaps to Rosa Navaro. She had even thought about going to the authorities but didn't quite know how to begin. Perhaps when Michael saw that she was a fair match for his stubbornness, he would finally give in and tell her everything.

And if he didn't?

She would face that particular dilemma only if and when it became necessary.

⁓

The concert hall quieted. The lights dimmed as the crimson velvet curtains opened on the orchestra. Paul Santi, the concertmaster, rose with his violin and gave the other musicians the note of A, and dissonance reigned until all the instruments swelled to total agreement.

Then silence again descended, and Paul exited the stage.

"There he is! There's Papa!" Caterina tugged at Susanna's sleeve, then bounced forward on the edge of her seat.

Susanna looked from the excited child to the stage, where Paul Santi was escorting Michael to the podium. The collective hush that had fallen over the audience now gave way to an unrestrained burst of applause as Michael took his place at the conductor's dais.

She saw him touch the toe of his left foot to the metal strip he used as a marker. He acknowledged the audience's welcome with a small bow and the quick, youthful smile that never failed to catch Susanna unawares. She had caught only brief glimpses of that smile, yet every time she encountered the sudden, unexpected expression of boyishness and warmth, she felt the same stab of confusion she'd known at their first meeting.

As it happened, Michael's stage presence was even more unsettling than his smile. Up until now, Susanna had seen him in only weekend or informal attire—often in his shirt sleeves or a worn sweater, his dark hair carelessly tousled, his demeanor sometimes brisk, sometimes relaxed, but always distant. She had come to think of him as a very casual man in his preferences, not much concerned with appearances and seemingly more inclined toward the natural than the artificial.

But the man on stage this evening was anything but casual. In truth, he was downright resplendent. In black tails and vivid white linen, he had forgone the dark glasses. The black, shaggy hair had been brushed to some semblance of control, the dark beard neatly trimmed, and with his towering height and Tuscan bearing, he was positively regal.

Susanna's throat constricted as she knotted her hands in her lap, acknowledging to herself, albeit grudgingly, that perhaps it wasn't so difficult after all to understand how Deirdre might have been dazzled by this man.

"Didn't I tell you, Aunt Susanna? Isn't Papa handsome?"

Caterina's loud whisper brought Susanna's thoughts back to the present. With her niece's small hand clasped warmly in her own, she smiled, then turned her attention back to the stage.

As she watched, Michael turned to the orchestra and gave an almost undetectable tapping of the baton. Then, with an authoritative lift of his wide shoulders, he signaled the musi-cians, and the three majestic chords of the overture to Mozart's opera *The Magic Flute* sounded.

The orchestra followed this overture with another, Gluck's *Alceste*, an intense, surging work of great nobility and depth. Then, with the assistance of Paul Santi, Michael again exited the stage, to return after only a moment or two.

He bowed again, then lifted his baton, and the first notes of the introduction to Beethoven's Seventh Symphony ascended and filled the hall. Susanna loved the Seventh but had been somewhat surprised at Michael's choice for the major work of the evening. She would have expected him to opt for the better-known and more ambitious Fifth or even the monumental Ninth. The Seventh was a more impetuous, emotional work, at times lively and deceptively lighthearted, then building to a frenzied, almost volcanic explosion of energy and power. It was also one of the tortured composer's more controversial, less predictable symphonies.

Critics often sought to offer an analysis of the work, but Susanna shared Michael's recently voiced opinion that the Seventh went *beyond* explanation, that perhaps the fact that it could not be explained or analyzed was actually a fundamen-tal part of the work's appeal.

Now, watching him, it struck Susanna that the man on stage was quite possibly as unpredictable, as inscrutable, as the capricious symphony itself.

By the time the music reached the driving, marchlike second movement, Susanna had temporarily suspended her misgivings about her brother-in-law.

Indeed, she had almost lost sight of Michael and the orchestra as separate entities. The two had somehow become one, melding into a single mighty instrument of rhythm and motion and sound, sweeping the hall with a somber but heroic processional that made her pulse thunder and her spirit sing with the magnificence of it all.

"Is he using a score?" she whispered to Rosa Navaro, unable to comprehend how such a herculean work could possibly be transcribed to Braille.

The older woman offered her opera glasses to Susanna, saying, "Michael doesn't need a score. It's all here," she said, lightly tapping her own forehead, then her heart.

Incredible.

Susanna lifted the opera glasses to her eyes. Under the direction of a less brilliant conductor, the *Allegretto* could easily have become a funeral dirge, but Michael and his musicians had honed it to a persistent, exultant paean of praise.

She became aware that Caterina was gripping her hand more tightly, but when she looked, she saw that the child's gaze was riveted to the stage. The sight of the little girl so completely absorbed in the music gave Susanna an inordinate sense of pleasure, perhaps because it had been the same with her. She couldn't remember a time when music hadn't been an overwhelming, even spiritual experience for her.

Out of the corner of her eye, she noted that Rosa Navaro, to her left, was blinking furiously, as if trying to hold back tears of emotion. Indeed, many among the audience seemed to be fighting to keep their feelings in check as the orchestra unleashed the full force of Beethoven's colossal work.

She could see from Michael's profile that his eyes were closed, his face damp with perspiration. Susanna sensed that so absorbed was he in this bold epic of musical struggle and celebration that he was no longer a *conductor* of the music . . . he had in some incomprehensible way *become* the music.

As the insistent, driving pulse of the *Allegretto* finally gave way to the more exuberant *Presto*, a faint, collective sigh rose up from the audience. Susanna expelled a long breath to relieve her own tension; at the same time she felt Caterina relax the grip on her hand.

She could not help but be transfixed by the man at the podium. Not one of his movements was superfluous, from the slightest roll of the wrist to the powerful shuddering that seemed to run the length of his tall frame as he demanded—and received—the ultimate in musicianship from his orchestra.

There was no melodramatic posturing, no obvious air of self-aggrandizement or showmanship. Instead he appeared to be a man lifted out of himself, transported to a higher plane as he reached for some sublime but elusive splendor, some unseen touch of glory, while the music gathered force and became a power in and of itself.

By the time the orchestra had plunged into the *Finale*, an energized, abandoned outburst of power and exhilaration, Susanna felt certain that the entire audience, herself included, had been left breathless. Watching Michael, seeing the unmistakable signs of the intensity, the physical and emotional demands this particular work placed upon a conductor, she would not have been surprised had he collapsed before his final bow.

She leaped to her feet with the rest of the audience as a violent explosion of cheers and applause erupted. For an instant, Michael seemed to hesitate where he stood. When he turned to face the delirious crowd, he appeared almost stunned for a moment, as if he might be struggling to place his surroundings. But then the familiar winning smile broke forth, and he made a deep, sweeping bow of tribute to the orchestra.

He and Paul shook hands, and then at last he lifted his face toward the box and, smiling even wider, gave a deferential bow in their direction.

"Papa always bows to me at the end," Caterina said with obvious pride. Bouncing on the balls of her feet, she blew a kiss to the father who could not see her.

Flowers were flung wildly onto the stage, an enormous bouquet was presented, and the demand for an encore went up like a roar. Finally, Michael gave a consenting nod and turned back to the orchestra.

The piece they plunged into was new to Susanna. Her first thought was of a folk tune or an old world dance, but the music suddenly shifted to a medley that might have been martial in quality, had the rhythms not been so unrestrained. It ended with a hymnlike theme of great beauty, its final cadence sustained by the trumpets and horns and timpani. The entire work virtually shouted of something new, something distinctly and utterly American.

Again the audience rose to their feet in a wild ovation. Rosa Navaro touched Susanna's hand. "That was one of Michael's own compositions," she said. "Part of a larger work, a symphonic suite."

"Did you like it, Aunt Susanna?" Caterina piped in.

"It was wonderful," Susanna replied in all sincerity. "Your papa is a very gifted man."

The little girl's face dimpled in a wide smile as she gave a vigorous nod. "He's the cleverest man ever. And the best papa in the whole world, too!"

Susanna studied her niece for a moment. Caterina obviously adored her father. Might her own feelings of distrust be unfounded after all? Could a man capable of such transcending emotion and brilliant artistry—and such obvious devotion to his child—also be capable of the kind of treachery of which she had long suspected him . . . and of which Deirdre had accused him?

Michael returned to the stage for two more encores. As Paul Santi led him to the wings for the final time, he seemed to falter and even stumble. Instinctively, Susanna lifted a hand out as if to steady him.

She caught herself, but not before Caterina had seen. "It's all right, Aunt Susanna," the little girl said, her features solemn. "You mustn't worry about Papa. He trips sometimes, but he never falls. Even if he should, everyone will pretend not to notice. They wouldn't want to hurt Papa's feelings, you see."

Susanna looked at the girl, sensing the total conviction with which she spoke. For one bittersweet moment she could see a reflection of herself in her niece's eyes. Like Caterina, she had adored her own father, had placed in him the same total, unshakable confidence, and had held the same childlike belief that others naturally revered him as she did.

But *her* father had been entirely worthy of a daughter's faith and devotion. For the sake of the trusting little girl beside her, she fervently hoped the same could be said of Michael Emmanuel.

Yet, somewhere at the outer fringes of her mind a dark, familiar whisper taunted her with the possibility that Caterina's confidence might just possibly be misplaced.

—

It was late when they boarded the night ferry. Only Rosa Navaro accompanied Susanna and Caterina up the river. Michael had stayed in the city, in preparation for the following night's concert.

They had barely settled themselves when Caterina, lulled by

the darkness and the rocking of the boat, curled up next to Susanna and fell asleep.

In the dim glow of the lanterns, Rosa, seated across from them, smiled and nodded toward Caterina. "It seems that you have become very important to her."

Susanna smiled down at the sleeping little girl. "And she has become very important to me. She's really quite wonderful."

Rosa nodded. "The child needs you in her life, Susanna. It's good that the two of you have taken to each other so quickly."

Rosa's accent was mild, not nearly so pronounced as Michael's, but even in the soft shadows of the night, her strong, distinct features and snapping dark eyes were unmistakably Mediterranean. She lifted a hand to pat her hair, setting off a delicate chiming sound from the heavy gold bracelets encircling her wrist. Not for the first time, it occurred to Susanna that Rosa was really a very striking and exotic woman in appearance.

But it was Rosa Navaro's kindness she appreciated most. The opera diva had a warmth, a comfortable way about her that made her easy to be with and seemed to invite the confidence of others. Although Susanna hadn't forgotten some of the unpleasant things Deirdre had written about "that Navaro woman" in her letters, she chose to form her own conclusions—and she had decided to accept the friendship that Rosa seemed more than willing to offer.

"So, Susanna—did you enjoy the concert?"

Susanna blinked, hoping she hadn't been staring. "Oh, yes, very much."

Rosa nodded. "Nobody understands the Beethoven like Michael, I think. He is a brilliant musician."

Susanna studied her. "I wonder, though—doesn't he miss the opera? It must have been very difficult to give up such an illustrious career."

Rosa glanced away for a moment. "Michael finds his work with the orchestra fulfilling. He seems content."

"Did he stop performing because of his blindness?" Susanna knew she was pressing, but her curiosity overcame her customary reserve.

Rosa turned to look at her. "Only Michael could explain his reasons." She paused, then added, "I do know he wanted more time for his own music. Composing is very important to him."

"Yes . . . I'm sure it is."

Susanna deliberated over whether to raise any further questions. This woman was, after all, a good friend to Michael. She clearly doted on him, much as an older sister might. No doubt she would resent any attempt to pry into his personal life.

But what about *Deirdre's* life?

"Rosa?"

The older woman's expression had become somewhat guarded.

"Would you mind—I was hoping you might tell me more about Deirdre's accident. I've never really understood what, exactly, happened the night she died."

Rosa's normally open countenance now took on an unfamiliar, closed appearance. "But surely you already know about the accident, the buggy overturning—"

"Yes, I know about the buggy," Susanna said, catching a breath in an effort to curb her impatience. "What I *don't* know," she went on, choosing her words carefully, "is what Deirdre was *doing* in the buggy, at that time of night—in the middle of a thunderstorm."

The lantern light flickered, bathing Rosa's face in shadows as she turned her gaze downward. "You should ask Michael about this, Susanna."

"I *have* asked Michael about it—"

Caterina stirred just then, and Susanna broke off. But the child showed no sign of waking up.

"There never seems to be a . . . a *convenient* time for him to talk with me," Susanna continued. Even to her own ears, she sounded petulant, but Rosa's features remained unreadable. "He always insists it will have to wait until later."

"You must try to understand," Rosa replied. "No doubt it is still very difficult for Michael to speak of the accident. I think you will need to be patient, to wait."

"It seems to me that I *have* been patient," Susanna said, swallowing down her resentment. "I've been here for nearly a month now. How long should I have to wait?"

She realized her voice had risen, but although Caterina moved slightly, she slept on.

"Rosa," she tried again, "was my sister . . . happy? In the marriage, I mean?"

The older woman regarded Susanna with a studying look, then lifted a hand to smooth her hair. "How well did you know your sister, Susanna?"

Surprised by the question, Susanna stared at her. "I . . . we were sisters."

Rosa's gaze never wavered. "But there were a number of years between you. And you had been separated for some time, no?"

"Yes, that's true. But she *was* my sister. I cared about her. That's why I want—why I *need* to know what happened."

"These are not questions for me to answer, Susanna," Rosa replied, her tone firm but kind. "I'm sure Michael will explain. In time."

The ferry was docking now, and Caterina began to stir again. Susanna was surprised when Rosa reached to take her hand. "Give Michael time, Susanna. As difficult as it was for you to lose your sister, you must remember that he lost his wife."

In the carriage on the road home, they maintained a polite but meaningless exchange. Rosa's obvious reluctance to talk about Deirdre had only sharpened Susanna's suspicions. Where else could she go for the truth? She was beginning to feel as though she were locked outside a door to which there was no key—perhaps a door to which someone had deliberately *hidden* the key.

She stared out the carriage window into the thick darkness of the night, then glanced at the drowsy little girl snuggled against her. If only Caterina were older. Perhaps then she could learn the truth from her, the truth about what had really happened to her mother.

And *why* it had happened.

Suddenly weary, Susanna leaned her head back against the seat. She could feel Rosa's watchful gaze on her, but she closed her eyes and pretended to doze until she felt the carriage slow in its approach to the Navaro mansion.

Susanna straightened, careful not to rouse Caterina, who slept curled up like a kitten, her head in Susanna's lap. Rosa was smiling at both of them, but as she started to step from the carriage, she turned back and again reached to clasp Susanna's hand.

"Try to trust Michael, Susanna," she said, her dark eyes intent. "I'm sure that in his own time, he will tell you what you want to know. But if I may, I would caution you to be absolutely certain you want your questions answered."

She paused, still gripping Susanna's hand. "Sometimes," she said, "the answers to our questions are so painful to hear that we end up wishing we had never asked."

Then she was gone, leaving Susanna more disturbed than ever as she absently stroked Caterina's hair the rest of the way to Bantry Hill.

SEVENTEEN

Physicians in the City

YOUR GREATEST CHALLENGE WILL NOT

NECESSARILY BE THE ATTAINMENT

OF THE TITLE, "PHYSICIAN,"

BUT INSTEAD MAY WELL BE THE OVERCOMING

OF THE OPPOSITION—

ESPECIALLY THAT OF YOUR "MANLY" COLLEAGUES—

ONCE YOU ATTAIN THAT NOBLE TITLE.

IN A LETTER FROM DORSEY COLE TO HIS GRANDDAUGHTER, BETHANY

A cold autumn rain began early Monday morning, and by now Bethany Cole had begun to question her own common sense.

Although Uncle Marsh had offered a carriage, so far she had managed to get around the city just fine either by walking or using public transportation. Last night's change in the weather, however, reminded her that winter would be upon them in no time, and the walks she usually enjoyed would no longer be so pleasant.

Bethany enjoyed being self-sufficient—up to a point. She insisted on living in her own flat rather than rooming with her aunt and uncle, not only because she valued her privacy and wanted to fend for herself, but also because she was keenly aware of Aunt Mildred's feelings about "women who worked." Her aunt's resentment of Bethany's career included any attempt on the part of Uncle Marsh to make things a little easier for her. As far as Aunt Mildred was concerned, if Bethany wanted to be an "independent woman," she would be *completely* independent, with no assistance of any kind from her family.

Of course, Aunt Mildred was an incurable skinflint, so Bethany wouldn't have expected anything else.

Still, the Scriptures did counsel against pride. Being on her own was all well and good, but a day like this served to remind her that there might be such a thing as too *much* independence. At the moment, her umbrella was doing little to ward off the wind-driven rain, and by the time she reached the corner of Seventeenth and Fourth, her skirts were soggy, her boots were leaking, and she was chilled all through.

Without her small savings, she would have had to swallow her pride and accept a loan from her uncle—at least the loan of a carriage. Her inheritance from her grandparents was far more modest than Aunt Mildred probably thought, but at least she had something of her own to dip into, if necessary.

As she struggled to anchor the umbrella against the wind, Bethany scanned her surroundings as best she could. The neighborhood was reasonably pleasant and might even have been fashionable at one time. Now there were unmistakable signs that its more well-to-do residents had moved else-where—more than likely, farther north. Commercial establish-ments seemed to have taken over many of the spacious brick and stone houses.

Stormy as it was, the streets nevertheless teemed with Monday morning traffic, both pedestrian and carriage. A mix of workers and businessmen hurried along, darting in and out among the buggies and omnibuses, while the pungent smell of rain, sodden leaves, and horse droppings permeated the air.

Throughout the three-block walk from her apartment, Bethany had tried not to be too optimistic about Dr. Carmichael's invitation to stop by his office. It wasn't as if he had spoken of anything specific, after all. Still, she hoped she hadn't misunderstood him. He *had* alluded to the possibility that he might be able to help her in her efforts to set up a private practice, as well as in her ongoing struggle to obtain hospital privileges.

Hadn't he?

The hope of hospital privileges alone would have been enough to bring her calling long before now, but circumstances had intervened, and she'd found herself working almost around the clock for three weeks running. Influenza had drastically reduced the Infirmary's staff, and Bethany had more or less been living there, grabbing an hour's sleep whenever she could, eating whenever she thought of it.

In spite of the long hours of hard work and the lack of acceptance—or outright contempt—of many of her male colleagues, Bethany couldn't remember a time when she hadn't wanted to be a doctor. As a child, she had made patients of her baby dolls and every stray animal that happened to venture into the backyard. By the time she was in her teens, she had read all the way through her grandmother's household medical manual, going on to cajole her physician-grandfather into allowing her free access to *his* bookshelves. Within another year, she was pressing him to make her his assistant.

Wise man that he was, Dorsey Cole had gently but firmly

resisted his granddaughter's badgering. "Bethany, these days anyone can become a doctor. At least anyone can become a quack. But not just anyone can become a *good* doctor. If you really want to hang out a shingle alongside mine, then you must first equip yourself with a good education."

In his usual unhurried manner, he'd gone on to emphasize that a physician's knowledge should not be limited to diseases and injuries. "If you want to be a good doctor, you need a keen understanding of your patients' minds and hearts as well. To attain that kind of insight, you need to learn as much as possible about *people*, about life, and the world we live in."

Bethany adored the grandfather and grandmother who raised her after the train accident that killed her parents. She wanted to make them proud, and so, despite her youthful impatience, she had taken her grandfather's advice to heart. After the prerequisite education at Miss Haverhill's Feminine Academy—where she would have doubtless succumbed to total boredom had it not been for the good-humored mischief she and her companions foisted upon their roommates almost nightly—she left for the Women's Medical College of Pennsylvania.

She graduated first in her class. But as it happened, her grandfather had not lived long enough to take her into his practice. His health had been failing for some time even before she entered medical college, and shortly before graduation, he passed away. Not long after, her grandmother followed.

With both of them gone, Bethany couldn't imagine returning to the home where she'd grown up, much less taking over her grandfather's practice, which had diminished considerably with his poor health. Instead, she decided to settle in New York, not so much because her only surviving aunt and uncle lived here, but more because she believed the prospects for a woman physician might be greater in such a highly populated city. Almost immediately, she found a position at the New York Infirmary for Women and Children, allowing her to further expand her training under the founder, Dr. Elizabeth Blackwell, and other excellent women physicians, such as Dr. Mary Jacobi.

Even as both women encouraged Bethany in her efforts to establish her own practice and gain hospital privileges, they urged caution and patience. But Bethany had begun to realize that it was going to take something more than patience to achieve her goals here in New York. And that realization had driven her out on this wretchedly cold, wet morning. If there was any chance that Andrew Carmichael might be able—and willing—to help her, she was definitely going to listen to what he had to say.

As she approached the entrance of the aging brick building on Seventeenth Street, however, it occurred to her that after all this time the best she could probably hope for was that he hadn't completely forgotten about her by now.

—

Andrew Carmichael lifted a shoulder to catch the perspiration on his forehead, then tied off the last stitch at the corner of Charlie Duffy's left eye.

"You're very fortunate, Mr. Duffy," he said, adopting a stern tone. "You might have easily lost your eye, you know. That cut was way too close for comfort."

The old man nodded vigorously, his almost toothless grin breaking even wider. "Ah, but it was a grand fight, Doc! And wasn't that black-hearted scallywag more than a little surprised when I trounced him?"

Andrew suppressed a smile at his feisty patient. "Mr. Duffy, I'm not sure that a man of your years ought to be taking up a challenge, don't you see? Especially when it involves someone with a name like Dukes Neeson."

His patient cackled. "Call me Charlie, Doc! And don't you fret yourself a'tall about *me*. I can handle the likes of any knock-a-kneed Kerry-man! No doubt you're thinkin' I took the worst of it, but that would be because you ain't seen Dukes."

Andrew shook his head, no longer able to keep a straight face. "All the same, sir, the next time your bluff is called, I'd strongly suggest you walk away."

Charlie Duffy was sixty-five if he was a day and no bigger than an adolescent boy, but he clearly thought himself a man to be reckoned with. And perhaps he was at that, Andrew thought with wry amusement.

"No self-respecting Irisher ever walked away from an honest fight, Doc, no matter his years. Why, that good-for-nothing blackheart accused me of chatin', don't you know?"

The wizened little man sat up, and Andrew winced as dirty fingers traced a line over the wound he had just stitched.

"Nobody gets away with callin' Charlie Duffy a chate," his patient proclaimed, jutting out his chin. "And me who's never so much as dealt a false hand in me life."

Andrew helped the wiry little man off the table and shook his hand, taken aback by the surprising strength of the other's grip. "All the same, Mr. Duffy, in the future I hope you'll take care."

Charlie Duffy beamed up at Andrew as he touched his wound again. "You can count on it, Doc. And that's the truth."

He lifted a grimy paw in a kind of salute, then swaggered across the room.

———

Bethany Cole stepped into the waiting room, stopping just inside the door. Her first sense was one of confusion and disorder. Two long benches along the walls were lined with patients, leaving many others to stand. There were several children, some whimpering in their mother's arms, others scurrying back and forth across the room. None of the youngsters paid any heed to her as she entered, but their mothers took her measure with undisguised curiosity.

The odors of formaldehyde, alcohol, and other familiar chemicals hung over the room. There was also a strong indication that some little person was in serious need of a diaper change. A tall counter divided the modestly furnished waiting room from the reception area and examining doors. Bethany caught a glimpse of an unoccupied reception desk behind the counter. The windows were narrow and dusty, the wooden floor bare but reasonably clean. In the far corner, against an outside wall, an iron stove gave off an acrid odor of smoke, but a welcome warmth.

Bethany caught the sense of a much used, very *busy* room that suffered from a dearth of attention. A place where time, not necessarily money, accounted for the lack of neatness and attractive furnishings.

Clearly, she had come at a bad time. She chided herself for not thinking. First thing on Monday morning was definitely not the optimal hour to "drop by" a busy physician's office.

She felt a twinge of envy at the sight of the crowded waiting room. With all her heart, she longed to know both the burden and the blessing of an office filled to capacity with patients—*her* patients—waiting for her to employ her skills in their behalf. Out of habit, she had brought her medical case, and her fingers on the handle now itched to open it and go to work.

Annoyed with her own bad timing, she turned, intending to leave, then stopped when one of the surgery doors opened to reveal a spry looking little man with a black eye over which a row of neat stitches had been drawn. Right behind him stood Andrew Carmichael.

The physician saw her right away, his face registering surprise and, to Bethany's relief, recognition.

"Dr. Cole!"

The doctor's lab coat was wrinkled, the sleeves noticeably too short. A shock of dark hair fell over one eye. He appeared slightly rumpled and somewhat bemused. But at the moment, the only thing that mattered to Bethany was that he seemed genuinely pleased to see her.

He came the rest of the way into the waiting room, watching while his patient, a small, spindly-legged man, gave a jaunty wave and went out the door. Then he turned to Bethany. "Well, it's good to see you again, Dr. Cole. Nasty morning, though, isn't it?"

"I'm so sorry," Bethany burst out. "I can't believe I was foolish enough to come by on Monday morning. I wasn't thinking—"

"No, no, this is fine! I'd almost given up on your coming at all." A faint flush crept over his features, as if he'd suddenly realized he might have said too much.

Even on the day of the fire, when they'd first met, Bethany had sensed an unexpected awkwardness in this man. Not shyness, exactly, but something akin to it, and she'd wondered why that should be.

Andrew Carmichael looked to be in his mid to late thirties, and although he wasn't exactly a handsome man by contemporary standards, his long, clean-shaven face held a definite appeal and hinted of a strong, but pleasant character. According to the staff members at the Infirmary, he was held in high esteem, not only by his peers among New York's medical community, but by many of the missionary organizations throughout the city as well.

During the years since he'd settled in New York, the Scottish physician had apparently established himself as a brilliant and totally dedicated doctor, albeit somewhat unconventional in his lifestyle and treatment methods. Without exception, his name was spoken with the kind of respect and admiration usually reserved for much older, more elitist physicians.

He was also known to be a man with a heart for the under-privileged, taking the sort of unlikely risks most other physicians of his reputation would never have considered. It wasn't uncommon, her sources at the Infirmary told her, for Andrew Carmichael even to venture into the Five Points—the most abominable, dangerous slum area of the entire city—where he freely offered his skills to the poor wretches who threw themselves upon the mercy of the rare mission clinic in the district.

Bethany thought it peculiar that such a man would appear so unassuming and found herself liking him all the more for his lack of pretension.

She was also uncommonly pleased by the warmth of his greeting—he seemed utterly delighted to see her. She wasn't accustomed to others responding to her so spontaneously. She was aware of her natural reserve, especially with those outside her family or small circle of acquaintances. Admittedly, she tended to keep others at arm's length.

All the more reason she didn't want to impose. "Really," she began again, mindful by now of the unconcealed interest of the patients watching them, "I can see how busy you are. Why don't I come back another time?"

"Please don't leave." He came to stand a little closer to her. "You brought your case," he said, inclining his head toward her medical bag.

"I . . . yes. Force of habit, I suppose."

He nodded, studying her. "I . . . ah . . . don't suppose you'd like to lend a hand?" he said, giving a tip of his head to indicate the waiting patients.

Bethany stared at him. "You mean—*now?*"

His face creased in a smile that seemed to make the years drop away. "Of course, you'll have to use the dispensary," he said as if he had suggested the most natural thing imaginable. "Which is also the supply room. I've only one examining room, I'm afraid."

Bethany looked from Andrew Carmichael to the patients waiting for his attention: the restless infants and children, some clearly feverish; the elderly man and woman who sat holding hands at the end of the room; the little girl standing by the window, her right leg noticeably shorter than the left.

She turned back to him. "You're serious?"

He regarded her for a moment. "I've been told that you're an excellent physician, Dr. Cole," he said, his expression holding what looked to be both challenge and expectation. "Would you agree?"

Bethany tightened her grip on her medical case, cast another glance at the crowded waiting room, then faced Andrew Carmichael, who was watching her intently. "Perhaps you might want to judge that for yourself," she replied.

Another disarming smile broke across his features as he made a sweeping motion of the waiting room with one hand. "Then choose your patient, Dr. Cole, and follow me."

EIGHTEEN

REVIVAL IN BROOKLYN

THIS IS MY STORY, THIS IS MY SONG,
PRAISING MY SAVIOUR ALL THE DAY LONG.

FANNY CROSBY (FROM "BLESSED ASSURANCE")

October

Sergeant Frank Donovan couldn't think of anything he'd rather *not* be doing than attending a revival meeting, especially a revival meeting in Brooklyn.

To begin with, he didn't hold with revivals—not that he knew all that much about them, or needed to. Moreover, he didn't like Brooklyn. And he *did* know a good deal about Brooklyn. More than he wanted to.

He kept his peevishness to himself, however, as he led Miss Fanny Crosby down the aisle. Miss Fanny, of course, had no way of knowing that their encounter this evening was not mere chance. On this particular occasion, Eddie O'Malley had "accidentally" run into Miss Fanny in front of her Varick Street apartment and squired her to the ferry, where Frank—who "just happened to be going across to Brooklyn on police business"—escorted her the rest of the way to the revival.

Miss Fanny had become a special duty to the police force—and to the fire department, the railroad men, and a host of other city workers who had taken a serious interest in the well-being of the little lady who for years now had ministered to them all. No matter the weather, no matter how busy or exhausted she might happen to be—if indeed Miss Fanny even knew the meaning of the word *exhaustion*—she always had time for "her boys."

And they in turn looked after her safety, as well as they could without her knowing it. Frank doubted that, strong-willed and independent as she was, Miss Fanny would appreciate anyone fussing over her. No matter. It simply would not do to have the woman roaming about on her own in a crowd such as this, and her without the means to see what was going on right under her nose. So, with his captain's permission, he would be keeping an eye on her for the rest of the evening.

As far as Frank was concerned, if ever there was a saint walking, it was Fanny Crosby.

The woman seemed to be everywhere at once. Even the boys on the force were hard pressed to keep up with her. In spite of the fact that she couldn't see, Fanny Crosby was the liveliest, busiest woman Frank had ever met up with. If she wasn't scurrying about one of the Bowery missions, teaching a Bible study or telling stories to the children, she could be found visiting the sick at Bellevue or the orphan home or, more worrisome still, bustling here and there about Five Points—a leprous, disgraceful sore on the entire city of New York, and a place Frank Donovan would like to torch in its entirety.

Miss Fanny also was reputed to spend a great deal of time—

although Frank could not imagine where she *found* the time—writing her poems and hymns. It was said the woman had written so many hymns that even *she* had lost count, and Frank could believe it. Those who knew her best claimed she gave away to the poor just about everything she made from her writing. And from the looks of the neighborhood where she lived, that might well have been so.

She had a husband, Miss Fanny did—a blind musician named Alexander Van Alstine. But theirs did not seem a conventional marriage, not in Frank's estimation. Miss Fanny continued to use her maiden name, and, even though she and her husband shared an apartment, they were seldom seen together socially. Apparently, they went about what they called "the Lord's work" in different ways, in different places.

That was their affair. For his part, Frank had resigned himself to tonight's event, which was being held, of all places, at a skating rink. It seemed that none of New York's churches were large enough to hold the mobs that packed these Moody/Sankey meetings.

As he might have predicted, Miss Fanny insisted on sitting as far down front as possible. "I might not be able to see what's going on," she explained cheerfully as they continued down the aisle, "but at least I'll be able to hear everything."

Frank found it necessary to flash his badge a few times, and more than once he had to shoulder their way through the crowd, but at last he delivered his charge safely to the third row center. When he would have taken his leave, however, with the excuse that he should stay in the back to keep an eye on the crowd, Miss Fanny gripped his hand and insisted he sit down beside her.

"Now, Sergeant, you told me yourself that you've never had the experience of hearing Mr. Moody preach."

"And that's the truth, Miss Fanny, but—"

As if she hadn't heard, she went right on. "Well, it's high time we remedied that, it seems to me. You'll be blessed, I promise you, by Mr. Moody's inspired preaching and Mr. Sankey's wonderful music." She smiled. "Oh, I'm so glad we ran into each other tonight! This is the Lord's doing; I'm sure of it."

For a little woman, Fanny Crosby was powerful strong. Frank tried in vain to remove his hand from her grasp. "The thing is, Miss Fanny, I'm on duty tonight, you see, so I really ought to stay where I can watch what's going on."

"Nonsense! Brooklyn isn't your jurisdiction, but even if it were, I'm sure the other men could handle things just fine without you. There's not going to be any trouble here tonight," she assured him. "This is a *revival* meeting, Sergeant! These are God's people. It may be a skating rink, but tonight it's the house of the Lord. Now you just sit yourself right down here beside me and prepare for a blessing. My other friends will be along any moment, and I want you to meet them."

Frank had yet to figure out why he found it so difficult to refuse a middle-aged blind woman. True, it was a rare occurrence entirely when Miss Fanny requested a favor. But when she did, it was sure to be accompanied by that sweet-mother smile of hers, and Frank knew right then and there he might just as well give up and do whatever she asked.

So with a somewhat exaggerated sigh, he plunked himself down onto the seat beside her. "I'll stay long enough to meet your friends," he said, "but then I'll need to be up and about."

He kept his tone firm, all the while hoping neither George Tully nor that weasel-faced Nestor Dillman from the Brooklyn force would witness his humiliation. Frank Donovan, perched right down front in a revival meeting, where no doubt some Protestant preacher was about to whip the crowd of thousands into an amen-shouting, hellfire-and-brimstone frenzy. He scarcely believed it of himself.

With that thought, he slid a little lower in his seat.

At the same time, Miss Fanny gave him yet another bright smile and a motherly pat on the hand.

―

With Michael at her side, Susanna stood in the aisle about halfway toward the front of the building, trying to catch a glimpse of Miss Fanny Crosby, whom they were to join this evening.

She could not have been more surprised when Michael asked if she'd like to accompany him tonight. A revival meeting wasn't exactly the kind of event with which she would have associated her bewildering brother-in-law, although his invitation didn't surprise her quite as much as it might have a few weeks ago.

As time passed, however, she found it increasingly difficult to believe that Michael's faith was superficial or somehow contrived for the sake of appearances. At first, Susanna, who had been raised Protestant by both parents, had assumed that Michael and his household would be Catholic. But according to Rosa, Michael's upbringing had been somewhat untraditional. Apparently his father, a practicing Catholic, and his mother, a Protestant from Northern Ireland, had exposed their son to each of their beliefs. Over the years he had explored both faiths for himself, eventually deciding on Protestantism, although he obviously maintained a wide circle of acquaintances among the Catholic faith.

In all aspects, he appeared to live an exemplary life, and his friends and associates—at least the ones Susanna had met— seemed genuinely fond of him, as did his small household staff. Certainly, there was no question but what he was a good father to Caterina. He was openly affectionate with his daughter and generous almost to a fault. Indeed, Susanna thought he might on occasion indulge the child just a little too much. Still, he seemed inclined to be firm and consistent in matters of discipline.

All things considered, Susanna supposed she shouldn't have found it peculiar that he'd be interested in a revival meeting. In any event, she had been pleased no end when he invited her to come with him tonight. Not only was she looking forward to hearing Mr. Moody preach again, but she hoped to spend at least a few minutes with the Moodys and Skankeys after the meeting.

She turned to again scan the rows of seats behind them, then looked toward the front, wondering how they would ever find Miss Fanny in such a crowd. The building, which was actually a large skating rink, was packed with people, most already seated but many still milling about. There were few vacant seats to be seen, even though it was still early.

"Michael, perhaps you'd rather wait while I go and see—"

Just then, Susanna caught a glimpse of Miss Fanny's be-ribboned little hat and her dark glasses. "There she is. Close to the front. And it looks as though she's managed to save seats for us. This way," she said, taking Michael's arm to direct him.

Gus, the wolfhound, and Paul Santi had stayed at home tonight with Caterina, who was still recuperating from a nasty cold, so it was up to Susanna to serve as Michael's guide. She led him through the crowd as best she could, increasingly aware of how difficult this sort of situation must be for him. Even though he wore the dark glasses that should have alerted others to his disability, he still had to depend on someone—in this case, Susanna—to "part the waters" for him.

At first it had unnerved her a little, acting in this capacity. But Michael seemed inclined not to take himself—or his blindness—too seriously, and within minutes had managed to ease Susanna's anxiety by making light of her iron grip on his arm and her erratic stops and starts.

She was surprised to find Miss Fanny seated next to a uniformed policeman, whom she introduced as "Sergeant Donovan, my escort for the evening."

The policeman stood, his dark eyes flicking over Susanna, then darting to Michael with a sharp, inquisitive stare even as they shook hands. But their greetings were brief, for on the platform Mr. Sankey was already seating himself at a small, modest organ, ignoring the much larger and finer instrument nearby. Any chance for further conversation was lost when Mr. Moody entered the auditorium, along with an enormous choir which appeared to be at least two hundred voices strong.

Mr. Moody was just as Susanna remembered him: a burly, bearded figure of a man with extraordinarily kind eyes. He now walked directly to the platform and, with an upraised hand, led the assembly in prayer. Shortly afterward, Mr. Sankey began playing the organ and leading the crowd in the hymn "Hold the Fort."

From that moment on, the evening belonged to D. L. Moody, Ira Sankey, and the Lord.

—

Frank Donovan quickly excused himself to Miss Fanny as the man at the organ began to play and sing. He didn't go far, just off to the side at the end of their row.

Leaning against the wall as he listened, he had to admit that the music wasn't all that bad. The man Sankey had a big, rich voice and a way of delivering a song that was beginning to bore a hole in Frank's discomfort.

He glanced over at Miss Fanny who, as if she sensed him watching her, turned slightly and smiled in his direction. Frank sighed. It was hard to believe a saintly woman like herself would resort to such deviousness, but he couldn't shake the feeling that she'd known all along this evening's events weren't altogether accidental. Considering her subtle but ongoing concern for the state of his soul, she might well have engineered the whole evening herself, simply to get him under the roof with this pair of traveling evangelists.

He wouldn't put it past her. Not at all.

He shook his head, smiling to himself. He had a clear view of the blind man and the Fallon girl, whom Miss Fanny had introduced as Emmanuel's sister-in-law. Susanna Fallon was more than a little attractive, in a quiet sort of way. She was slender and fairly tall for a woman, with dark, soulful eyes and an interesting face, all framed by a tidy arrangement of heavy, chestnut hair shot with gold. She was young. *Too* young, Frank reminded himself ruefully. Obviously a churchgoer like the rest of the crowd, she held her songbook open, but she seemed to know the words mostly by heart as she sang along with everyone else.

Frank saw no resemblance to her deceased sister. Emmanuel's wife had been the bold, dramatic type who could snare a man at twenty paces and leave him babbling in the dust as she passed on by.

He would wager the girl was down on her luck. Her black dress appeared a bit worn, and there were no jewels. He wondered why her brother-in-law had brought her across. Perhaps with the intention of making her the next Mrs. Emmanuel?

Frank thought that unlikely, given her youth and decidedly unsophisticated appearance.

On the other hand, would a man who couldn't see be all that concerned with how a woman looked?

But Emmanuel's first wife had been a stunner, he remembered. He'd seen them together one night a few years back when he had duty on Broadway, near the opera house. They'd been surrounded by a crowd of admirers, but Frank had been close enough to get a good look at them and had asked Johnny Keenan who they were. At the time, he'd thought them a handsome pair, although the woman had appeared overly flashy, decked in her finery and enough jewels to light an entire city block. Still, she'd been a looker, no doubt about it.

Rumors had run rampant after the accident in which she died, but then rumors always ran rampant about theater people. Still, there *had* been talk of something strange. For one thing, you didn't find her kind driving her own buggy. She would have been *driven*. And taking off in the middle of the night during a fearsome thunderstorm—well, a number of the boyos had felt there was something wrong somewhere.

One thing was certain: the poor woman had met an ugly fate. Bernie Kehoe, one of the officers at the scene of the accident, told Frank that the buggy must have plunged a good twenty feet down before crashing against the rocks. According to Bernie, the Emmanuel woman had been thrown several feet from the buggy. Bernie said she'd looked for all the world like a busted doll when they found her.

Frank studied Emmanuel, wondering what a thing like that would do to a man. But his curiosity was quickly replaced by a surge of amazement as he saw Emmanuel suddenly throw back his head and begin to sing along with all the others.

Never in all his days had Frank Donovan heard anything like the sound that came out of that blind man's mouth. It was a wondrous thing entirely.

The familiar hesitation had begun to plague Michael as he stood listening to what had to be thousands of voices lifted in unrestrained praise. He seldom sang in public anymore, and even when he did, there was always that initial hesitancy, that springboard of indecision, until, no longer able to constrain himself, he gave in to a need which was, for him, as basic as food or drink.

Tonight's music had drawn him in with the force of a magnetic field. It was music that virtually *demanded* to be sung. The first time he had heard the new "gospel music," as some were calling it, he had been surprised by the strength of his own response. Far removed from the classical forms he knew and loved so well, it nevertheless held a unique appeal all its own. It was a music without class or ethnic distinctions, a music seemingly without sectarian ties or the confines of some of the older, more traditional structures. And yet in its rhythms and melodies, Michael could hear the wail and the cadence of the exile, the sorrowful lament and the plea for deliverance of the black slave, and the vigor, the ecstatic joy, and the call to glory of the camp meeting preacher.

This was a music evolved from diverse roots and mutual needs: a music of the common people who sought to worship, to praise, to plead, and to be one in the freedom of Christian love. Some called it heathenish. Others found it too personal, too self-centered. Many thought it nothing more than "message music," a trend that would never survive in the established church.

But Michael loved its lack of restraint and self-conscious convention, its spontaneity and free-flowing emotion, its inclusive embrace of the old and the new. This was the sound of *America*.

He had heard—only in part—a hint of this music years ago, when he had been but a boy, about to depart New York Harbor from his first visit to America. Something had happened to him that day, something too wondrous, too enormous for a child to grasp. Only years later had he finally come to accept that he had been given a kind of vision. Somehow he knew, without understanding how such a thing could be or why, that his Creator had given him a glimpse of a mighty, matchless music, a music that was as elusive as it was beautiful.

Ever since that day on the deck of the ship, he had been seeking the fulfillment of that early vision. And despite the years of frustrations and failures, the disappointments and defeats, he remained resolved to capture that divine spark, that it might ignite a flame and breathe its glory into his own work. It rang through his soul and echoed in his spirit, seeking—*demanding*—its own voice. This body of music would be his magnum opus, his greatest achievement—and the reason God had gifted him.

But for now, he was engulfed by the music at hand, a music that demanded to be sung.

And he simply could no longer resist its call.

—

". . . This is my story, this is my song . . ."

"Blessed Assurance"—written by Miss Fanny—was quickly becoming one of Susanna's favorite hymns. She loved to sing it, and she loved to hear it sung. But the unexpected sound of Michael's voice as he joined the other voices filling the meeting place quickly silenced her.

She could not help but turn and stare. Before tonight, Susanna had only heard about the "Voice of the Century," the voice that was said to fill an amphitheater and thrill even the most world-weary audiences.

She had read of Michael's triumphs, but with nothing more than the curiosity of any other music lover. And of course in the early weeks of Deirdre's and his courtship, her sister had

raved about her new suitor's "magnificent talent" and the un-
paralleled success that greeted him everywhere he performed.

But now, as she stood watching Michael, listening to him,
her very soul shaken by his incredible voice, Susanna realized
that neither the critics' reviews nor her sister's glowing accounts
had been adequate to convey the wonder, the uniqueness of his
extraordinary gift.

The truth was that mere words, no matter how eloquent or
impassioned, couldn't possibly begin to express the inconceiv-
able power—the *phenomenon*—of his singing. If God had
arranged to give *glory* a voice, it might have sounded very
much like the voice of Michael Emmanuel.

Vaguely, she was aware that others nearby had also stopped
singing, some turning to look. Even Miss Fanny, although she
didn't miss a note of her own, turned toward Michael with a
broad smile of obvious delight, squeezing Susanna's hand as if
to share the moment.

Michael, for his part, was absorbed by the music, completely
unaware of the attention he was getting.

Susanna thought that the experience of being in the midst
of thousands of voices raised in collective praise to their
Creator would have been enough by itself to overwhelm her.
But the sound of that glorious voice at her side as it lifted
and soared above the entire auditorium was nothing short of
breathtaking.

Transfixed, she could do nothing but stand and watch him.
With his head thrown back, he looked as if his every sense was
alive and ablaze with exultation.

Questions hurtled through her mind. With such a gift, how
could anything—*anything*—have driven him from the world
he had once conquered and made his own? What could possibly account for his turning away from the vast international

audiences who had adored him, practically *enshrined* him, above all other musicians of his time?

Even as the questions gripped her, Susanna felt a sudden sickening—and wholly unexpected—wrench of dismay for all this man had lost. She fought to shake off the emotion. How could she feel so strongly for this baffling brother-in-law who had yet to provide her with even the most cursory of explanations for her sister's death?

Besides, she was quite certain he would not welcome her sympathy. On the contrary, he would most likely find it anathema. From what she had seen of Michael Emmanuel so far, she would expect him to have no desire, no need, for *anyone's* sympathy. As for her natural feelings of compassion for the man, she told herself firmly that it would be far more appropriate to sympathize with him for the loss of his wife—and, of course, the loss of his vision—rather than the loss of his career, no matter how spectacular it might have been.

But what about Michael himself? Susanna studied him, again recognizing the look of some profound and unfathomable joy enlivening his features. And she wondered—which among his many devastating losses had been most grievous to *him?*

NINETEEN

DARK REMEMBRANCE

AND, EVEN YET, I DARE NOT LET IT LANGUISH,
DARE NOT INDULGE IN MEMORY'S RAPTUROUS
PAIN . . .

EMILY BRONTË

They visited with the Moodys and Sankeys for nearly half an hour, then took a late ferry. By the time they started for Bantry Hill, it was well after eleven. In the meantime, a cold wind had blown up, and with it a soaking rain.

In spite of the lateness of the hour, Susanna was still too exhilarated from the excitement of the evening to give in to fatigue. Michael sat in silence, his head resting against the back of the carriage seat, but Susanna knew he wasn't dozing.

She had become accustomed to his silences by now. There seemed to be no pattern to them, no predictability. They were just as likely to come in the midst of a crowded room as when they were alone together, which was rarely the case. He was never exactly rude. He would simply grow very still, occasionally for several minutes at a time. Although he seemed to be aware of his surroundings in a peripheral sense, it was obvious that for the most part he had distanced himself from those nearby.

Just then, the carriage bumped over a deep pit in the road, and he stirred. He straightened a little in the seat, stretching his arms out in front of him. "It's just as well that Caterina stayed behind tonight, no? She would be exhausted."

Susanna agreed, especially given the chill rain that had set in. "It's probably best that she stay in another day or two, I think, until her cold is completely gone."

Michael nodded, but said nothing more as he again leaned back and crossed his arms over his chest.

Just when Susanna had begun to think they would pass the rest of the drive in silence, the carriage took another jolt. She gave a sharp intake of breath. Michael uttered a sound of disgust and shook his head. "This road—*un disonore!* A disgrace."

Susanna looked at him, a coldness spreading over her. Did she only imagine that he winced, as if he'd realized that by mentioning the condition of the road he might have opened a door he would have preferred to leave closed?

"Michael—"

He cut her short. "I know," he said, giving a flick of his wrist. "We have not yet talked about the accident."

Susanna braced herself for another attempt on his part to evade the subject. "Don't you think it's time?" she ventured.

"*Sì,*" he said, surprising her. There was a long pause, then, "We will talk now, if you like."

His voice was low and tight, as if he were steeling himself for a dreaded ordeal. Susanna waited, still half expecting him to evade.

But apparently that wasn't his intention.

"We are very close to the site of the accident," he said quietly.

Susanna instinctively glanced out the window into the darkness. "How can you tell?"

His eyebrows lifted. "I know this road, of course. Every turn, every rise and fall of it. I know the exact place where it happened."

"What . . . *did* happen?" Susanna felt as if her throat were swollen shut. It was all she could do to force the words out.

As she waited, he drew in a long breath, leaned back, and turned his face slightly toward the carriage window. "It was raining," he said, his tone now more pensive than strained. "Even harder than tonight. A terrible storm. Thunder. Lightning. And wind—I remember the wind was particularly vicious. The road was already deeply rutted and slick from a week of much rain. In some places, large chunks had simply washed away."

He pressed a hand against his bearded face. "Deirdre drove the buggy herself," he went on, his voice thin. "She was not used to doing so. The police said she must have lost control in the turn." He paused, then added, "It's just ahead."

The hand against his face trembled slightly. "The buggy went over the side and crashed . . . down onto the rocks. Deirdre—"

He broke off, removed the dark glasses, and wiped a hand over his eyes as if caught up in the throes of some memory too excruciating to voice.

At that moment, they entered the deadly turn. Susanna held her breath until they came out of it. As if he, too, had been waiting until they passed the dreaded place, Michael dropped his hand away from his face and knotted it into a fist against the door panel.

"She was thrown from the buggy," he continued, his voice scarcely more than a murmur. "The police said she died instantly, from the impact of the fall."

A hot surge of nausea rose up in Susanna's throat. "But *why* was she alone?" she choked out. "You said she wasn't used to driving. What possessed her to do such a thing? And in the middle of the night, in such a storm—"

His expression was shuttered, revealing nothing of his feelings. He began to tap his fist against the door.

So long was his reply in coming that Susanna feared he meant not to answer at all. But finally he brought his hands to his knees as if to steady himself. "We had . . . an argument. A terrible argument."

For the life of her, Susanna couldn't imagine an argument so fierce that a woman would leave the house in a raging thunderstorm and drive off alone on a treacherous road.

As if he had read her thoughts, Michael hurried on. "Deirdre was very angry. I tried to reason with her, but—"

He stopped, making the slight turn of the wrist Susanna had come to recognize when he either couldn't find the words he wanted, or when no words seemed necessary.

"As I said, she was very angry." Again he straightened, replacing the dark glasses as he turned his face toward the window.

Susanna sat watching him, her mind racing. Obviously, raking up the memory of that awful night had been very difficult for him. And his explanation, as far as he'd taken it, seemed candid enough. Her instincts, however, told her he was leaving out as much as, if not more than, he'd divulged.

"But whatever were you arguing about that could have upset her so much?"

The moment the words escaped her lips, Susanna could

have bit her tongue. She had no right to ask such a question, and she knew it.

He turned toward her, one eyebrow lifting in obvious annoyance.

"I'm sorry," Susanna said quickly, wringing her hands in her lap. "That was—that's none of my business. But, Michael—I'm only trying to understand what happened, what drove Deirdre to do such a reckless thing."

The line of his mouth tightened. "Married couples sometimes argue, Susanna. That is not such an uncommon thing."

"But their arguments don't usually end up with one of them dead!"

In the flickering light from the carriage lantern, he seemed to pale. "You wanted to know what happened, and I've told you. As for what we argued about, that is something I'm not willing to discuss."

Susanna stared at him, her impatience heating to frustration. "Michael—I already know Deirdre was unhappy, that your marriage was far from perfect. It's no great shock to hear that you fought. I'm simply trying to understand what happened, but it seems you don't want me to know!"

She hurled the words at him like stones, but he seemed unmoved.

The wind shook the carriage. The rain was coming in torrents now, beating against the roof and battering the doors as if trying to gain entrance. There were repeated crashes of thunder. Lightning streaked along the tree branches bending and whipping in the wind.

Susanna shuddered, unable to shut out the thought of Deirdre abroad on such a night as this, undoubtedly frightened, perhaps even terrified, as she fled the stone monolith of Bantry Hill in an effort to escape—

Escape *what?* Susanna studied the dark-featured man across from her who had again retreated into silence, his features set, his head bent low. Clearly, he had said all he meant to say.

Anger renewed itself and slammed through her as she groped for words to launch an attack on his stubborn silence. But just then, she realized the carriage was slowing. She turned to look and saw that they had already passed through the gate and were almost at the front of the house.

Something didn't seem right. She stared, at first unable to determine what was amiss. Then she realized.

"The lights," she said, more to herself than to Michael.

"What do you mean?"

"The house—there's too much light. It looks as if every lamp—"

She broke off as a blazing bolt of lightning cast the entire front of the house in an eerie incandescence. At the same time, the carriage quaked, slammed by a brutal gust of wind.

"Caterina—" The word was little more than a whisper on his lips, but even before the carriage came to a complete halt, Michael's hand was on the door.

The moment they stopped, he was out of the carriage, not waiting for Dempsey, hesitating only long enough to help Susanna down.

Susanna grabbed his arm, Dempsey following behind them.

Wind drove the rain against them, lashing their skin and clothing. Michael stumbled in his haste, but Susanna steadied him, and they went on.

By the time they reached the top of the porch steps, Moira Dempsey stood framed in the doorway. "Thanks be to God!" she burst out at the sight of them. "I thought you'd never get here!"

Paul Santi brushed by the housekeeper and took Michael's arm to hurry them inside. "It's Cati, Michael," he said without preamble as they shook the rain off their hair and coats onto the floor of the vestibule. "She seemed all right earlier, but now—she's very ill."

Michael raked both hands through his wet hair. "But she was better. What happened?"

Paul met Susanna's eyes for just an instant, and the worry she saw there chilled her far more than the water dripping down her face and hair.

Before Paul could answer, Moira Dempsey burst out, "'Tis the lung fever; I'm sure of it!" The woman stood wringing her hands, her mouth trembling. "She started in with the cough not long after you left, and she's scarcely stopped since, God help her. There's a wicked fever on her. She's that sick, lad. I did all I know to do, but it hasn't helped."

Michael paled. Then, throwing off his wet coat, he started for the stairway.

TWENTY

A LONG NIGHT

TILL HER EYES SHINE,
'TIS NIGHT WITHIN MY HEART.

RICHARD BRINSLEY SHERIDAN

They heard the hard, hacking cough before they even reached the landing.

Upstairs, the wolfhound was lying outside the door to Caterina's bedroom. The minute he saw them, he whimpered and got to his feet. Absently, Michael put a hand to the dog's head, ordering him to stay as they entered the bedroom.

Caterina was awake, pillows propped behind her. "Papa—" Her attempted greeting set off a hard spasm of coughing.

Susanna went to one side of the bed, Michael to the other, where he scooped Caterina into his arms, holding her close and putting his cheek to her forehead.

"I'm sorry, Papa." The child's voice was hoarse and thick.

"Sorry?" Michael stroked her hair. "Why would you say such a thing?"

"I don't like to make you worry," Caterina managed between bouts of coughing.

Michael's composure seemed to slip for an instant as he rocked his daughter gently back and forth. "Papa isn't worried, *cara*. We will have Dr. Kent come and see to your cough. He will give you some medicine, and you will be well again. So why should I worry, eh?"

Caterina turned toward Susanna. "You look funny, Aunt Susanna," she said with a feeble smile. "You, too, Papa. Both of you are wet . . . like the ducks on the pond."

The few words seemed to exhaust her, and Michael drew her even closer as she was seized by yet another fit of coughing.

A knot settled in Susanna's chest at the familiar sound of that cough. She thought she recognized it.

She hoped she was wrong.

"Pauli?" Michael was saying. "Send Dempsey for Dr. Kent, please. Right away."

Paul started for the door, then suddenly turned back. "Michael—Dr. Kent is in hospital himself. Do you not remember? The stroke?"

Susanna saw Michael blanch. Caterina gasped and began to cough again, a loud, barking cough. Carefully, Michael lowered her to the bed and sat down beside her, stroking her forehead.

"She's so warm," he said, his voice low. "Too warm. We must have a doctor. But who?"

Paul gave a quick shrug of frustration. "We will have to find someone from the city."

Susanna's mind raced. A thought struck her, perhaps

implausible. But Michael was right. They had to have a doctor.

"Michael—"

He turned toward her.

"I think I know what this is. The cough—it sounds like croup. I'm almost certain."

He frowned. "Croup? What is that?"

"It sometimes follows a bad cold. One of the Maher twins was susceptible to it. I remember what Mrs. Maher used to do. You understand, we'll still need a doctor, but perhaps we can ease the cough a little and make her more comfortable for a time. I'll just need a few things—"

"Pauli," said Michael, "help Mrs. Dempsey collect whatever Susanna needs. We will never get a doctor this time of night, but tell Liam to plan to leave first thing in the morning for the city, as early as possible."

On impulse, Susanna laid a hand on his arm. "Actually, Michael, I think I know a doctor who *might* come tonight." She sent Paul to fetch the items she'd need, then told Michael about Dr. Carmichael, the physician she'd met during the crossing. "He seemed such a good man, and the Moodys spoke so highly of him. He might remember me. Perhaps if I were to send a note, he would come."

Michael's strained expression seemed to ease slightly. "Where would Dempsey find this man?"

Susanna had to think a moment. "Seventeenth Street . . . yes, that was it. He mentioned that he was considering moving from East Seventeenth Street to somewhere with more office space."

"But surely he would not be in his office at this time of night."

Susanna frowned. "But he lives upstairs, over the office! I remember, because Mrs. Moody was often fussing at him that he ought to live somewhere else, where his patients can't find him at all hours."

Michael nodded. "Write the note, please, Susanna."

―

Within minutes Dempsey appeared at the door to get the note for Dr. Carmichael. "I'll be leaving for the city now," the gruff Irishman announced. "Best not to wait. Even if the ferry's not running, there's always some fellow hanging about the dock, looking to make himself some extra money. I'll find a way."

"Grazie," Michael replied, his voice strained. "Pay whatever you must, Liam. Paul, get him some money; would you please?"

When Dempsey was gone, Susanna made a tent of one of the bedsheets and explained to both Caterina and Michael—who of course couldn't see for himself—what she intended to do. By the time Paul returned with the bucket of hot water and lime she'd sent for, she was ready to begin.

"Now, Caterina, I'm going to get inside the tent with you, darling, and we'll breathe in the steamy fumes from this bucket, the two of us. I think it will ease that nasty cough."

For the next half-hour, Michael kept the fire going in the fireplace and Paul added hot water to the bucket every few minutes. Susanna held Caterina's hand as the child inhaled the vapor from the lime water.

The steam finally helped to lessen the coughing spasms enough that Caterina fell into a fitful sleep. Paul helped Susanna dispose of the wet sheets, then went downstairs to fetch some tea for all of them, leaving the room quiet for the first time since their return.

Susanna got up and took a towel to her wet hair. She could see Michael in the mirror, seated close beside the bed, holding Caterina's hand. His face was haggard with worry and fatigue.

Whatever else she might think about her cryptic brother-in-law, Susanna had to admit that there was no doubting his love for his little girl. Clearly, Caterina was the heart of Michael's life, the most important part of his world, and she could not help but feel a measure of softening toward him when she watched him with his daughter.

She could tell that he was praying. Susanna added yet another of her own silent pleas to his. The little niece with the ready smile and merry nature had become infinitely precious to her in a very short time. She couldn't imagine a single day without Caterina. If the child didn't make it—

She shook off the thought, refusing to give in to her fear. Caterina would be all right. This was only croup, after all. A common illness among young children, and one from which they almost always recovered.

Almost always. Unless it turned out to be what the old women back home called "the bad croup."

"I'm very thankful you were here, Susanna," Michael said softly from across the room. "You knew just what to do."

Susanna became aware that she'd been staring into the mirror, the towel still swathed around her hair. "This may not last, Michael. You understand that it's only a temporary measure?"

He nodded. "*Sì*, but it is something." He was silent for a moment, then said, "You care deeply for Caterina." It was a statement of fact, not a question.

Susanna swallowed, still watching his reflection in the mirror. "I love her as if she were my own."

"It would make Caterina so very happy to hear you say that." He paused and smiled a little. "It pleases me, too."

Susanna was unprepared for the warmth that stole over her at his words. She realized for the first time that in some inexplicable way, she *wanted* his approval, wanted to please him.

It was an entirely unexpected thought, and one that left her shaken and confused.

Why should she care whether Michael approved of her? This was the man who had somehow managed to make her sister so miserable that she'd referred to her marriage as a "disaster." Moreover, everything Susanna had learned so far led her to believe that Deirdre might well have been running away from Michael—and her marriage—the night she died.

She studied him in the mirror. It occurred to her that she still knew little more about Deirdre's accident than she'd known before she came here, other than the fact that there had been an argument—a particularly ugly one, apparently—and that Deirdre had driven off to her death. Up until tonight, Michael had managed to evade even the most superficial of explanations. Now, with his earlier account interrupted, she couldn't help but wonder how long it might be before he would again be willing to take up where he'd left off.

But before she could pursue her troubled thoughts any further, Caterina was gripped by a new, and even more violent, fit of coughing.

And this time, she seemed to be fighting with all her strength simply to breathe.

—

There was nothing unusual about a knock on Andrew Carmichael's door in the middle of the night. In fact, it was a rare night indeed when he managed more than four or five hours sleep. Fortunately, he had discovered while still in medical college that he could get along surprisingly well on very little sleep—a quality that had proved exceedingly valuable for one in his profession.

At the sound of someone pounding, he came instantly

awake, fully alert. Quickly, he lighted the lamp on the table beside the bed. A glance across the room to the clock on the fireplace mantel showed that it was almost one-thirty.

It was still raining, a persistent, drumming rain that held little promise of slackening soon. Chilled, the doctor shivered a little as he threw on his bathrobe and half stumbled downstairs to the side entrance.

He felt uncommonly irritated—more so than usual—at being disturbed at such a late hour. The lingering effects of what he thought must have been a very pleasant dream clung to him like a subtle fragrance, and for a moment he resented the unknown intruder. Even so, he could hardly ignore the relentless pounding and go back to bed.

On the way downstairs, he became aware that the dream in question was of Dr. Bethany Cole. Now, there was an intrusion! The woman had been invading his mind at the most inopportune moments almost from the first day they'd met.

The thought of his attractive new associate fled, however, when he opened the door. The man standing on the stoop bore a strong resemblance to a walrus. Yes, definitely a walrus, complete with the heavy mustache. He was a hardy, thick-chested man, probably in his late fifties, with a bit of a droop to one eye.

"The name is Dempsey, sir," he said in a voice as rough as gravel. He thrust a piece of paper into Andrew's hand. "I was to deliver this note from Miss Susanna Fallon."

Andrew frowned, looking from the man with the Irish accent to the note in his hand. For a moment he couldn't think. Then it came to him. "Miss Fallon . . . oh, of course! Why, whatever is wrong? She's not ill, I hope?"

Even as he spoke, Andrew unfolded the stationery and read what appeared to be a hastily written note.

"Please forgive this imposition, Dr. Carmichael. I don't mean to

presume on our brief acquaintanceship, but my four-year-old niece—the daughter of Mr. Michael Emmanuel—is very ill with what would seem to be a severe case of croup. I believe it is most critical that she receive medical attention right away, and Mr. Emmanuel's family physician is himself hospitalized. I do apologize for asking, but if you would be good enough to accompany Mr. Dempsey upriver, we'd be most grateful. We desperately need a trustworthy physician, and I naturally thought of you right away."

"Upriver?" Andrew questioned, glancing at the man called Dempsey.

"Aye, sir. Between Tarrytown and the Military Academy, it is. You know Mr. Emmanuel, sir?"

Andrew nodded, still studying the note. "The musician . . . yes, of course. That is, I know *of* him. That's right, now I remember, Miss Fallon told us about him and her niece."

He hesitated only a moment. "Well, step in out of the rain, man. I'll have to dress and get my bag."

The Irishman seemed relieved—and somewhat surprised. "You'll be coming, then, sir?"

Andrew cut a look at him. "Why, yes, of course." In truth, he hadn't thought of *not* going.

The sturdy Irishman stepped inside, cap in hand. He seemed unaware of the fact that he was thoroughly drenched.

"Come on up if you like," Andrew said, already starting up the steps.

"Thank you, sir. I'll be fine right here."

The man Dempsey was obviously a fellow of few words, which was just as well. This hour of the night Andrew wasn't much inclined toward conversation himself.

Rain on the River

If it be stormy,
Fear not the sea;
Jesus upon it
Is walking by thee

JOSEPH SHERIDAN LEFANU

Susanna had tried everything she knew to do, but Caterina's racking cough only grew worse. She glanced across the room at the clock on the mantel. Nearly three-thirty. It seemed as if Dempsey had been gone all night.

Only with the greatest of effort had she managed to avoid utter panic. Michael, too, was clearly distraught. His hair was wild from raking his hands through it, and he had pulled at his tie so fiercely that both the tie and his collar hung askew.

"Michael, you should try to rest," Susanna said, raising her voice to make herself heard above Caterina's coughing.

He shook off the suggestion and got to his feet for yet

another round of pacing the room. After a moment, he stopped in front of Susanna, extended a hand to her, and said, "Will you pray with me? Pray with me for Caterina."

Susanna studied him, her throat tight. For the first time since they'd come upstairs she could see him struggling with his faith. By now his fear seemed almost palpable, as was her own increasing dread. On impulse, she took his hand and went to stand with him beside Caterina's bed. With the rain drumming a relentless rhythm against the house and her heart hammering in painful counterpoint, they pleaded together for the child they both loved with all their hearts.

At some point, Susanna felt Michael's hand tighten on hers. At first she resisted, but only for an instant. His hand was strong and warm, and her growing panic, plus the need to be in harmony as they prayed, made it possible for her to put aside, at least for the moment, her misgivings and her doubts about him. For now, all that really mattered was Caterina, and it seemed vital that they join their thoughts and their hearts as they approached the only One who could bring healing into this room tonight.

A few minutes later, Susanna went for a fresh pitcher of water. The rain had slackened by the time she made her way back to the bedroom, and the house had grown quiet, except for Caterina's continual hacking. The strangling cough pierced the night, sending one stab of pain after another shooting through Susanna.

The wolfhound saw her from his watchful position outside the room and lifted his great head in appeal. Even Gus was looking for a reassurance she couldn't offer. She stopped long enough to rub his ears and give him a word of encouragement.

She started to enter the bedroom, then hesitated. Michael had lifted Caterina from the bed and sat cradling her in the rocking chair by the window. His arms were wrapped securely around his daughter to help support her against the brutal coughing. Even as he hummed a soothing melody against her hair, his own face was a mask of despair and helplessness.

The sight of his stricken countenance and his unmistakable love for his daughter was almost Susanna's undoing. Something twisted inside her, and for a moment, forgetting that Michael could not see her distress, she turned away to collect herself before crossing the room to set the pitcher on the table.

The sound of voices downstairs startled her, and she sloshed water over the side of the bowl as she set it in place. Michael was already on his feet, still cradling Caterina in his arms.

"That must be Dempsey!" Susanna said. "I'll go."

Outside the room the wolfhound was poised at the top of the steps. He barked once, then turned to Susanna, as if waiting for a command from her.

"Quiet, Gus." A wave of relief swept over Susanna at the sight of the tall, rangy Dr. Carmichael ascending the steps while Paul waited in the vestibule with Dempsey, watching.

"Miss Fallon." Andrew Carmichael gave her a quick smile as he reached the top of the stairway.

"I can't thank you enough for coming, Dr. Carmichael! I know what a terrible imposition this is, but I couldn't think what else to do."

He waved off her apology and, at the sound of Caterina's coughing, glanced toward the bedroom. "Sounds as if she's having quite a time of it," he said, already starting down the hallway as Susanna hurried to keep pace with him.

"How long has she been this way?"

"All night," Susanna replied. "Mrs. Dempsey said she started not long after we left for Brooklyn, for the revival."

He looked at her. "You were at the meeting? So was I. In the wings, actually. One of the workers wasn't feeling well, so I stayed close by. Just in case."

They stopped just outside the bedroom door. "Now, then—tell me what you've done for her so far."

Susanna gave him a hasty account of her efforts, to which he nodded approval. "Good. Very good thinking. Well, let's go in."

Upon entering the room, the doctor stopped for only a moment before crossing to where Michael stood with Caterina in his arms.

Susanna quickly introduced them, and with great care Dr. Carmichael took Caterina from Michael. "Let's have a look, if I may," he said, lifting her onto the bed.

The child's frenzied coughing and unfocused gaze set off yet another spasm of alarm in Susanna. But Andrew Carmichael's good-natured features creased into a smile as he bent over the bed.

"I'm Dr. Carmichael, Caterina. I need to have a look at your throat, is that all right? It won't hurt a bit, I promise."

The girl's cheeks were stained with crimson, her eyes sunken, but she managed a faint smile and a nod. Even that small effort seem to ignite another round of hacking.

Susanna watched Andrew Carmichael closely as he checked Caterina's throat. She saw his expression turn somber, and in the stillness of the room she imagined everyone could hear her own heart pounding with apprehension.

—

The child's cough was so relentless it was all Andrew could do to manage even a cursory examination. But he was vastly relieved to find that it wasn't membranous croup, as he had feared when he first heard the cough. No, this was the plain old ordinary stuff—just an unusually severe case of it. More than likely the result of a bad cold but, hopefully, still treatable.

The girl's condition concerned him, however, for she was a slight little thing and clearly exhausted. When he listened to her heart, he knew at once the coughing was overtaxing it. He needed to get that cough under control, and at once.

Without turning, he asked Susanna Fallon to bring him a bowl of boiling water and a funnel. While she was gone, he gave the child a dose of quinine mixed with a little sugar. The quinine would do nothing for the cough, of course, but it would help to support her strength.

The girl's father stood beside the bed in silence, his hands knotted in fists at his sides. Reminding himself of the man's blindness, Andrew commenced to explain what he was doing. Emmanuel seemed eager to understand.

As soon as Susanna Fallon returned with the boiling water, Andrew mixed a tincture of benzoin in it and helped the child inhale it through the tin funnel. "We're going to repeat this in a few minutes," he told them. "I should caution you that she might throw up at any time, but it's just as well if she does, so don't be alarmed."

Over the next hour, Andrew applied the benzoin treatment twice more, but saw scarce evidence of relief. Since Miss Fallon had already administered a steam tent, there was little else to try. The child was already much too weak; he wished he could have treated her sooner. He knew that to let this go on much longer would involve real risk to her heart and lungs.

There was only one other remedy left to him. In itself it contained an element of risk, but at this point he had no choice but to try.

He waited a few more minutes after the last inhalation of benzoin. Finally, when no relief seemed imminent, he stood. "All right, then," he said. "Let's wrap her in blankets. I'm going to take her outside."

The girl's father took on a look of horror, as if Andrew had threatened to drive a stake through his daughter's heart. *"Outside?"* he repeated, his voice strangled.

Susanna Fallon also went pale and opened her mouth as if to object.

Andrew understood their inevitable protests but tried to ignore their shock. There was really nothing else to do.

"It's a perfect night," he said by way of explanation. "The rain has stopped, but the air will still be moist. And this close to the river, we'll have fog. Those are excellent conditions. Just what we need right now."

He took in their faces, still frozen in doubt. "In extreme cases, such as Caterina's," he said carefully, "when nothing else works, quite often the night air will help. Now, there's no sign as yet of bronchitis or pneumonia, you see, so I think the risk is minimal. I strongly suggest we give this a go, Mr. Emmanuel. Quite frankly, there's little else left to do."

The girl's father seemed to be waiting for something more, while Susanna Fallon was studying Andrew closely. He met her gaze straight on, but gave a lift of his hands to show that he could not promise anything.

Meanwhile, the child took up another seizure of coughing.

Miss Fallon finally broke the silence. "Michael, we should at least try, don't you think? We can trust Dr. Carmichael."

At last the man nodded. But Andrew had the distinct feeling that if this didn't work, Michael Emmanuel—in spite of his blindness—would somehow make him pay. And it would not be a pleasant experience.

—

Outside, the night had grown calm. The rain seemed to be over, at least for the moment, and, just as Dr. Carmichael had predicted, a heavy fog was moving in.

The physician carried Caterina, bundled securely in blankets, onto the front lawn, where he stood, holding her and speaking softly of the beauty of her home and the night around them.

"I hope this is not a madman you have brought to our house," Michael said under his breath.

Susanna looked at him, but he didn't appear angry, merely skeptical.

"If you think about it," she said, "it makes perfect sense. The moist air, the fog—"

"Please, God, it will work," he said quietly.

Susanna heard the tremor in his voice and knew that he was trying his best to conceal his fear.

They stood that way, in silence, for what seemed a very long time, engulfed by the cool damp air. They could smell the river. The fog, acrid to the throat but somehow calming, drifted in and out among them and the trees. There was no sound except the faint rustle of leaves and the steady panting of the wolf-hound, who stood at Michael's side, alert and seemingly poised for action.

It was a lonely, forsaken kind of silence, and Susanna shivered a little, not from the night air, but more from the sense of isolation that sometimes seemed to hang over Bantry Hill and this entire Hudson River Valley.

Andrew Carmichael had grown quiet now, too. Watching him as he stood with Caterina bundled securely against him, Susanna could see his lips moving only slightly.

She couldn't be sure, but she thought he was praying.

She had seen enough of the Scottish physician's interaction with the Moodys and the Sankeys to know that he was a deeply devout man. Still, it both surprised and comforted her to realize that a man of science and medicine looked to a higher power for the ultimate healing.

She seemed to lose all track of time. They might have been standing there for minutes or hours when she realized that Caterina had finally stopped coughing. Indeed, the child had grown completely silent.

Panic overtook Susanna. She heard Michael's sharp intake of breath and took his arm, as much to steady herself as him. But then she saw Andrew Carmichael's face in the flickering glow from the lantern, the slow smile breaking over his features as he studied Caterina.

After a moment, he lifted his face to the night sky and whispered something Susanna couldn't quite make out.

Suddenly the night no longer seemed lonely or forsaken. "She's all right, Michael," Susanna said, hurrying to reassure him. "Caterina is going to be all right."

He was trembling, and for a moment Susanna feared that he, too, had taken ill. But then she saw the dampness on his cheeks.

Moved, she reached for his hand, and when she did, he wrapped it securely between both his own, bringing it to his lips just for an instant. Taken completely off guard, Susanna would have yanked her hand away, but he restrained her with a gentle, firm clasp as he murmured something in Italian, then in English.

"You are a gift to us, Susanna. A gift of God. And I could not be more thankful for your presence in our lives."

Susanna swallowed hard. Her resolve to dislike—and distrust—this man began to bend like a slender reed in a windstorm. Even as the old emotions inside her rose up in protest, she felt an unaccountable desire stir within her, a longing for things to be different between them.

For one yearning moment, she found herself wishing she could simply give up her suspicion, surrender her doubts, and put all the old questions to rest for once and for all.

Carefully then, he lowered her hand, loosening his grasp so that Susanna could move away if she chose. Instead, she lightly pressed his fingers with her own, took a deep breath, and led him across the grass to Dr. Carmichael and Caterina.

TWENTY-TWO

FAITH IN THE FACE OF FEAR

OUR FEET ON THE TORRENT'S BRINK,
OUR EYES ON THE CLOUD AFAR,
WE FEAR THE THINGS WE THINK,
INSTEAD OF THE THINGS THAT ARE.

JOHN BOYLE O'REILLY

Aboard the Jonathan Nye *on the way to America*

"Am I going to die, Mum?"

Vangie MacGovern dabbed the forehead of her fevered son with a damp cloth, forcing a smile for his benefit. "Ah, James, and what kind of talk is that, now? Of course you're not going to die! You've a cold in your chest, is all. Why, no doubt you'll be the first among us to see the shores of America. Here, now," she said, laying the cloth aside, "take a bit more of this broth."

She put the cup of barley water to his lips, but the boy turned his head away. "I don't like it, Mum. It smells."

Tears stung Vangie's eyes. "Please, James. You *must* take it. I know you don't like the taste, but just take a bit for Mother, won't you?"

He made no response to Vangie's coaxing, but simply closed his eyes. The boy had taken nothing since yesterday morning except a few sips of broth, and Vangie was at her wit's end. She had no enticements to offer him, no choice victuals that might tempt him. What with the dampness and lack of ventilation, even their basic provisions had spoiled long before they should have.

Grieved by her own helplessness, she turned to Nell Grace, who sat holding the sleeping Baby Emma in her arms. "Put the baby in her cradle and go and find your da," she told her daughter. "I can't think where he's wandered off to this time, but I'll wager if you follow the music, you'll find him."

The strains of a fiddle and a squeezebox could be heard coming from the dank compartment some called the galley. This was where many of their foodstuffs were stored, and where the women, disgusted with the foul fare served by the ship's cook, occasionally cooked their own meals over the fireplace. It was also where some of the steerage passengers had taken to gathering during the long days of the voyage to make their music and tell their tales in an attempt to ease the monotony of the journey and the growing despair that hung over them like a fetid cloud.

Some felt the merrymaking out of place, woefully inappropriate among the dark shadows and putrid stench of the ship's bowels. Conn, however, contended that the people must find their own escape from the relentless distress of the crossing, or else many would go mad.

Vangie agreed with him, but at the moment she felt as if she might be going mad herself.

She watched Nell Grace wind her way through the crowded

passages between the bunks. A body could hardly navigate from one berth to the other without either bumping into a stranger or tripping over a protruding foot on the way.

It occurred to her that she had lost track of time. Their quarters were always dark, with nothing but a few flickering lanterns to scatter the shadows. Without a change in light to mark the hours, it was easy to become disoriented.

Here, too, Conn took the brighter side. They were fortunate, he said, to be among those sailing on an American ship rather than aboard one of the disgraceful British vessels. "At least our bunks won't be falling off the wall, and the water closets won't collapse with the first high wind."

He often compared their lot to that of the poor souls who made the crossing during the Great Hunger in the forties. "They were half-dead already when they boarded, but even if they hadn't been, the infernal British coffin ships would have finished them off. It is our good fortune, don't you see, to be making the journey in our full strength."

No doubt he knew whereof he spoke—and of course he meant well, trying to keep their spirits up. But at the moment, Vangie was feeling anything but fortunate. During the first week aboard ship, both she and Nell Grace had suffered fiercely with the seasickness; even Baby Emma had not been able to keep much on her stomach. Not long after, Conn and the twins had come down with colds and dysentery, along with half of the other steerage passengers. Now James had been taken with a fever.

It seemed as if the busker girl, Renny Magee, was the only one of them to escape the ravages of sea travel. Conn claimed the girl's devilry kept sickness at bay.

Lately, Vangie paid little heed to her husband's crankiness when it came to Renny Magee. Hadn't she seen the way his mouth twitched when the girl went barreling across the hold to retrieve the baby's rattle, or the faint creasing about his eyes when he came upon the lass entertaining the twins with one of the old tales about magic pigs or the great hound of Cuchullin?

The girl amused him, Vangie could tell. For her own part, she had to say that she was growing fond of Renny Magee. The busker girl had been as good as her word, not causing a bit of trouble, in fact bringing more help than harm to this odious voyage. She was especially good with the twins and Baby Emma.

Of course, Conn never much cared for admitting he was wrong, so it wasn't likely he would willingly concede any real virtue to the girl, certainly not until more time had passed. Even Vangie couldn't help but wonder what Renny might do once they left the ship. Would she keep her pledge to stay and work for them as they'd agreed, or would she simply disappear into the city, having accomplished the adventure she'd contrived for herself?

Vangie sighed and wrung the cloth in the basin. Only time would reveal the girl's true mettle. They wouldn't know what to expect from her until they arrived in America—which, according to some of the crew members, ought to be soon now. Within days.

There were things she ought to be doing in preparation, but she couldn't bring herself to leave James's side, sick as he was. She looked at her ailing boy, his face so thin and pale that even the band of freckles across his nose appeared to have faded. Drenched in perspiration, he jerked once, then again, in his troubled sleep.

Vangie shook her head as if to free herself of the panic clawing at her and began to sponge the boy's brow with renewed determination. "You must be getting well now, son," she murmured, speaking for her own benefit as much as for her son.

"You must be strong and fit for your first sight of America. Soon we will be leaving this terrible ship for our new life, and you'd not want to be missing a minute of that, would you? You must be brave and not give in to the fever, love. Our Lord will be taking the sickness away from you; I'm sure of it. God's healing hands are upon you at this very minute. You will be well, James. You will . . ."

Merciful Savior . . . I've already lost my firstborn son. Not another of my boys, please . . . not another . . .

Vangie knew she dared not give in to the ever-present fear that nagged her day and night. From the time she was a child, fear and its ugly accomplice, worry, had circled over her like buzzards waiting for their prey to drop. Only her faith had kept her a step beyond this plague of the spirit.

Even now, and her a woman with children grown, she could still fall victim to an entire host of fears that, unchecked, would all too easily freeze her spirit and paralyze her soul. Her husband credited her with far more grit than she actually possessed. Not for the world and everything in it would she have Conn or the children know that she was less than they thought her. In their eyes, her faith was unshakable, her strength inexhaustible.

And that's what she wanted them to believe, what she *needed* them to believe. Her only defense against this hidden weakness was her faith in the Almighty and the strength her family thought her to possess. As long as she could cling to God, and as long as her loved ones continued to confer on her the qualities she only wished she possessed, then Vangie could go on being everything they believed her to be, everything they needed her to be.

But God help her—and perhaps her family as well—if they should ever discover how slender was the thread that held her strength and faith intact.

❧

Earlier, Conn had wandered across to the small galley next to steerage, where a few of the more able-bodied men had taken to making their music at night.

He was not a musician himself, but he could never resist the sound of a happy fiddle or a good Irish song. There had been a time when he and Vangie had danced with the other young people at the crossroads, and he had no doubt at all but what his wife could still outstep the best of them.

Shea Sullivan was fiddling a set of jigs when Conn ducked his head to pass through the doorway. One of the young McCormick lads was doing his best to keep up on the squeeze-box, and in spite of the heaviness in Conn's chest, he couldn't stop his foot from taking up a tapping to the lively rhythm.

Except for two or three of the children, no one was dancing tonight. No surprise, that. Conn figured few had the energy or the heart left in them to dance.

His gaze traveled to the far end of the room, where Renny Magee sat, amusing a circle of youngsters. With her worn old cap crushed atop her head and a bit of flour dusting her features, the busker girl was giving forth the nonsensical lyrics and motions to a song about a constable and a goat that was smarter than the law.

More truth than lie in that particular song, Conn thought with a wry grin.

The lass was a natural mime. Indeed, Conn would concede that Renny Magee was likely adept at most any amusement, be it rendering a song or dancing a jig or playing a ditty on the tarnished tin whistle she carried around in her pocket. The girl was as cunning as a gombeen man and had as many tricks as a cart of monkeys, and that was the truth.

He knew the children—his own and the others aboard as well—did fancy the girl. And nothing would do Vangie but to defend the young hoyden. So, in order to avoid his wife's barbed remarks about his being such a hardhead, Conn had learned to restrain his sharp tongue about the little busker. Most of the time.

Besides, despite his misgivings about bringing her along, Renny Magee had proven to be quite a lot of help, not only to Vangie and their own brood, but to the other children in steerage as well. The girl was a constant source of entertainment. Her mercurial mind seemed to hold a limitless supply of diversions, and her energy was as boundless as her imagination.

Too bad, Conn told himself with grim amusement as he watched her, that the young scamp's code of honor was not honed nearly so fine as her inclination toward mischief.

He turned just then, catching sight of Nell Grace as she appeared in the doorway. In that moment, Conn was seized by an unexpected thought of Vangie at the same age. His daughter's hair was the same dark red, though easier tamed, and she had the same finely molded, sharply chiseled features as her mother. Though her loveliness was quieter, more subdued, than Vangie's fiery good looks, at seventeen the lass already carried herself with the same grace and lissome movements. As she stood there, her hand lifted to beckon him, she might have been Vangie herself, twenty years past.

Of all his children, this sweet daughter evoked in Conn a tenderness, a fierce protectiveness that almost bordered on the obsessive. He loved them all, but he feared most for Nell Grace. Her delicate beauty, her gentle nature, the innate goodness and innocence he had seen in her since childhood would make her easy prey for the vultures and despoilers of the world. Sometimes he wished he could shut her inside the fortress of her family's love and keep her there forever.

When he prayed for his children, he invariably found it harder to surrender Nell Grace to the good Lord's care than he did the others. It seemed that every plea for her safekeeping was accompanied by a wrenching anxiety, almost as if he must convince even the Almighty that the girl had greater need of

God's protection than did the other, sturdier MacGovern off-spring.

He didn't like to think what this said about his faith. Sure, Vangie would call him to task for his weak-kneed prayers. But then Vangie would not understand about doubting, especially about doubting their Lord.

All these thoughts coursed through him as he made his way across the room to his daughter. Her shadowed eyes betrayed her own fears and the reason she had been sent, and Conn chided himself. This night it was not Nell Grace who most needed the sheltering arms of their loving God.

—

Renny Magee watched MacGovern and Nell Grace leave the room. She knew at once why the girl had come for him, but forced herself to turn back to the children long enough to pull a comical face and make a hasty bow. Then she sped from the room.

As she plowed along the dark corridor that led to the bunks, it occurred to Renny that up until recently, any task she might have done for one of the MacGoverns, even Vangie, as the missus insisted she call her, would have been done with the thought of increasing her standing with MacGovern himself.

That was no longer the case. Now she did what was asked of her because of her feelings for them all. Unfamiliar feelings to which she could not give a name, but which seemed to be growing stronger—and more bewildering—with each day passing.

She had never known folks like the MacGoverns. These were people who seemed to actually *want* to be together, as if they found each other's company grand fun. They talked a lot and laughed a lot—and they seemed to hug a lot as well. Even when they scrapped—which the twins did with regularity—

any one of them would defend the other in a heartbeat, should some rascal aboard the ship pose a threat.

Renny had noticed that the MacGoverns—especially Vangie—also spoke of "The Lord" as naturally as if the Almighty sat with them at table. They said their prayers *aloud*, not seeming to mind who else might be listening. They were keen on saying things such as "blessed" and "thanks be" and "if The Lord wills."

Why, MacGovern and his missus—Vangie—were so free with their conversation that they sometimes even said "I love you" to each other, not just to the children! Indeed, the man couldn't seem to walk across the room without smiling at his wife, and didn't he call her "my beauty" and hold her hand, even give her a squeeze when he thought no one else was about?

It seemed to Renny that the family treated her with un-common decency, instead of haranguing her as if she were just another stray alley cat nobody wanted around. Well, except for MacGovern, of course, who still eyed her as if he half expected her to stick a shiv in his back every time she ventured within a hand's-breadth of him.

Now that she thought of it, though, even MacGovern tended to treat her well enough these days.

So perhaps it wasn't all that curious that she actually liked doing tasks for them, and found herself eager to be helping out more and more, instead of just seeing to what was expected of her.

Renny wished she could do something now. She wished with all her heart she could manage a way to help poor James get well and at the same time banish that awful look of terror from his mother's eyes.

Perhaps Vangie thought no one else had seen the way she held the boy with her eyes, as if he might slip away from her at any minute. She had a way, Vangie did, of not letting the others know she was afraid.

But Renny had seen enough fear in her time to recognize it for what it was. And Vangie was scared. Bad scared.

And with good reason, Renny allowed. The fever had wee James in a fierce grip, all right, and she didn't like the looks of the boy. Not at all.

Earlier today, she had heard Vangie praying for the boy, praying as if her heart might fly to pieces if The Lord didn't answer. So far, Renny had seen no sign of a reply.

It struck her that perhaps the Lord needed to be reminded about James a bit more often—perhaps as much as every hour or so. But Vangie had an awful lot to do as it was.

Renny was tempted to try her hand at the praying, but from the little she had heard, The Lord might not have any truck with a sinner like herself. Of course, she had only resorted to thievery when she was so hungry she couldn't bear it any longer, so hungry her stomach felt like the rats had been at it. Still, would the fact that she'd been near famished be an acceptable excuse to The Lord for the pockets she picked now and then? And what about the wrappers of fish she sometimes filched when the opportunity presented itself?

Vangie claimed God knew everything, that there was no keeping secrets from The Lord. If that was the case, no doubt he would turn a deaf ear to the words from the mouth of one such as herself.

Worse still, what if her boldness vexed him and he took it out on the MacGoverns, them being associated with her as they were? Sure, she wouldn't want to do anything that might hurt James's chances for getting well.

No, Renny decided, she'd best not bother the Almighty with a sinful busker girl's prayer. She'd do better to keep her silence and stick to helping out in other ways, however she could.

She had reached the door to their quarters now, but stopped when she saw the whole family standing around James's bunk, holding hands and praying.

Renny Magee had been alone most of her life. She had lived on the streets of Dublin ever since she could remember. Even among the other buskers she had always been known as a loner. It had never much bothered her, being on her own. It was all she knew, after all.

But at this moment, watching from a distance as the MacGoverns joined ranks and prayed for their own, she had never felt more alone in her life.

TWENTY-THREE

Just One Touch

Prayer is the burden of a sigh,
The falling of a tear,
The upward glancing of an eye
When none but God is near.

James Montgomery

Throughout the long night, Renny did everything she could to help the MacGoverns. She changed the water beside James's bed as needed, fetched whatever they asked, and watched over Baby Emma so that Nell Grace could relieve Vangie.

No one, however, could coax Vangie into leaving the boy's side for more than a few moments. It seemed to Renny that Vangie was beginning to look almost as pale and wan as poor James.

Apparently, there was no ship's doctor aboard. One of the sailors had given MacGovern the excuse that the physician who would normally have traveled with them had to stay behind in

Liverpool, due to some sort of emergency. When MacGovern demanded that one of the crewmen try to locate a doctor among the passengers above, he was told in no uncertain terms that they could not bother the first-class passengers with "the likes of a filthy Irisher."

MacGovern, of course, not one to swallow this sort of abuse easily, had made a terrible scene. Only Vangie's pleas—and the threat of lockup for the duration of the trip—had kept him from flying berserk at the man. Ever since then, he had done nothing but pace, his face set in a terrible fierce scowl.

Renny would warrant that MacGovern was not a man used to being scotched, and he was having a hard time of it, being helpless to aid his boy. Had it not been for upsetting Vangie even more, no doubt he would have been pounding the wall— or a crewman's head—with one of his big fists long before now.

At the moment, he had stopped his stomping back and forth to once again join Vangie and Nell Grace, who stood heads bowed, continuing their prayers for James. Some of the other steerage passengers, those not wary of infecting themselves, had come to add their petitions to those of the family.

Apparently, Christian folk believed that it took a great number of prayers from a large contingent of people to get anything worthwhile accomplished.

Renny was sitting between Johnny and the makeshift cradle of rags and straw that held Baby Emma. Both the boy and the baby were sleeping. Renny figured it must be two or three in the morning by now, if not later. Her view was blocked by the prayer circle, so she could not see James. But she knew all too well how he looked.

Her last sight of him had sent a creeping dread over her heart, for she realized with near certainty he would be gone by first light. She had seen the mask of death on others, had seen it often enough to believe the boy was only a short distance away from breathing his last.

Her eyes went to Vangie, and she could have wept at the raw fear and desperation ravaging the woman's face. Vangie knew. She knew her boy was dying, knew there was nothing to be done for him now.

There was no help to be had for James, and that was the truth. And yet she went on praying, Vangie did, as if any minute the door to heaven might open and pour out some wondrous potion on the boy that would rouse him from his fatal stupor and take the sickness away.

Renny sat watching a few minutes more, hammered by an entire riot of emotions. Suddenly, she knew what she must do. She could not—*would* not—put it off any longer. Taking pains to move quietly, she stood and, after reassuring herself that Johnny and the baby were still sound asleep, tiptoed down the aisle and out the door.

She went straight to the galley, which she knew would be deserted at this late hour. As she'd hoped, she found the place unoccupied. For a long time, Renny stood in the shadows, mustering her nerve. Finally, the blood pounding in her ears and her heart rising to her throat, she dropped down to her knees and propped her elbows on top of a small keg.

At first, she hesitated, uncertain and even fearful of what she was about to do. Would The Lord be offended by someone like herself having the cheek to come begging? Vangie and Nell Grace were big on talking about God's love and kindness, but so far Renny had seen little of either from him. What if she angered him? Would he strike back at her, punish her?

What if she prayed and James took even worse?

She shook off *that* thought after only a second or two. James couldn't possibly take worse. Wasn't he already dying? The worst that could happen was that The Lord might penalize *her* for being so bold where she had no right.

But even if she did rile him, she had to try. She *had* to, for James's sake. And for Vangie's.

And so kneeling there in the shadows, on the cold, damp floor, she took a deep breath, bowed her head, and closed her eyes.

"Please, Lord . . . your Honor . . . my name is Renny Magee. You don't know me, any more than I know you, and I'm begging your pardon ahead of time for bein' so bold, but I'd like to ask you a favor. Not for myself, you understand, but for James. James MacGovern. And perhaps I ought to tell you straight off that the favor is a big one . . ."

———

Conn stood in the dark corridor between their quarters and the galley, feeling more desperate than he had ever felt in his life.

They'd lost the two wee babes—one before she ever so much as saw the light of day, the other while only a few days old. Even so, bad as it had been, at least they had loved them but a brief time before their passing.

But Seamus, their wee James—eight years he had been with them now. Eight years of loving him and his brother, Johnny. Loving them and dreaming bright dreams for them and holding the highest of hopes for them.

And now to lose one of them? Was that how it was to end?

Dear God, it would be grief enough if he didn't have to look at Vangie's face and watch her heart break, piece by piece— what was left of it, that is, after leaving Aidan behind.

Two babes taken from her. One grown son as good as dead. How could she endure the loss of another?

He tried to pray, found that he had no words, could not

summon enough strength or hope or faith to give voice to yet another supplication for his boy.

He knew he was not trusting as he should, not "clinging," as Vangie would say.

Never had he known such a terrible weakness before, such a hollowness in his soul. All this night he had felt as though *he* were the one who was slipping away, his life draining from him, little by little, like drops from a well going dry.

And Vangie—ah, he could no longer bear to meet her eyes. He felt the great failure of his life each time he looked at her, for he had brought her to this place and now could do nothing for her, not even comfort her.

Their son was dying. He knew it, and so did she. And yet Vangie went on hoping, went on praying and pleading and even *praising* the One who in an instant could stop this madness and give them back their James, their precious boy.

Aye, the Lord could do that.

If only he would.

Vangie had not as yet given up her hope. Nor would she, Conn knew, not until James had exhaled his last labored breath.

Conn hated himself for not being able to match his wife's faith with his own. He ought to be drawing on every shred of strength left to him, every remnant of hope and faith he could muster. Not only for his son, but for Vangie. He should be strong for the both of them.

Instead, he was wandering about in the gloom like a man lost in a fog, aimless and without a thought of what to do. He was useless entirely.

He lumbered toward the galley, then stopped in the doorway at the scene that met his eyes. In the shadows, relieved only by the dim light flickering from the lantern beside the door, Renny Magee was kneeling.

It took Conn a moment to realize that the girl was praying.

Renny Magee, praying! He wouldn't have thought the little heathen even knew how!

He stood, scarcely breathing, not moving as he watched and listened in numb amazement.

"*The thing is, Lord Sir, Vangie has already had to give up her one boy, the oldest—and 'twas me who gained the good from her loss, don't you see? His staying behind in Ireland made it possible for me to come to America. And now that we're almost there, James— well, sure, he's dying. I can tell from the looks of him. And so Vangie will lose another son, and her not yet recovered from her first grief.*

"*Do you really think that's fair, Lord Sir? Not that Vangie blames you for any of this, mind! Nothing of the sort. Vangie would never do that, although I confess I don't understand how she keeps from it at times. But even after all that's happened, 'tis clear she doesn't fault you for her sorrows.*

"*She's a good woman, Vangie is. But I expect you already know that. She's good to everyone, even to me, and myself a total stranger to her, and her husband believing I'm nothing but a common thief.*

"*It just seems to me that Vangie is entitled to something better than what she's had so far. She's a good mother, as you know, the kind of mother I'd have wanted for myself. She does love her children fiercely, as anyone can see, and her husband, too, although he is a hardheaded man, if ever I met one.*

"*All things considered, I have to wonder if you couldn't see fit to make James well again? I heard Vangie say to Nell Grace that all you would have to do is touch him, and the fever would leave for good. James would be well again.*

"*He's on fire, don't you see? If it's true that you could touch him and take the fire away, well . . . would that really be asking too much from you? Sure and a touch wouldn't require all that much effort, would it? Just one touch?*

"And please, Lord Sir, I don't mean to rush you, but I'm afraid it might be too late even for you *to do anything unless you do it quick like—right away if possible."*

There was a long silence, and Conn thought perhaps she had finished. But then she started in once more, and even though he disliked himself for eavesdropping, he could not have moved away now if someone had tried to drag him.

"By the way, I expect it might be best if the family don't know I've talked to you. They might not like it, my speaking with you about James, what with MacGovern thinking I'm a heathen. And perhaps I am, so if it's all the same to you, could we keep this between ourselves?"

She went on, but Conn, overcome, quietly turned and walked away. Nearly blinded from the tears that had welled up in his eyes, he trudged back down the dim corridor toward their quarters. As he went, he carried with him the sight of Renny Magee on her knees in the darkness, the sound of her childish but determined voice pleading on behalf of his dying son.

Renny Magee, whom he had berated time and time again as a thief, an abandoned child of the streets. He, too, had abandoned her, had deliberately made her feel unwanted and unwelcome.

Renny Magee, who believed he thought her a heathen and altogether worthless.

All this time, when he should have been modeling for her the unconditional love and mercy of their Savior, he had instead shown her only reproach and condemnation.

Self-disgust ripped through him, and he had to stop for a moment as bitter tears of shame spilled over, nearly blinding his eyes. "God forgive me," he whispered in the darkness. "I have been the worst kind of man. A cold, unfeeling, *hardheaded* man. And a poor excuse for a Christian as well."

He shook his head at his own poverty of spirit. "I have failed that child, Lord, and that's the truth." He faltered, his whisper echoing along the damp, dark walls. "God forgive me, I failed young Renny Magee. But somehow I believe—Lord, I *have* to believe—that even though I let her down, you *won't*."

TWENTY-FOUR

RENNY MAGEE'S
WONDERFUL SECRET

OH COULD I TELL, YE SURELY WOULD BELIEVE IT!
OH COULD I ONLY SAY WHAT I HAVE SEEN!

FREDERICK W. H. MYERS

It was nearly four o'clock in the morning when James's fever broke. The fire left the boy so quickly it was as if a cool, healing hand had passed over every inch of his burning body, absorbing the heat unto itself.

Conn was half dozing, sitting upright on his berth and leaning against the wall, when he heard Vangie cry out for him. He sprang to his feet so quickly he slammed his shoulder against the iron brace that fastened the bunk, sending a knife of pain shooting down his arm.

He reached James's bunk in a heartbeat. Vangie was kneeling by the boy, and Conn put a hand to her shoulder to steady her as he stood staring down at his son.

So it had come, then. What they had feared for days.

He began to tremble. Cold . . . he was so cold. He couldn't stop the shaking as he stood studying James's inert form. It occurred to him that the boy looked strangely serene.

He had to get a grip on himself, for Vangie's sake. "So, is he gone then?" he choked out, putting a hand to her shoulder. "Ah, you should have called me sooner, love."

"No, Conn!" Vangie lifted her face to him, and Conn saw that her eyes were wide and shining, not with grief-stricken tears, as he would have expected, but with a kind of wonder and something else, some peculiar kind of excitement.

"The fever is *gone*, Conn! James is only sleeping just now. He's better. Much better!"

Conn stared at her, then turned his gaze back to the boy for a closer look. Only then did he realize that James was indeed alive. Breathing deeply, evenly—peacefully—without the dreaded death rattle he had been expecting to hear all night.

Vangie reached for his hand, and Conn dropped to his knees beside her. "You're quite sure?" he choked out. "The fever is truly gone?"

She was weeping now, but through the tears her tired eyes glistened with unmistakable joy. "'Tis true, Conn. James is going to get well! Our boy is going to be all right, after all! God has answered our prayers, don't you see?"

"Aye, glory be to God," Conn said softly, his voice rough with emotion, his heart slamming against his chest as he watched his sleeping son. "But I can scarce believe *what* I see."

By now, Nell Grace and Johnny had come to join them. Like her mother, the girl was crying with stunned happiness, and Johnny was grinning down at his twin brother—and best chum—with huge delight.

Something struck Conn, and he glanced toward Renny

Magee's bunk. The girl was simply lying there, watching them with those intense pale eyes of hers.

Conn couldn't be sure, for the lantern light was dim and flickering, but the lass appeared to be somewhat dazed. Her expression registered nothing except pure and utter amazement.

As Conn watched her, she met his eyes, but only for an instant before quickly glancing away.

She didn't want him to know, he realized. He remembered what he had overheard her as she prayed. Why, the foolish little scamp, she actually feared they would be offended at the thought of her going to the Lord in James's behalf!

Somehow Conn understood that even now, with James obviously past the dark hour, the girl would want to keep her secret. He could see the shock in her face, the look of incredulity, the glint of something akin to panic, and he almost smiled, to think that Renny Magee could actually be struck speechless.

But why would she keep silent *now?* Oh, if James had died, God forbid, then in her confusion and ignorance, the girl might have possibly feared their disapproval—though her apprehension would have been unreasonable entirely.

Or would it have been?

But James *hadn't* died, and the real surprise was that the lass apparently was not going to try to steal a bit of the credit for his recovery.

He turned back to James, studying his son with damp eyes for a long time.

He would keep Renny Magee's secret all right, if that's how she wanted it. But not from Vangie. At another time, when they were alone, he would tell Vangie. He could not keep such a thing from her, not such a strange, unbelievable thing as this.

Regret came washing over him at the thought that he could

not speak of this to the girl herself. He could not even thank her for caring so much about their boy that she would entreat a God she didn't know, a God who, Conn suspected, even frightened her.

But if he could not thank her directly, he could at least begin to treat her more decently. Perhaps he might even find a way to let her know that she was a heathen no longer in his eyes.

—

Later that morning, Renny sat holding Baby Emma, listening to the family's happy discussion about James.

He had awakened once and spoke with them, then almost immediately drifted off to sleep again. But there seemed no doubt that he was improving and would eventually be completely well again.

Renny did not know what to make of it. Certainly, it was no thanks to her. If MacGovern was right, she was a heathen, after all.

Perhaps it was nothing more than a . . . a *coincidence* entirely, James coming out of the fever as he had not long after she had prayed to the Lord.

It wasn't as if she were the *only* one who had prayed for the boy. In truth, the family had not *stopped* praying from the time the boy had taken ill, and a great number of others among the passengers—*good* people, *Christian* people—had prayed for James, too.

So she must not allow herself to make big out of little for her part in things. The fact that she had prayed, and in secret at that, could not possibly have had anything to do with James's recovery.

Indeed not.

But there was the matter of what James had said when he'd finally come round. The boy's words had left her head spinning.

"I felt the fire go out, Mum . . ."

When Vangie asked him what he meant, James told them of his dream.

"I dreamt I was on fire. It was like I was burning up, inside and out. It hurt awful bad, Mum! But then an angel came and touched me, soft-like, and took the fire away. Snuffed it right out of me! I could feel it going, I could. And all of a sudden, I felt . . . cool. Not cold, but just good, like when you come out of the river on a hot day and the wind blows on you while you're still all wet."

". . . then an angel came and touched me . . . and took the fire away . . ."

Renny swallowed, hard. Her throat felt tight. She had no way of knowing what exactly had happened to James. But *something* had happened; that much was clear. Something unlike anything she could have imagined. Something strange. Very strange.

After a moment, she closed her eyes. Even if she dared not let herself believe that she had contributed in some way—no matter how small—to James's recovery, she reckoned it would only be polite to say *thank you.*

And so she did.

TWENTY-FIVE

A MATTER OF TRUST

LAMENT FOR THE LAND WHERE THE SUN BEAMS
WANDER,
AND SHADOWS DEEPER THAN ELSEWHERE FALL . . .

JOHN SWANWICK DRENNAN

Bantry Hill

Today, Susanna decided, she would make the visit she had been putting off far too long.

Not that the delay had been entirely her doing. What with getting settled in and then Caterina's illness, there had been little time for anything other than managing the daily routine. But now there *was* time, and she intended to go while she could.

Shortly after breakfast, she went looking for Paul. She found him alone in Michael's office, putting some papers in order.

He looked up and, seeing her, broke into a wide smile. "Ah, Susanna! Come in! You are not taking your walk this morning?"

"Not yet," Susanna said, returning his smile. "Actually, I

have a visit I'd like to make, and I was wondering if you might have time to drive me."

"Of course! Where would you like to go?"

"To Deirdre's grave," Susanna said, watching his reaction, "but I have no idea where she's buried."

His expression sobered. "The cemetery is not far. And, of course, I will be glad to take you."

"I thought—" Susanna stopped, then went on. "I thought perhaps we could also stop at the site of the accident. If you're quite sure it's not too much trouble."

He studied her for a moment, his usually lively features now altogether solemn. "It is no trouble at all. When would you like to leave?"

"Would it be convenient to go early this afternoon? Perhaps while Caterina is napping?"

"*Sì*, that would be very good. I will bring the buggy around front, say, at one o'clock."

"Thank you, Paul. I appreciate it."

Instantly, his expression brightened. "But it is my pleasure, Susanna! You never ask for anything. Never. I am more than happy to do something for you."

He *had* seemed pleased, Susanna thought on her way back upstairs. Not for the first time, it occurred to her that perhaps she should make more of an effort to get to know Paul Santi. In time, they might even become friends. He had certainly gone out of his way to make her feel at home since she arrived, often stopping to chat with her, inquire after her day, or inspect Caterina's latest drawings.

Not that he had ever indicated any sort of interest other than friendship. To the contrary, his behavior couldn't possibly be construed as anything but the natural courtesy and kindness he would have extended any other member of Michael's family.

At another time and under different circumstances, Susanna thought she might have responded more readily to his overtures toward friendship. She did enjoy Paul's company, especially since he never made things awkward by flirting or displaying any hint of romantic interest.

She had to smile a little at the very thought. Her experience with men was admittedly limited, but she couldn't help but think it would be *Paul,* not herself, who would find the idea of a "romantic interest" awkward—if not positively alarming.

Most of the time, he reminded her of a mischievous boy who entertained himself by amusing the entire household. His high energy and zany antics often made it difficult to remember that as concertmaster for the orchestra, he was an accomplished musician in his own right, not just Michael's assistant.

No matter how much he enjoyed playing the court jester, Susanna was convinced that back of his puckish high spirits there was a keen intelligence and sensitivity rarely glimpsed by anyone except those closest to him. Yet even though she liked Paul a great deal, she deliberately kept a certain distance from him. In truth, with the exception of Caterina, Susanna supposed it was fair to say that she kept a safe distance from *everyone.*

Perhaps her self-imposed reserve had to do with the fact that she could not shake the feeling of *impermanence* about her situation. After more than two months at Bantry Hill, she still could not completely relax, would not risk allowing herself to be seduced into a false sense of security. While she longed to share Caterina's life—at least until the girl was fully grown—a part of her lived in dread that circumstances might somehow dictate otherwise.

Outside Caterina's bedroom, she stood listening for a moment to the child's chatter, which was, of course, directed to Gus, the wolfhound. As she stood there, amused by her small niece's one-sided dialogue with the hound, something inside her gave an unexpected wrench at the thought of just how painful it would be to have to leave Caterina now, after becoming so fond of her, so involved in her life.

In an attempt to shake the melancholy that had been stalking her since daybreak, she went to tidy up her room a bit, then stood looking out the window. It was a sunny October morning, almost crystalline in its brightness and clarity of view. And yet Susanna had come to realize by now how quickly that could change. In fact, she half suspected that the gloom which sometimes hovered over her own spirit these days had much to do with the landscape itself.

There was a certain brooding secretiveness about this entire river valley, and Bantry Hill was in no way exempt from it. This was a world of dark, moldering estates, dense forests, and always the mighty river that gouged and wound its way through an almost surreal vastness. Magnificent but primitive, spectacular but formidable. It was all too easy to imagine that Bantry Hill might harbor some awful truth or terrible secret that, once revealed, would prove to be more than she could bear. Something that might even drive her away from this place—and from Caterina.

She hugged her arms to herself, as if to press the miasma of dread out of her body, out of her soul. With a sigh, she told herself it was simply her Celtic imagination running amok. The prospect of visiting her sister's grave had cast a pall over the entire morning.

On a day like this, she chided herself, her surroundings should inspire her, not depress her. She had no excuse for this shadowed, nagging sense of foreboding that darkened in the recesses of her spirit. She had a niece she adored, work she enjoyed, and people—like Paul Santi and Rosa Navaro—who seemed to care about her. God forgive her, what more could she want?

Without warning, the thought of Michael—the image of his darkly bearded face, the quick, brilliant warmth of his smile—caught her unawares, striking her like a blow and leaving her to reach out a hand to the window frame in order to steady herself.

After a moment she opened the window. Perhaps the morning air would clear her head. Leaning forward a little, she could see Michael and Paul standing just in back of the house. They seemed to be having a brisk, even heated, exchange, with much gesturing of the hands and waving of the arms—mannerisms Susanna had come to associate with the two men as typical of the Italian male.

Her first inclination was to close the window, or at least to step away. But when she heard her own name mentioned, her curiosity overcame her reservations about listening in, and she edged to the side of the window so she could hear better without being seen.

—

"—but it is not right, Michael! You should tell Susanna the truth! You should have told her long before now!"

Michael checked the impatient retort that rose to his lips. "And what should I tell her, Pauli? What exactly do I say to her, to Deirdre's sister, eh?"

"That is exactly the reason you should tell her the truth, Michael. Because she *is* Deirdre's sister. She has a right to know!"

"She has no *need* to know!"

"How can you be so sure? Is it really for you to judge?"

"Who else but I?"

He could hear Paul's shallow breathing and knew he was debating on whether or not to continue. Michael gave him no chance. "You of all people should understand why I do not speak of this to Susanna. You were here, Pauli. You saw how it was with us."

There was a silence. Although Paul sounded more guarded, obviously he wasn't ready to desist. "Michael, you think you are protecting Susanna. But I wonder if it is not yourself you are trying to protect."

"And what is *that* supposed to mean?"

"Do you really not see what you are doing?"

"No, I do not *see* what I am doing," Michael shot back, his words laced with sarcasm. "Apparently, I must depend on you even for this."

Michael regretted his sharpness the instant the words left his lips. But he wasn't accustomed to criticism from Paul, except perhaps when it pertained to a difference of opinion over a music score, and he was surprised by how much it hurt. Paul was closer to him than a brother, yet he could not seem to understand why Michael had chosen to keep his silence about Deirdre. Instead, Paul saw his actions as unreasonable, even selfish.

"This is not right, Michael. It's not fair to Susanna! Why are you doing this? It is not like you to be deceitful."

Michael gave a long sigh, groping for patience.

"You are so intent on keeping the truth about that night— that one, terrible night—from Susanna, that you are keeping everything else from her as well, including—"

"Including *what?*" Michael bit out, losing the struggle to restrain his temper.

There was another silence. Then, "You care for her, Michael," Paul said quietly.

Michael tensed, knotted his fists at his side. "Enough, Pauli. You overstep."

"I see it, *cugino*. You care for Susanna, but you suffocate your feelings with your stubborn silence. And Susanna—"

"What about Susanna?"

When Paul finally answered, he sounded unexpectedly deflated. "Never mind. Perhaps you are right, I have spoken out of turn."

"*Sì, avete,*" Michael said tightly.

———

"Yes, you have . . ."

They had lapsed into Italian now, but even if Susanna hadn't understood their words, she could have detected the frustration in Paul's voice—and the tightly controlled anger in Michael's.

She waited another moment, then heard the back door slam as one or both of them came inside.

So Michael *hadn't* told her the truth about the night Deirdre died. At least not the *entire* truth. Indeed, it sounded as if he was hiding a great deal more than just the truth about the accident.

"You care for her. I see it."

Her heart leaped again, just as it had when she heard Paul speak those words. But obviously, Paul was wrong. If Michael really cared about her as something more than a friend—for that clearly was what Paul had insinuated—he wouldn't deliberately deceive her about her own sister. Would he?

"I wonder if it is not yourself you are trying to protect."

What had Paul meant by that accusation? At least, it had *sounded* like an accusation.

Suddenly, her every instinct urged Susanna to fly downstairs and confront Michael. She wanted to rip away those unnerving dark glasses and *demand* that he tell her everything. She wanted to lash out at him, to challenge him until that dark, inscrutable countenance finally showed some emotion, until he admitted that he had been in some way responsible for Deirdre's horrible death.

But of course she would do nothing of the kind. She could not face him and admit that she'd been eavesdropping, no matter how much she was tempted to do so. Nor could she go charging downstairs and provoke a scene that might prompt him to send her packing like the poor relative she was, leaving Caterina behind.

No, she could not risk arousing his anger to the point that he might actually banish her. Caterina had already lost her mother. God forbid that she should have to suffer yet another loss of one she loved.

And the child *did* love her. Susanna had no doubt of it.

She lowered the window, then began to pace the room. Could the truth, no matter how terrible it might be if fully known, really make all that much difference? She could not for the life of her fathom anything so horrible that it would prompt her to leave Bantry Hill—leave Caterina—of her own volition.

Finally, she sat down on the side of the bed, still struggling with the question as to whether anything—*anything*—she might learn about Michael himself, or Deirdre's death, could possibly be so heinous that she would allow it to drive her away from Caterina.

In the midst of her attempt to make a way through the quagmire of unanswered questions, yet *another* question—this one even more unsettling—came hurtling out of nowhere, startling her with its almost brutal force:

Was Caterina really the reason, the only *reason, she was so resolved to stay at Bantry Hill? What part, exactly, did Michael play in her unwillingness to leave?*

Shaken, Susanna sat unmoving, scarcely breathing, as she clasped and unclasped her hands. She must not, dare not, commit the folly of trying to answer that question.

Not now. Not ever.

TWENTY-SIX

THE DOCTORS ARE IN

'TIS THE HUMAN TOUCH IN THIS WORLD THAT
COUNTS . . .

SPENCER MICHAEL FREE

New York City

Today was the first day the Drs. Carmichael and Cole would be seeing patients at their new location.

Loath to think that she might have been in any way responsible for Andrew's decision to relocate, Bethany finally accepted her new partner's insistence that the move had been inevitable for some time now, that she had merely provided the needed impetus for his taking action.

There was no denying that he had outgrown the building on East Seventeenth, and even though the new quarters were situated in a less desirable area, they were far more spacious. Besides, this was where Andrew Carmichael wanted to practice.

Bordered by Bleecker Street, Thompson Street, and the Bowery, the rambling brick building was located in the very heart of an immigrant district. Although many of the older structures in the area had once been homes to city merchants and businessmen, by now most had become commercial establishments and, more recently, settlement houses. Among them could be found temporary housing, as well as class-rooms and workshops where English was taught and instruction provided in sewing, cooking, and other basic skills. Occasional clinics were set up for the poor, but these were makeshift at best and usually open to patients only a few days a month.

It hadn't taken Bethany long to realize that Andrew Carmichael had an intense burden for the underprivileged, especially the countless poor immigrants who spilled onto the shores of New York by the thousands. He had actually purchased the entire building on Elizabeth Street with the express purpose of moving both his office and his living quarters. His intention was clear: not only would he be available to his patients, he would also be living among them.

Bethany had been a little puzzled by the acquisition of the building, if not by the man's commitment. Andrew Carmichael couldn't be much past his midthirties—hardly old enough to have accumulated any real wealth. Besides, he kept his fees far too low to generate a lucrative income. Perhaps he was just unusually adept at saving. From what she knew of his lifestyle, it was modest, altogether unpretentious.

In fact, they had this in common; Bethany had never felt the need to own more than the basic necessities, except for her one extravagance—books. Nor had she ever been ensnared by the love of "things," desiring instead the freedom to practice medicine where the need was greatest, not necessarily where she could earn the most money. It seemed that here, too, her goals were highly compatible with those of her partner.

Her partner.

The fact that she could actually think of Andrew Carmichael in those terms was entirely his doing. Less than a month after they'd begun to practice together, he had informed Bethany that he preferred to acknowledge her as his *associate* rather than as his *assistant.*

The truth was, Bethany would have been *grateful* to serve as his assistant, at least for a time, so eager was she to set up a practice and secure hospital privileges. Andrew, however, refused to discuss it, pointing out that she had worked just as long and as hard as he had to gain her education and training—"most likely harder, considering the obstacles you've had to overcome in the medical community itself."

He insisted his need wasn't so much for an assistant as it was for a full-time partner, someone willing to carry an equal share of the increasing patient load. "Much as I dislike admitting it," he told her, his speech rhythmic with the faint Scottish burr Bethany had come to find rather charming, "I cannot seem to manage the work as I need to. So you see, there will be none of this 'assistant' business. You're my associate, and that's how it will be."

Even now, as Bethany stood scrutinizing the examining room—*her* examining room—she had to remind herself again that all this was real. She had worked so hard and had waited so long for her own private practice that she could scarcely take it in.

She heard Andrew clattering about in the adjoining examining room and smiled a little. Perhaps she ought to go offer to help him. The poor man did seem inclined toward disorder, even clumsiness at times.

She had worked until early evening the day before, arranging her instruments just so, stocking the cabinets with tins and bottles and boxes all neatly labeled, then lining the drawers with clean paper before filling them with an adequate supply of dressings, bandages, and towels. Now, with her white ticking apron starched and pressed, her hair tucked firmly into a knot at the nape of her neck, she was ready for whatever the day might bring.

Andrew, on the other hand, had made late calls on two patients the night before and consequently was only now readying his office and examining room. From the sound of things, he was *throwing* supplies in place rather than arranging them.

Bethany knew before she entered that she would most likely find him in a clean but rumpled laboratory coat, with a shock of dark hair falling over his forehead. As always, he would appear somewhat harried and impatient, although his impatience never seemed to be directed at her, only himself.

In fact, he was still in his shirt sleeves and down on his knees, scooping up an armful of bandages off the floor. He looked up as Bethany entered, giving her one of his diffident smiles as he scuttled to his feet, his free hand knocking an entire row of tin containers off the cabinet shelf in the process.

With some effort, Bethany kept a straight face as the tins went clattering to the floor. Andrew stared at the disarray, then, red-faced, gave a quick little shrug and a quirk of his mouth as he heaped the bandages on the examining table and bent to retrieve the scattered tins.

When Bethany knelt to help him, he muttered, not looking at her, "I should have done this last night, I expect."

"You were seeing patients last night," she reminded him. "I'll help you finish up."

Something about his lean profile, the dark head bent so

seriously to his efforts—and so close to her—made the breath catch in Bethany's throat. More peculiar still was the sudden inclination to brush that rebellious wave of hair away from his forehead.

He turned to her then, their eyes meeting for an instant.

Bethany quickly averted her gaze, but not before her pulse gave an unexpected leap.

"I'm really quite pathetic, aren't I?" he said.

Surprised, Bethany turned back to him, unable to stop a smile at the sight of his undue look of self-disgust.

"Don't be silly," she said, hurrying to scoop up the remainder of the tins. "It's just that you're in a rush, that's all."

It was then that she noticed his hands. His fingers were swollen, his knuckles red and inflamed, his movements stiff as he went on collecting the containers.

Bethany's stomach knotted. So there was more to Andrew's ungainliness than haste or preoccupation. Suddenly anything but amusing. The slow, stiff gait as he ascended a flight of stairs, his tendency to drop things, the unusual paleness and fatigue that occasionally seemed to overtake him now took on new significance.

She said nothing, however, as she got to her feet. With a deliberate effort to keep her expression clear, she set the tins back in order, then refolded the towels and stacked them in the cabinet drawers.

When she turned, she found him watching her. He had donned his lab coat, its sleeves nearly an inch too short above his wrists. Not for the first time, it occurred to Bethany that with his considerable height, his long arms, and somewhat prominent nose, Andrew Carmichael was almost Lincolnesque—albeit more handsome-featured than the late president—in his appearance. Perhaps he was also just as stoic in his character.

She forced a smile. "Well," she said brightly, "it would seem that all we need now are some patients."

As if on cue, the bell above the entrance door rang, alerting them that someone had come into the office. They looked at each other, and both of them started for the door at the same time.

——

They had discussed the likelihood that they would see at least three or four new patients on their first day. Before noon they had ushered no less than a dozen through the doors.

By agreement, Bethany had seen to the women, while Andrew tended to the men. They had taken turns, also by agreement, in treating the children.

Andrew stood watching Bethany escort the last of their morning patients—a small girl dressed in little more than rags and her cadaverously thin mother—out the door. Word that a woman doctor had set up practice in the area seemed to have traveled fast, and Andrew suspected that after today the news would spread like a brush fire. Women simply did not want a male doctor attending them, especially in the more delicate female matters, such as gynecological problems and childbirth.

In deference to those women who did subject themselves to an examination, he always tried to be sensitive and exceedingly careful, even to the point of using a longer stethoscope than usual to maintain his distance from the patient. But these cursory physical examinations were unsatisfactory, to say the least.

Bethany had brought a solution to this dilemma. She seemed to easily gain the confidence of their female patients, even the most hesitant ones. A steady stream of women had already begun to show up at the old offices before the move, and Andrew had no doubt but what the same thing would happen here as well.

All told, there was simply no reckoning the difference she had made in the practice, not only by gaining the trust of the women patients as she had, but in the considerable workload she'd assumed all along. Andrew could not help but recognize a certain irony in the situation.

If he were to be altogether honest with himself, he supposed that in the beginning of their relationship, he might have entertained a fanciful thought of himself as some sort of modern-day knight, "rescuing" Bethany Cole by helping her obtain her hospital privileges, and at the same time secure a patient list of her own.

Saint Andrew. He smiled at his own foolishness. The fact was that *he* had been the one who needed rescuing.

And it seemed that the lovely Dr. Cole had done a fine job of it, in a very short time.

In any event, it was an immeasurable relief to know that entire families could now receive the medical treatment they needed and deserved. He had tried to do his best for *all* his patients, of course, but there was no denying an ongoing frustration in never being able to provide adequate care for the ever-increasing numbers who needed it, especially the women.

Of course, the truth was that he had never been all that comfortable with women, professionally or personally. His mother had died giving birth to him, leaving Andrew to be raised by his middle-aged clergyman father. There had been only an older brother, no sisters to bring even a touch of feminine influence to his youth. With the exception of his aging Aunt Cecily and a grandmother who died before he even reached his teens, nearly all the people in his life had been men.

He had been in love once, in his late twenties. Tragically, his somewhat frail Evelyn had died during a diphtheria epidemic before they could marry. After that, Andrew had withdrawn to his profession, the church, and his travels. More recently, of course, his own physical condition had become an issue, making him reluctant to even consider a new romantic interest.

Not that the opportunity had presented itself. Indeed, Bethany Cole was the first woman to evoke more than a passing interest in all that time.

In many ways, Bethany was a puzzle. At twenty-seven, she had gained an impressive education and quite a lot of experience. She seemed to attack any task she undertook with the same competence and conscientiousness she brought to every patient under her care. Yet she was an extremely feminine, attractive young woman with a bright, appealing personality.

More than once, Andrew had marveled that she hadn't married and wondered if there was someone in her life. A fiancé, perhaps? And if not, then *why* not?

He came to himself and realized she was standing with her back to the door, watching him with a faint smile.

"Well—it seems we managed our 'three or four' patients for the morning, Dr. Carmichael," she said.

"It does seem so, Dr. Cole," he replied. He became aware that he had been rubbing his hands together, kneading his fingers—an involuntary, almost mindless effort to assuage the pain. Quickly, he lowered them to his sides.

"Since the waiting room is finally empty," he said, "why don't we get away for lunch? There's just the place down the street."

Bethany looked dubious. "In this neighborhood?"

"I can see that I need to acquaint you more thoroughly with your new surroundings. You might be surprised at what's out there."

"I don't doubt that for a moment."

Andrew leaned against the counter, studying her—the fine,

clearly drawn features and delicate complexion, the slight lift
with which she carried her head, the always-correct posture—
all of which virtually shouted upper class and breeding.
"Whatever possessed you to do this, Bethany?"

She frowned. "Do what?"

Andrew took in the room with a quick sweeping motion of
his hand. "Medicine. More to the point, why would you agree
to practice in the thick of a settlement district, where you'll
never earn anything more than a modest living, at best?"

"What possessed *you* to do it?" she countered.

He shrugged. "That's different altogether. I didn't have to
fight the prejudice and resistance of an entire establishment.
And I don't come from an upper-class background."

He hadn't meant for the last to slip out, and he could tell the
remark had caught her unawares—and quite possibly annoyed
her as well. "I'm sorry," he said quickly. "That was uncalled
for—pure assumption on my part."

She was studying him with one uplifted eyebrow.

Again, Andrew attempted to apologize. "I *am* sorry, Bethany.
As I said, I just assumed—"

With relief, he saw the ghost of a rueful smile touch her
lips. "I'm not rich, if that's what you're thinking, Andrew."

"No, really, I didn't mean—"

She laughed. "It's all right. As I said, I am definitely not
wealthy, although there was a time, I suppose, when my grandfather was. He came from a long line of bankers and philan-
thropists. Most of his family tried to discourage him from
medicine. They thought it too *common*. Ultimately they more
or less disowned him." She paused, smiling a little. "It didn't
seem to bother him much. He was generally considered to be
one of the finest surgeons and researchers in the country, but
he had a distinct tendency to give away his earnings."

"What about your parents? I don't believe I've ever heard you mention them."

"They died in a train accident when I was very young. My grandparents raised me."

She said this without a trace of sentimentality, and Andrew sensed she had said all she meant to say about her family. Before she could change the subject, however, another thought struck him.

"Bethany—" He paused, thinking, then musing aloud. "Bethany *Cole* . . . your grandfather isn't Dorsey Cole, by any chance?"

She looked surprised, but pleased. "You knew my grandfather?"

"No, but of course, I know *of* him. I studied his papers on narcotics addiction after the war. In fact, I attended one of his lectures once when he visited Columbia. A brilliant man. Does he still practice?"

The light in her eyes dimmed slightly. "No, he died before I finished medical college."

"I'm sorry," said Andrew. "He must have been very proud that you chose to follow in his footsteps."

Her smile returned. "Yes, I think he was." She started for the door into the examining area, tugging at the ties of her apron. "He even permitted me to do an apprenticeship with him, which was probably the best—and definitely the most strenuous—part of my training."

She stopped, glancing back at the waiting room. "If this morning is an indication of things to come, Andrew, I think we may have to consider hiring a receptionist soon."

"Quite right. And if you don't mind, I'll let you handle the interviewing. My last receptionist was a huge mistake. Perhaps you'll do better."

"I'll take care of it," she said briskly. "And now—about that lunch?"

Her gaze traveled down the front of his lab coat, at the blood spots left by a policeman with a stab wound.

Andrew tried to ignore the annoying way his heart had begun to race at the prospect of an hour alone with her, an hour without a room full of patients waiting for their attention. "I'll just change, and we'll go," he said.

He fumbled at the buttons on his coat, for once unable to blame his clumsiness on his swollen fingers.

TWENTY-SEVEN

AMONG FRIENDS

TWO ARE BETTER THAN ONE,
BECAUSE THEY HAVE A GOOD RETURN FOR
THEIR WORK . . .

ECCLESIASTES 4:9 (NIV)

These are quite possibly the best potato pancakes I've ever tasted," Bethany declared, bringing the last bite to her mouth.

So much for her resolve not to finish everything on her plate.

"Didn't I tell you?" Andrew said, his tone smug as he stabbed another piece of German sausage. "The place may not look like much, but Axel's is a legend."

They sat on benches across from each other at a scarred wooden table. Bethany glanced around the small, dim room, the air of which was heavy with too many rich aromas to distinguish one from the other. Earlier, when they had come in, they'd had to wait for a table. Now she knew why.

Amid the clink of glasses and clatter of silverware, a variety of diners talked and laughed. Most of the patrons were dressed in business attire, but some men wore the work clothes of laborers, too.

A waiter in a butcher's apron appeared just then to suggest dessert. Bethany groaned aloud. "Do people really eat dessert after a meal like that?"

"Not I," Andrew said, waving off the waiter. He pushed his plate out of the way and leaned forward, folding his elbows on top of the table. "Tell me about Dr. Blackwell," he said. "What's she like?"

"Dr. Blackwell," replied Bethany, "defies description."

Elizabeth Blackwell had been the first woman in the United States to receive a medical degree. She had also created quite a scandal with her insistence on attending a male-dominated medical school because, at the time, the women's colleges didn't provide as high a quality of medical training as did the traditional universities. After finally graduating from Geneva Medical College—at the head of her class, no less—she had gone on to do advanced studies in London. When she returned to New York, with the help of her sister she established her own hospital: the New York Infirmary for Women and Children, where Bethany had received a part of her training while also serving on staff.

"Actually," Bethany said, "I've only met Dr. Elizabeth once, when she was here for a visit. She spends most of her time in London now. I know her sister, Dr. Emily, much better. And Dr. Jacobi as well."

"Yes, I know Dr. Jacobi, too. An excellent doctor. She's still teaching at the Infirmary, then?"

"Oh, yes. In fact, I more or less functioned as her assistant until recently. She's really remarkable, you know. In addition to her practice and her teaching, she's been busy setting up a children's dispensary at Mount Sinai. I've learned more from her about children's diseases than I ever did in medical college!"

"Good. I can promise you you'll put that knowledge to work sooner or later in our practice."

Bethany studied him. "Andrew," she said, "why haven't you told me about the rheumatism?"

A look of pained surprise darted over his features. As if by instinct, he dropped his hands to his lap, where they couldn't be seen, and glanced away. "I didn't realize you'd noticed."

"I wasn't sure until today," Bethany said. "So I'm right? It *is* rheumatism?"

"Rheumatoid arthritis, actually."

Bethany swallowed. "Acute?"

He tossed his head a little to flick the stubborn shock of hair away from his face. "No, chronic. With all the predictable symptoms."

"I'm sorry, Andrew."

"It doesn't interfere with my work," he said quickly, almost irritably. "You needn't worry about that."

"I'm not worried. But it must make things difficult at times." Bethany was careful to allow no hint of anything resembling sympathy to slip into her tone. She sensed he would be appalled if he suspected she felt sorry for him.

His shrug seemed casual enough, but he avoided meeting her eyes. "I apologize, Bethany. I know I should have told you before you agreed to come into the practice with me."

"Why didn't you?" she asked quietly.

He raised his head and looked at her. "That's fairly obvious, isn't it? I was afraid I might frighten you off."

"Oh, Andrew! Surely you don't believe that."

He sighed. "I wasn't being entirely selfish, Bethany. At least,

I hope I wasn't, although I could hardly blame you for thinking otherwise. I really *did* believe I could be of help to you in your own efforts rather more quickly than if you tried going it alone." He paused. "Naturally, I'll understand if you want out."

Bethany frowned at him. "Don't be ridiculous. This makes no difference whatsoever."

His relief was unmistakable as he leaned forward and brought his hands back to the table. "You can't imagine how glad I am to hear you say that. And it truly *doesn't* affect my work."

"Stop apologizing, Andrew. Your work is exemplary. I should know that if anyone does. So . . . how long have you had it? The arthritis?"

He took a sip of water. "Several years, actually. It started when I was still in medical college. Although looking back, I think I had symptoms of it even before then."

"What do you do for it?" Bethany had no intention of prying, but her interest wasn't entirely professional. She had come to like Andrew Carmichael. She liked him a lot. She also admired him a great deal. Knowing how his particular disease could ravage the body, she hated to think what might lie ahead for him if the affliction progressed.

Again he shrugged. "I'm sure you already know there's not much one *can* do. Heat. Massage. The new salicylate treatments seem to help more than anything else. Of course, there are two schools of thought on whether exercise is helpful or harmful. I tend to think activity is best. At least that's been my experience."

"What about new research? Is there anything available?"

"Not very much, I'm afraid. I haven't run across anything lately that I didn't already know. The problem is, there seems to be a disadvantage for every potential benefit."

"What about these ocean crossings, Andrew? Don't you

worry that being on the water so much might aggravate your condition? The dampness and cold can't be good for you."

He made a gesture with one hand as if to minimize the question. "I suppose it doesn't help, but I can't imagine giving up the traveling altogether. "

"It's that important to you to be a part of the Moody campaigns?"

"It's a way I can help in the work." A faint smile tipped the corners of his mouth. "I'm no preacher, but I can at least help to take care of those who are."

"You feel that strongly about it?"

He regarded her with a look that made Bethany wonder if he thought she was being critical. She simply did not understand Andrew's commitment to these international "revivals."

The more she knew of Andrew Carmichael, the more she realized that something about Andrew's faith was different from her own. He tended to be reserved, even shy, in some situations, but there was a bedrock steadiness and strength to the man, both as a person and as a physician. In contrast, he displayed a kind of abandonment in his life that she could easily envy. As a believer, he was almost childlike. Enthusiastic. Even joyful. Devout. And completely nonsectarian. His interest and concern for people went beyond mere tolerance.

Andrew loved people. He loved them quietly, and sometimes even with a wry amusement. But he loved them. The impartial, unconditional treatment he extended to those around him on a daily basis exemplified a quality of life that Bethany had never before witnessed, except possibly in her grandfather.

His voice jarred her out of her thoughts, and she realized he was answering the question she'd asked.

"I know I'm not explaining this very well," he said, smiling a little. "No doubt you've noticed that I'm not all that good with words. But you see, traveling with D. L. began as my way of giving something back. There's always a need for a doctor's services during such a large, extended campaign. But D. L. Moody and Ira Sankey are doing their own kind of healing, it seems to me—an even more important kind of healing than I can offer as a physician—and it's gratifying and fulfilling for me to be a part of it, no matter how small a part. So if I'm uncomfortable for a few weeks as a result"—he gave a light shrug—"it's relative. It doesn't matter all that much."

Bethany found herself responding to his candor, his humility. "I must say, I admire you for it, Andrew. Even if I don't quite understand."

He frowned, then shook his head. "Don't admire me. The truth is that I gain far more from the Moody-Sankey campaigns than I could ever possibly *give.*"

"Goodness, Andrew, it's not such a bad thing to be admired."

He regarded her with his usual warmth and good humor for a moment. Then his expression sobered. He reached across the table, and although he withdrew his hand at almost the same instant as he touched hers, the effect on Bethany was immediate—and unsettling.

"Believe me, Bethany, I covet your good opinion," he said softly. Their eyes locked for another second or two before he finally looked away.

"I didn't mean to embarrass you," Bethany said, feeling a need to lighten the moment. "I suppose I have a bad habit of sometimes saying what I think—*before* I think."

"No need to apologize," he said softly. "It's just that I wouldn't want you to think more highly of me than I deserve. You don't . . . there's a lot you don't know about me, Bethany."

"Secrets, Andrew?"

His entire expression changed, and she immediately wished

she hadn't teased him. "I expect we all have our secrets," he said, his eyes darkening with some unreadable emotion.

Was it sorrow she saw reflected in his gaze? Bethany felt a sudden urgency to reassure him, though for what she couldn't have said. "Andrew, I just wanted you to understand that I respect you. As a physician. And as a person. And I want to be very clear on the fact that the arthritis makes absolutely no difference in our partnership." She paused, then added, "Or in our *friendship*."

Bethany was surprised by the ease with which the word rolled off her lips. But it was true. He was becoming more than a colleague. Even before today, she had sensed a subtle change taking place in their relationship, as if they'd moved beyond a professional alliance toward something more personal, something deeper . . . something that held a kind of promise.

A promise of what?

"You're quite sure?"

Bethany looked at him, and the softness of his gaze made her fumble for words.

"Yes. I'm quite sure."

His eyes held hers, and he swallowed with some difficulty. "I'm glad," he said. "And very relieved."

They sat quietly for a time, the companionable silence between two people who were becoming comfortable with each other.

"Bethany?"

She looked up.

"Are you . . . is there someone in your life? You've never said, but I've wondered. Are you engaged? Do you have a . . . commitment of any sort?"

His face was crimson, his hands occupied with wringing his napkin into a rope.

"Engaged?" Bethany stared at him. "No. No, I . . . there's no one."

He suddenly looked both relieved and embarrassed. "I confess that I find it nothing less than amazing, that some fellow hasn't put a ring on your finger by now."

"Well, there was someone, once. A long time ago."

He watched her closely. "What happened?"

Bethany hadn't expected that the memory would still hurt. Even so, she forced a note of lightness into her reply. "I finally realized he loved medicine more than he loved me." She paused and took a breath. "Not to mention the fact that a certain young debutante's father was only too willing to finance such a promising physician's career—if that promising physician happened to be his son-in-law."

He looked stricken. "I'm *sorry*, Bethany."

Bethany gave him a long, level gaze. "I'm not."

There. He could interpret that however he chose.

He finally mustered a smile, and it occurred to Bethany how dramatically even the faintest of smiles seemed to alter his entire countenance. Andrew wasn't exactly a handsome man. She supposed his face was a little too lean and long for classical good looks. But when he smiled, it was like the sun breaking through a stand of trees. She was increasingly coming to esteem that smile.

Later, outside the restaurant, he offered his arm, and Bethany took it. "Andrew?"

"Yes?"

"Will you be traveling again anytime soon?"

He looked down at her. "Why, no. Not for some months, actually."

"I'm glad," Bethany responded.

"Please don't be concerned about the workload, Bethany. I'll make certain that when I do travel, someone will be available to help with the practice. I wouldn't expect you to carry the entire patient load by yourself."

"It's not that," she said evenly, tightening her grasp on his arm just a little.

"No?" He gave her a quizzical look.

"I'm not concerned about the workload. I'm just glad you're not going away again soon."

"Oh," he said softly.

After a long pause, he cleared his throat. "I believe I'm glad, too."

With that, he tucked her arm a little more snugly against his side, and they walked down the street together toward their new office.

TWENTY-EIGHT

Lingering Shadows

For the vision of hope is decayed,
Though the shadows still linger behind.

Thomas Dermody

Bantry Hill

But I'm not sleepy, Aunt Susanna. Why must I take a nap? Naps are for babies. And I am *not* a baby. I am four years old."

"Yes, I know, *alannah,* but remember what Dr. Carmichael said? A nap every day until he tells us otherwise. He wants to see you strong, even stronger than you were before your illness."

Susanna tucked the quilt snugly about Caterina's shoulders, then kissed her lightly on the forehead. "And you are quite right, miss, you are not a baby. You are growing up even as I watch, it seems."

Caterina, who never sulked for more than a moment or two, looked up and smiled. "Am I really, Aunt Susanna? You can *see* me growing?"

"Oh, indeed. I sometimes wonder where my wee girl has gone. Do you suppose someone might have taken her away and left a garden plant in her place, one that seems to be shooting up in front of my very eyes?"

The child giggled. "You're teasing, Aunt Susanna! I'm right here. And I don't feel any bigger than I was when you came."

Susanna smiled back at her. "Ah, but if you don't have your rest as Dr. Carmichael ordered, you might not grow at all, don't you see?"

"Couldn't I have another story first?"

Susanna could see the beginning signs of drowsiness in those deep blue eyes, so she shook her head firmly. "You have had two stories already, young lady. Perhaps tonight before bedtime we'll read another."

Caterina's expression turned solemn. "Papa is leaving. I don't like it when he's away."

"He won't be gone long. And didn't he promise to come say good-bye before he goes?"

"Yes. But I still wish he would stay home." She yawned. "I suppose I don't mind his being gone *quite* so much since you've come, though. I like having you here, Aunt Susanna."

The girl's eyes grew heavier, and Susanna touched another kiss to her forehead. "Thank you, sweet," she said quietly.

"Do you like it here with us, Aunt Susanna?"

The question was entirely unexpected, especially given the fact that the child could scarcely keep her eyes open.

"What kind of a question is that, Caterina? Of course, I like it here! I like being with you more than anything else I can imagine."

"I'm glad," said the little girl, her voice even thicker now. Her lashes fluttered as she closed her eyes. "Mama didn't, you know."

Susanna tensed. So rare was any reference to Deirdre by her daughter that the girl's words took her by complete surprise. "Whatever do you mean, Caterina? I'm sure your mother *loved* being with you."

Caterina didn't open her eyes, and Susanna had to strain to hear her reply. "No . . . she didn't . . . Mama didn't like us . . . very much . . ."

Susanna straightened. She felt suddenly chilled, as though the room itself had lost all warmth. She stood watching the sleeping child for another moment, then started for the door.

Susanna wished Paul had suggested two o'clock rather than one.

After getting Caterina settled, she'd gone to freshen her hair, then exchange her shoes for boots, in case the graveyard happened to be muddy. Consequently, she was in such a rush on her way out that she bumped into Michael, who was just coming inside.

The memory of the conversation she had overheard between him and Paul that morning caused her to feel even more awkward than usual in his presence. Awkward—and angry.

"I'm sorry, Michael," she said, an edge in her voice that even she could hear. "I didn't see you."

"Nor I you," he said with a smile.

"No, really—"

Susanna stared at him. As always, it took her a moment to realize that he was teasing. Although a touch of levity was hardly out of character for him, he never failed to surprise her when he made light of his blindness.

"And where are you off to in such a hurry?" he said, still smiling.

"I—" Susanna hesitated. She was reluctant to tell him where

she was going, perhaps because of the way his facial expression typically altered at the very mention of Deirdre's name.

"I asked Paul to take me to the cemetery. I haven't had a chance as yet to visit Deirdre's grave, you see."

For a change, he wasn't wearing the dark glasses, although his eyes remained closed. Susanna watched him closely, and sure enough, his features tightened, if ever so slightly.

There were times when it almost defied belief, that this man—always so quiet-spoken, so gentle in his treatment of others, and, on the surface at least, so accepting and at peace with his own misfortune—could possibly be guilty of the deception she suspected. Other times, such as now, however, given his immobile countenance and the hard set to his mouth, she thought it might not be so unimaginable after all.

His tone was distant, impersonal when he replied. "You should insist that Paul take the buggy instead of the carriage. It is a most pleasant day."

On impulse, Susanna said, "Would you like to go with us?"

He was very still, and for a moment Susanna thought he wasn't going to answer. Then, averting his face slightly, he said, "No, you should be alone, I think."

Susanna waited, but he offered nothing more.

"Mrs. Dempsey will check on Caterina from time to time," she told him. "I won't be long."

He turned back to her. "Take as long as you like, Susanna," he said quietly. "I will be here until later this afternoon. Just so you know, I may stay in the city overnight, depending on how late we rehearse."

He hesitated as if he might add something more, but instead turned and started down the hall toward his office.

Susanna watched him walk away. Part of her seethed at his seemingly unshakable self-control. Another part tried in vain to ignore a stab of disappointment at the reminder that he would be leaving later.

What sort of madness was it, she wondered, to be continually torn by these opposing feelings about a man who, even after two months of living under his roof, remained a mystery? Was she ever to learn whether he was indeed the saint those closest to him believed him to be . . . or the fiend his wife had made him out to be?

—

The graveyard rested at the very top of a high hill, no more than a mile distant from the house. It was one of the loveliest pieces of ground Susanna had ever seen. And one of the *loneliest*.

So this is how the wealthy bury their dead . . .

An unexpected swell of resentment rose up in her as she regarded the broad expanse of land, the ornate monuments, the grave sites decorated with extravagant floral arrangements or even objects of art. The hillside itself was rich and unmistakably fertile ground, planted with thick grass, its color now dulled by the approaching end of autumn. Broad, rolling reaches of land lay totally unused, but obviously well cared for.

Susanna found the place offensive, almost as if it had been desecrated by pagan symbols. In Ireland, land meant survival. At home, a piece of ground this large and opulent would have fed countless starving families. With such land as this, her parents could have made a comfortable living for a lifetime! Here in America, it was left to lie fallow, its only purpose to serve as burial grounds for the dead.

At one corner of the cemetery, just ahead, there was a small chapel that looked as if it would hold no more than thirty people. Either the services held there must be limited to a very few mourners, or else the building was used only as another empty memorial.

"This way, Susanna." Paul took her arm and led her to a grave near the far side of the cemetery.

Susanna stumbled on the uneven ground as they approached the monument. It had been hewn from marble, with an inset of an intricately embellished Celtic cross.

She was somewhat surprised to find a solitary grave rather than a family crypt. Given Michael's apparent wealth, she had half expected a more imposing burial site. Her sister's grave was one of the least pretentious she had seen so far. Not that she would have favored a more ostentatious stone; to the contrary, she found Deirdre's resting place more tasteful than many of the other more elaborate grave sites.

Paul continued to support her with his arm as they stopped beside the grave. Susanna's eyes locked on the words engraved at the base of the cross:

DEIRDRE FALLON EMMANUEL

WIFE AND MOTHER

1843–1874

Something about the stark simplicity of those few words, so utterly lacking in emotion or sentiment, tore at Susanna's heart. For the first time, the reality of her sister's death struck her full-force, and like a string under the tension of a tuning peg, she felt herself grow tight, tight to the point of snapping. Then the trembling began, a brittle, spasmodic shaking she couldn't control. She would not have been surprised if her very bones had fractured under the force of the tremors quaking through her.

Paul tightened his grasp on her arm. Offering no words, he simply stood beside her, lending his support in silence.

"The flowers?" she questioned, pointing to the simple arrangement of wildflowers decorating the grave.

"Michael sees to it that there are always flowers here. Dempsey maintains the grave at his direction."

There it was again, one of the many inexplicable contradictions that seemed to make up Michael Emmanuel's character. The man who could not bear to mention Deirdre's name was the same man who saw to it that fresh flowers adorned her grave.

She shook her head as if to clear away the confusion.

Until this moment Deirdre's death, although all too real in Susanna's mind, had never actually penetrated the depths of her emotions with its dreadful, irrevocable finality. But now, standing here beside this lonely mound of earth, beneath which rested the lifeless body of her only remaining family member, she seemed to hear, for the first time and the last, the thud of the coffin as it closed, signaling the end of her sister's all too brief life.

Deirdre . . . Wife and Mother . . .

Dead at thirty-one years of age. Survived by a husband who seemed hard-pressed to speak her name, and a daughter whose childish memory of her would soon wither and drop away like the flowers that adorned her mother's grave.

"If you like, I will leave you alone," Paul said quietly, giving her arm a reassuring squeeze. "Take as much time as you want."

Susanna nodded, and he walked away, turning down the path from which they had come. For a long time, she stood staring at Deirdre's monument. Finally, she knelt in the soft grass, warm in the afternoon sun. Her throat swollen, her heart heavy, she whispered a prayer for her sister.

When she got to her feet, she stood looking around the graveyard, then turned her attention back to the monument. Why hadn't Michael made more of an effort to personalize the stone? Had he cared so little that he hadn't even bothered to have a more loving memorial engraved—if not for his own consolation, then for Caterina's sake? Was this austere inscription yet another sign of his indifference to Deirdre?

The gravestone seemed too cold to Susanna, too austere. And yet wasn't it somehow in keeping with Michael's obvious resistance to Deirdre's memory, his attempts to shut out all evidence of her existence and their life together?

In the midst of her musings, Susanna searched for her own grief. What, exactly, did Deirdre's death mean to her? How did she really feel about the loss of the sister she had never known all that well?

With so many years between them, they had never been close. They had been sisters, but never friends. Susanna had been little more than a child when Deirdre had left home to pursue her dream of becoming an important singer. She'd returned some months later, discouraged and without further hopes, only to leave again, this time as a member of a small traveling musical company out of Dublin.

She had gone on to become a part, albeit a rather insignificant part, of the opera world. After that, she had never come home again to stay, only to visit, and then for a few days at most. When she *did* visit, it was always in the midst of a whirlwind of rapturous accounts of her latest role, or her latest male conquest—or, on occasion, in the throes of depression because a role was not going well or because there *was* no recent male conquest.

She had met Michael in London, married him in Italy, and from there accompanied him to New York. Long before then, any real affection or closeness she and Susanna might have shared had eroded during the long periods of separation. Only when her marriage began to go bad had Deirdre renewed her letter writing, penning one grim post after another to Susanna, each filled with her growing unhappiness and despondency—as well as tales of her husband's bad temper and selfishness.

Susanna surveyed the forlorn grave and the cemetery, its rows of solemn monuments and crypts so at odds with the bright, sunny afternoon. Most of the grief she was now experiencing, she realized, was due less to any real affection she might have once held for her sister than to a bitter sense of all that had been lost. The fleeting years apart, the hours and moments wasted, the irretrievable opportunities for growing closer. All the times they had never had . . . and now never would.

The sad reality was that she missed Deirdre more for what they had *not* been to each other than for what they *had* been.

In any event, all she could do for her sister now was to take care of her child and, at the same time, continue her search for the truth behind Deirdre's tragic death. That much she could do, *would* do.

The sun-swept graveyard had begun to darken with lengthening shadows. Finally, with unshed tears stinging her eyes, Susanna touched her gloved hand to the stone cross. "Goodbye, Deirdre," she murmured. "God give you peace."

An Unveiled Truth

Even the truth may be bitter.

Old Irish saying

"Does Michael bring Caterina to visit her mother's grave?"
Susanna asked as they drove away from the cemetery.

Paul glanced at her, then turned quickly back to the road.
"No, not often."

"Does he come at all?" Susanna pressed.

Paul's face took on a pinched expression as he clicked his
tongue to step up the horse's pace a little. "No . . . I do not
really know, Susanna."

"I see," she returned evenly. She was not in the least surprised that Paul would equivocate. More than likely, Michael
didn't visit the cemetery at all.

They drove on, the silence between them thick with tension. Paul seemed different from his usual self this afternoon:
quieter, more sober, as if he had much on his mind, and none

of it pleasant. She wondered if he was still disturbed by his earlier argument with Michael.

As for herself, she felt completely drained, and her earlier melancholy had returned in force. She would have to shake off this dreary mood before going home to Caterina. It wasn't easy to conceal her feelings from her precocious niece; the child was uncommonly sensitive for one so young.

First, however, there was one last stop to make—this one, perhaps, even more difficult than the visit to Deirdre's grave.

—

The buggy slowed as Paul turned into a clearing on the left side of the road, just inside the turn.

Susanna looked around, a chill brushing the base of her neck. "This is where it happened?" she said, her voice low.

Paul nodded, and she started to get out.

"Wait," he cautioned, jumping down and hurrying around the buggy to help her.

Taking her arm, he led her across the road, where Susanna stood looking down the deadly drop. The rock-faced bluff pitched straight down for at least twenty feet or more before leveling off onto a kind of shelf, from which the ground again fell away to nothingness.

Instinctively, Susanna stepped back, and Paul's hand tightened on her arm. "The road was very muddy and slick that night, because of all the rain we'd had," he said, his voice tight. "Part of it had already washed away in a mud slide. The buggy went over here"—he inclined his head—"and landed there." He gestured to the shelf below.

"The ledge was enough to keep the buggy from going the rest of the way over the cliff, but even so—"

He didn't finish. He didn't have to. Susanna could imagine

the rest. She could almost hear in her mind the clatter of the wheels, the shriek of the terrified horse, the sickening crunch of metal, Deirdre's screams . . .

The horror of that night came roaring in on her, and she shook her head as if to throw off the nightmare. Feeling ill, she turned and walked quickly away.

Paul followed. Back inside the buggy, they sat in silence, both of them staring straight ahead. The sun had slipped behind thickening clouds. No longer bright, the afternoon was tinged by what her mother had called "the long light," that wistful lengthening of shadows that hints of autumn's passing and winter's lurking.

A shudder seized Susanna, and for a moment she thought the same trembling that had gripped her back at the cemetery would overcome her again. She sat up straighter, stiffening her back as she tried to force from her mind the image of the cliff and what had happened there.

"They were very unhappy together, weren't they?"

He glanced at her, then looked away, his expression clearly uncomfortable. "That is not for me to say, Susanna."

"Apparently, it's not for *anyone* to say," Susanna shot back, provoked by the inevitable resistance that greeted any question she might ask about Deirdre.

"I'm well aware that Deirdre wasn't happy, Paul," she persisted. "She wrote to me often. Especially the last year, before . . . the accident. There was no mistaking her misery."

Paul sat in stony silence, his gaze straight ahead, as if he hadn't heard her.

"Why won't *anyone* tell me what happened?" Frustration pushed Susanna to the edge of her composure. "Deirdre died in an accident as inexplicable as it was tragic. She left her home—and her child—in the middle of the night in a terrible rainstorm! *Something* happened that night, something that must have made her take leave of her senses!"

She leaned toward him even more, and finally he turned to look at her as she went on. "She was my *sister!* I have a right to know what happened, yet no matter who I ask, I'm made to feel guilty *because* I ask! No one will tell me *anything.* Her own husband seems to choke on the very mention of her name! Why, Paul? Why should that be?"

His dark eyes behind the glasses were plainly troubled. "Susanna, I am so sorry," he said. "I know you must have many questions, but it should be Michael who answers them, not I. Still, it is so very difficult for him. Please try to understand."

By now Susanna's pulse was thundering, her head throbbing. "*Understand?*" she burst out. "I'm supposed to understand that it's difficult for Michael? Deirdre is *dead,* but I'm supposed to feel sorry for *Michael,* even though he refuses to tell me the truth about what happened to his own wife—to my *sister!*"

She heard the shrillness in her voice and groped for restraint, but she was shaking so badly her words spilled out in a staccato stammer. "I already know their marriage was troubled. You're not going to shock me. Deirdre told me in her letters how difficult Michael was to live with, how unreasonable he could be—"

Without warning, Paul swung around to stare at her, and whatever else she might have said froze on her lips. His face was white with fury, his eyes blazing.

"I should have known!" he ground out. "So—Deirdre told you that Michael made *her* unhappy?"

Momentarily stopped by this lightning change in him, Susanna could only sit and stare in astonishment.

"She said this?" he demanded.

"I . . . yes," Susanna admitted. "She was . . . wretchedly unhappy."

"Because of Michael," Paul repeated, his voice like that of a stranger in its hardness.

"Yes."

"And did she—"

Unexpectedly, he broke off, turning away from her. Susanna watched him drag in several long, uneven breaths and knot both hands into fists, bringing them to his temples as if to squeeze out some unbearable emotion as he stared mutely down at the floor of the buggy.

Her own anger temporarily deflected, Susanna managed to keep her tone level, even calm, when she spoke. "Paul, I understand your loyalty to Michael. He is your cousin, and you're very close, I know. But can't you try to understand what this is like for *me*? All I'm asking for is the truth. Not just bits and pieces of it, which is all Michael has ever offered me, but the *entire* truth. I'm not trying to pry. I don't mean to intrude on anyone's privacy. But is it really too much to ask that *someone* tell me what happened to Deirdre? And *why* it happened?"

At last he raised his face to look at her, and in that moment the pain she saw reflected there made Susanna question if she had gone too far.

"Michael has suffered, too, Susanna," Paul said, his tone quiet now. "He has suffered more than you can ever imagine. More than he would ever want you to know."

Susanna looked at him, wanting him to be right. She wanted to believe that Michael had indeed suffered because of Deirdre's death. She wanted to believe that he had cared enough to grieve for her, to agonize over his loss of her.

And yet how *could* she believe it, when everything Deirdre had written in her letters contradicted Paul's words? And when Michael himself seemed so intransigent in his silence?

She clutched at the rough wool of her skirt. Obviously,

there was nothing more she could do to sway him. Like everyone else, Paul was determined to protect Michael.

She was about to suggest they leave when his voice cut through the quiet.

"I can see that I must tell you," he said, his tone heavy with resignation.

Susanna caught her breath at his words. A bleak, solemn look settled over his countenance. All light seemed to have fled his usually animated features as he faced her.

"God forgive me," he said, "for no doubt Michael will not. But this has gone on long enough. Too long. I think I must tell you, not only for your sake, but for Michael's sake as well." He paused, studying her. "But how much should I tell you, Susanna? How much do you really want to know?"

"Everything," she said firmly. "I want you to tell me everything."

He shook his head, and an expression of sorrow passed over his face. "No, I cannot do that. There are things of which only Michael can speak. But I will tell you what I can, and I warn you, Susanna, that even *that* may be more than you will want to hear."

THIRTY

IN THE EYE OF THE STORM

WHEN WORDS ARE SCARCE, THEY'RE SELDOM
SPENT IN VAIN;
FOR THEY BREATHE TRUTH THAT BREATHE
THEIR WORDS IN PAIN.

WILLIAM SHAKESPEARE

From the difficulty Paul seemed to have framing his words, Susanna was beginning to think that whatever he was about to say held the potential to either confirm her worst suspicions—or replace them with an entire set of new ones.

She watched as he removed his glasses and rubbed a hand over his eyes in a gesture of infinite weariness. When he finally spoke, even his voice sounded tired and leaden. "So . . . you knew the marriage was not good, that there was trouble between them—"

Susanna nodded. "Deirdre was very frank in her letters. More than once she told me their marriage was a failure."

His lips thinned. "The marriage was a *disaster*. A battlefield. And for a very long time."

"But *why?* Deirdre was so happy in the beginning—"

Paul looked at her. "Please, Susanna, you must let me tell you this in my own way, as best I can. And first, you must try to forget anything Deirdre may have written to you. There will be much you do not understand. Even after I have finished, you will no doubt have questions, but please realize that I can only tell you what I know. What I witnessed for myself. You are already aware that Michael will say nothing. Even now, he is not willing to speak against Deirdre. For Caterina's sake— and for his own reasons—he will keep his silence."

Reluctantly, Susanna nodded, indicating that he should go on.

"There was much trouble between Michael and Deirdre," he said heavily. "Much trouble. Always they fought. Deirdre, you see, was always angry with Michael, and she would try to make him angry, too. She provoked him. Deliberately."

Susanna found it nearly impossible to remain silent in the face of such gross overstatement about Deirdre, an exaggeration that Michael surely must have fostered. But sensing that too many interruptions on her part would only distract Paul from the accounting he had begun, she resisted the temptation to object.

As if he could read her thoughts, Paul made a rueful smile. "You think I exaggerate about Deirdre, that I defend Michael and tell you only his side of things." He shook his head. "I am telling you the truth, Susanna. I know this is most difficult for you, but you must try to understand. Deirdre *hated* Michael."

At that, Susanna couldn't stop herself. "That's not true! She *never* wrote me anything of the sort. To the contrary, she said—"

Again he smiled, but it was bitter and utterly without

humor. "That she was afraid of him, no? And what else? That Michael mistreated her? That he was a madman, with a vicious temper, and she lived in terror of what he might do to her?"

A terrible coldness began to seep through Susanna as she sat staring at him. The truth was, Deirdre *had* written those very things . . . and worse. Much worse.

"How—"

"How do I know what she told you?" His mouth twisted as though he had bitten down on something foul. "Because that's what she told *everybody!* Anyone who would listen." He glanced away. "Especially when she was drinking. As she almost always was."

Shock and outrage streaked through Susanna. "I won't *listen* to this! This is all Michael's doing, isn't it? He put you up to this—"

"Why would he do that?" Paul's retort was sharp, almost angry. "Why would Michael tell me what to say, when in truth he will be furious with me for saying *anything?*"

Then his expression gentled. He reached to touch her hand, but she pulled away.

"Susanna . . . I am so sorry. I know this must be very difficult for you. But you wanted to know . . ."

"I wanted the *truth,*" she bit out.

"And that is what I am trying to tell you," he said evenly. "But if you prefer that I not go on, I understand."

Susanna hesitated. Here, finally, was her first glimpse behind the door that up until this moment had been firmly shut to her. If she stopped him now, she might never have an opportunity like this again. And yet his words had already stirred up such a maelstrom of disbelief and doubt, such a tempest of anger and resentment in her, she couldn't imagine how she would deal with it all, much less whatever else she was about to hear.

But wasn't *not* knowing worse? And even if Paul's perspective had been colored by his affection for Michael, he was at least making a sincere effort to be honest with her. So absolute was the integrity that emanated from Paul Santi that there could be no question of his deliberately twisting or tainting the truth. Not even for Michael.

So she swallowed hard and turned back to him, waiting. "Go on," she said. "Please."

He nodded. "Before I say more, I think I should tell you that Michael has always believed Deirdre had a . . . a *sickness*. That she was ill." He put a hand to his head. "In her mind."

"Are you saying he thought she was mentally ill?"

He delayed his reply, obviously considering his words. "*Sì*, but not because he meant to make . . . ah . . . the *excuse* for her, you see. He truly did believe this. And perhaps he was right. Perhaps to do the things Deirdre did, she would have had to be ill. Michael said that Deirdre was . . . that she could not control the drinking. And when she drank, she did things—she became very difficult. She hurt many people—especially Michael."

He paused, his voice dropping. "You say that Deirdre wrote to you of how Michael had hurt her. But the truth, Susanna, is that Deirdre hurt *Michael*. And Caterina. She hurt Caterina as well."

Despite the mildness of the day, a chill shuddered through Susanna. Questions and doubts came rushing in on her. And yet watching him, seeing her own hurt reflected in his eyes, sensing how difficult, even *painful*, this was for him, she found it impossible not to believe him.

"The fights were terrible," he went on in the same strained voice. "And Michael is a man who, I can tell you, resists an argument. Always, he has sought peace in his life. But Deirdre would give him no peace."

"You're painting a very cruel picture of my sister, Paul," Susanna said, her voice thin.

"*Sì*, it must seem so to you, I know. But the truth is sometimes a bitter thing, Susanna. And I will not lie to you: Deirdre could be a very cruel person."

All the uneasy memories and reluctant recollections that had begun to crowd her thoughts of late now collided with Paul's bitter narrative, battering her with the force of a tidal wall. For a split second she thought she might suffocate under the weight of her own emotions. But she managed to nod an indication that he should continue.

"Michael tried—for a long time he tried—to save their marriage. To help Deirdre stop the drinking. But Deirdre, she did not want to be helped; she did not want to save the marriage. She wanted a divorce."

Susanna looked up. "A *divorce?* Deirdre never mentioned a divorce in her letters."

He shrugged. "Nevertheless, it is what she wanted. She asked him for a divorce often. All the time."

"But surely after his accident—"

He laughed, a short, strangled sound. "After Michael's accident, she *demanded* a divorce."

Susanna forced herself to take deep, steadying breaths, fighting off one wave of nausea after another. "But by then they had Caterina."

"*Sì*, they did." Paul's tone was almost plaintive. "But Deirdre never wanted Caterina, you see. She meant to leave both Michael and Cati."

"*No!*" The fierceness of her response surprised Susanna. "Deirdre wouldn't have abandoned her own child—"

"But of course she would have abandoned her! Caterina was little more than a nuisance to Deirdre!"

Paul's words cracked like the lash of a whip, startling Susanna. Her arms felt numb, and she began to rub them with a hard, bruising roughness.

"Susanna? I'm sorry, I think I must say no more. This is too difficult for you. I am hurting you—"

"I'm all right," Susanna said shortly. She wasn't, of course. She wanted to pummel him with her fists for inflicting these hideous images onto her, even as the entire sum of her own fears began to materialize in her mind.

The stone of pain in her midsection might crush her in half at any moment. But she couldn't let him stop. Not now. "I have to know," she whispered.

He sighed and started in again. "I will tell you what Michael believed. This he told me himself, that Deirdre had never loved him, not even from the beginning."

"No, I—that's simply not true, Paul! She absolutely *raved* about him in her early letters. She *adored* him—"

"Perhaps she adored what he represented to her," Paul interrupted, an edge to his voice, "but Michael is convinced that for Deirdre, it was nothing more than a brief infatuation, that in truth she *used* him. As she might have used a rung on a ladder to get where she wanted to go."

Susanna stared at him, struggling *not* to believe. "That's unfair! Deirdre wouldn't have married him simply to advance her career—"

She stopped. Her heart gave a hollow thud, and her own words echoed in her ears as she remembered a day in the past. A sweet, warm summer's day at the farm, when Deirdre had been about to leave home for a tour with a small theater company . . .

They had ventured down to the stream behind the old

Mannion place and were sitting on the bank, splashing their bare feet in the water. Deirdre had just announced, somewhat pointedly, that on this particular trip she would be traveling in the same company with Donal Malone, an older man from the village, fairly well known in the county as a gifted baritone and an above-average actor.

He had also been sweet on Deirdre for some time.

"You don't want to be telling Papa that old Donal Malone is going along," Susanna warned her, only half teasing.

"It's not as if we'll be traveling *alone* together," said Deirdre. "We'll be with all the other members of the troupe. Not that I'd mind being alone with Donal."

Susanna had responded like a typical adolescent, giving an exaggerated shudder and a curl of her lip. "Donal Malone is an old man!"

"He's just past *forty*, you little eejit. That's hardly old. Not that it's any of your affair."

"He has a belly, and his hair is always greasy. I'll wager he uses fish oil on it." When Deirdre didn't react, she pressed, "You wouldn't let him *touch* you, would you?"

Deirdre had simply given her a look of disdain—a look that made it clear Susanna was still a child and, at the moment, a tiresome one. "Donal is thick with Thom Drummond, the director," Deirdre said archly. "It never hurts to have a man of influence take a fancy to you. I'll let the poor fool chew on my ear all he wants if he can boost my standing in the company."

Susanna fervently wished she could dismiss the memory as nothing more than mere girlish foolishness. Instead, she found herself cringing with sympathy for Michael. Even then, her sister had displayed a blatant tendency to manipulate. Was it really so difficult to believe that Deirdre had refined her skills even more in that particular area as she matured? If that was the case, what an incredibly painful—and humiliating—discovery it must have been for Michael, to realize he'd been nothing more than a means to an end.

Paul was watching her. "I am only telling you what Michael believed, Susanna," he said. "And he believed that he had been—used. Especially when—"

He stopped abruptly, frowning as if uncertain how to proceed.

"When *what?*"

"When the affairs began."

"Affairs?" Susanna flinched as if she'd been struck. "She was *unfaithful* to him?"

Paul was staring at something in the distance now, his jaw tight. He had begun to pull at the frame of his eyeglasses so viciously Susanna expected them to snap in his hands.

Abruptly, he replaced the glasses and turned toward her. In that moment, Susanna encountered an expression of such bitterness, such misery, that she knew she had not yet heard the worst of it.

"There is no kind way to tell you something like this, Susanna, so I will simply say it: Deirdre was openly promiscuous. She cuckolded Michael almost from the time they came to New York."

Susanna felt the blood drain from her head. The cold that had earlier enveloped her now seemed to turn inward with a fierce, numbing blast. She felt Paul's eyes on her, watching her as if he feared she would faint.

"Do you have *any* idea how difficult this is for me to accept?" she choked out.

No matter what else Deirdre might have done, Susanna simply couldn't believe that her sister had actually been capable of such baseness, such . . . *depravity.*

And yet every instinct within her seemed to shout that Paul would never lie about such a thing. As unbelievable and vile as it was, he was telling the truth.

And so she sat, mute, her mind reeling, her heart aching, and listened to the rest of it.

THIRTY-ONE

A STORY TOLD

I WILL MY HEAVY STORY TELL . . .

W. B. YEATS

Susanna couldn't have said when she turned the final corner of her lingering suspicions and doubts. She knew only that she could now *see* the truth evolving, like a distorted collage being formed even as she watched, as pieces of her own unsettling memories converged with Paul's devastating narrative. One after another her fragmented recollections came together, finding their place among the heartbreaking images Paul was painting for her. Having accepted the irrefutable reality of her sister's shame, she now unlocked the closed places in her mind and prepared herself to hear whatever was left to be told, no matter how grievously it might wound.

Stunned and trembling, she listened to the evidence against a sister whose debauchery had eventually robbed her of all reason, morality, and self-respect, only to leave her a dissipated virago who ultimately brought the worst sort of scandal down upon her husband and herself.

She listened in silence, her heart breaking even as a part of her raged inwardly for the awful destruction wreaked by her sister upon the very ones who loved her most. She learned of the ways Deirdre had shamelessly used Michael and his influence in the operatic world to foster her own career, while all the time Michael knew her voice suffered the lack of brilliance and power that might have eventually brought her true greatness.

And when he left the world that Deirdre had been so desperate to conquer, she had viewed his abdication as a kind of personal betrayal, foisting upon him even more bitterness, more resentment, more vicious attacks.

She heard with shuddering revulsion of the ongoing trysts with other men that had continued right up to the disgraceful affair in which Deirdre had been involved at the time of Michael's accident . . . and her death.

She bled inside to hear that her sister had turned away from her own child. Having never wanted Caterina, she punished Michael by punishing his child with her sharp tongue and scolding derision, indeed punishing the girl so cruelly Michael had begun to fear she might actually resort to physical abuse.

When Paul was loath to continue, offering to spare her any further demoralizing details, Susanna insisted he go on. And so she sat listening with mounting horror as he told her of the sick and demented "pranks" Deirdre had perpetrated on Michael after he lost his sight—often just before an orchestra performance or a social event: despicable tactics which caused him such humiliation and embarrassment that eventually he could scarcely bring himself to leave the house.

She listened, she anguished, and she quietly wept. By the time Paul reached the night of Deirdre's death, Susanna felt stricken with such misery she thought she could not bear to hear the rest of it. But she knew she must. There was no way in the world she could live without knowing what had happened that terrible night.

"The night she died," she choked out, "had she been drinking?"

Paul nodded, his face engraved with the stark, grim lines of remembered pain. "Most of the day. Earlier in the evening, I heard her and Michael arguing. She was determined to go out, was demanding that Dempsey take her to the ferry so she could go to the city. But Michael had already alerted Dempsey and me that we were not to drive her anywhere, not under any circumstances.

"It was a terrible night," he went on. "A dangerous night. The roads were treacherous at best. But apparently Michael's attempts to keep her from leaving only made her that much more determined. I was in the back, in my office, but I could hear them. Some time later, Deirdre went upstairs, and I thought she had retired for the night."

He leaned forward on the seat of the buggy, his expression doleful as the mild breeze blowing over the mountain ruffled his hair. "I was wrong," he said. "Much later—I think it was nearly midnight—I was reading in my room when I heard them again. Downstairs, in the music room. Deirdre was screaming, and Michael was shouting—an uncommon thing for him. I heard a crash, the sound of something breaking. I got up and went to Caterina's room. Cati was terrified of those drunken rages," he explained. "I didn't want that she should wake up alone."

His face ravaged, he faltered in his account. Susanna very nearly told him to stop. Her heart ached, not only for Caterina, for the fear and bewilderment the child must have endured, but for Paul as well. She could see what this was doing to him, that it was as painful for him to relive as it was for her to hear for the first time. But he quickly regained his composure and went on.

"Caterina was awake and very frightened. I wanted to go downstairs, for by then Deirdre had gone wild, screaming like a madwoman, and we could hear glass shattering. I was afraid of what might happen—"

He stopped to take a breath. "Michael had instructed me I should never interfere. Deirdre never liked me anyway—she resented anyone Michael cared about—and I was afraid I would only make things worse if I tried to intervene. So I stayed upstairs with Caterina.

"A few minutes later, I heard Deirdre in the vestibule, raving, screaming at Michael, that he was trying to keep her a prisoner. Then I heard the front door slam.

"After a few minutes, Michael called for me and Dempsey."

"I left Caterina and went downstairs. Michael was beside himself. Dempsey and I left as quickly as we could get the carriage horses harnessed. Michael was insisting he would go with us, but we convinced him to stay at the house, with Caterina."

He looked at her. "Later, we were much relieved that he had stayed behind." He stopped, his expression bleak. He seemed to shudder, and his voice faded until Susanna had to strain to hear. "We were too late. She had gone off the road."

He motioned to the bluff. "She was dead by the time we reached her."

Susanna sat totally still, tugging at her hands, unable to breathe as she watched Paul, now hunched over, his hands gripping his knees.

His harsh words sliced through the silence. "She was going to another man that night. She told Michael so. She often did that, tormented him about the other men—"

He broke off, shaking his head. "Michael tried to stop her,

but he couldn't. He could never stop her when she was like that. No one could stop her . . ."

His words drifted off. Susanna was seized by a peculiar sense of unreality, as if she'd been caught up in the middle of someone else's nightmare.

Paul straightened, leaned toward her a little. He seemed calmer now, quieter. "Michael tried many times to help Deirdre. He took her once to a . . . a *sanitarium*. But she refused to stay. He also brought doctors to her, at Bantry Hill. But she defied them. Michael did everything he could think to do. But Deirdre—it was as if she did not want to be helped. Perhaps Michael was right, after all. Perhaps she was sick in her mind. I never understood. None of it. The drinking, the affairs, the . . . craziness. And all the time he never so much as lifted a hand to her. Some men—" He looked at Susanna. "Some men would have *killed* her!"

There was a question Susanna had to ask, although she thought she already knew the answer. "Did Michael . . . did he love her? Ever?"

Paul turned to look at her, his gaze steady—and exceedingly sad. "*Sì*, of course he loved her. Even at the end, he loved her, although perhaps . . . it was a different kind of love by then. One of pity, no? But without love, how could he suffer such abuse, such disgrace, and still stay with her, even try to help her? But his love . . . his attempts to help—nothing was enough. Nothing was ever enough for Deirdre."

When Susanna made no reply, he added, "I'm sorry, Susanna. So very sorry you had to learn these things about your sister. I can only imagine how painful it is for you."

"Well," Susanna said, her voice thick, "at least I finally know . . . the truth."

For a time she sat, unmoving, unable to speak. She glanced

away, too dazed to think, too numb to even try to absorb everything he had told her. Yet a grim certainty ran through her. He had spoken the truth.

Paul leaned toward her, his gaze seeking hers as if searching for evidence of further doubt on her part. "Susanna, what I have told you is the truth. I have exaggerated nothing. It is all true."

Slowly, Susanna raised her head. She saw reflected in his dark eyes his concern for her, as well as the fundamental honesty she had always recognized, and in spite of her reluctance to accept the terrible burden he had just shared with her, she knew she had no choice but to believe him. He wasn't lying. More than likely, Paul Santi wasn't even *capable* of deception.

"It's all right, Paul. I . . . need to thank you for telling me. I had to know."

Still, it was simply too much to take in, all at once. There was so much she couldn't grasp, so much she couldn't comprehend. She wondered if she would ever be able to understand what had actually happened to Deirdre, what had gone wrong, in her marriage . . . her life.

Did she even *want* to understand? Could she bear it?

"I will take you home now," said Paul, his tone gentle. He hesitated. "Are you all right, Susanna?"

Susanna looked at him, then managed a nod. But she wondered if indeed she would ever be all right again.

THIRTY-TWO

AT THE CROSSROADS

STILL HEAVY IS THY HEART?
STILL SINK THY SPIRITS DOWN?
CAST OFF THE WEIGHT, LET FEAR DEPART,
AND EVERY CARE BE GONE.

PAUL GERHARDT (TRANSLATED BY JOHN WESLEY)

They pulled up to the front of the house, but although the wind had turned much cooler, neither made any attempt to get out of the buggy.

Susanna glanced at the porch, then looked away. She was utterly exhausted, weary to the point of weakness, yet reluctant to go inside and face Michael.

"So," she said quietly, turning to Paul, "what made you finally decide to tell me?"

"I realized that Michael would not . . . *could* not," he replied.

Susanna slowly shook her head. "I still don't understand why."

"Michael meant only to shield you, Susanna," he answered. "To protect your memories of Deirdre and spare you pain. And I think . . . perhaps, without realizing it, he meant to protect himself as well."

Susanna frowned. "What do you mean?"

His expression became thoughtful as he studied her. "Have you not seen, Susanna, that Michael is coming to have much affection for you?"

Susanna tensed. At the moment, the last thing she wanted to hear was how Michael might feel about *her*. She had yet to get past his turbulent relationship with *Deirdre*. Even so, something stirred inside her at Paul's words.

She diverted her gaze, saying nothing.

"Perhaps," Paul went on in spite of her silence, "Michael has been blind in more ways than one."

She stared at him, surprised that he would refer to Michael's blindness in such a way.

"I believe you are becoming very important to Michael," he went on, his expression solemn. "And when I see the two of you together, I wonder if he is not becoming important to you."

Susanna suddenly felt as if she were suffocating. "Don't, Paul. Not now. I can't deal with anything more right now. Surely, you understand that."

He held up a hand, palm outward, shaking his head. "Wait—please, Susanna. I do not mean to cause you further distress. Naturally, any feelings between you and Michael are none of my business. I am merely trying to answer your question. I know, because Michael told me so, that he was determined not to damage your memory of Deirdre. But I think it is also possible that he was afraid—afraid the truth might turn you against *him*."

"That's ridiculous."

"Is it?" He searched her eyes. "Michael knew that Deirdre was writing often to you. Don't you think he at least suspected *what* she was writing? He sensed almost from the time of your arrival that you had distrusted him. Perhaps he thought that if you knew the truth, you would find it unforgivable, that he could not somehow help Deirdre, that he could not save his own wife."

As Susanna considered his words, uneasiness began to snake through her. What he was driving at seemed uncomfortably close to something she was reluctant to admit, to Paul, perhaps even to herself. "But his evasion only made me more suspicious," she said, not quite meeting his eyes.

"*Sì*, I understand that, and you understand it. But Michael did not. I think he might have been afraid you would even blame him for Deirdre's death. That you might think him somehow responsible."

"I *never*—"

The denial died on her lips. In truth, because of Deirdre's letters and Michael's entrenched silence, she *had* suspected Michael of deception at the very least, had even wondered if he might not have somehow played a part in Deirdre's death.

She framed her face with her hands, trying to knead away the pain drilling at her temples.

"Susanna, I have never gone against Michael," Paul said, his voice low. "Not until today. But when I realized that by withholding the truth from you, he was only fostering more and more doubt on your part, I felt I had to do something."

She sensed him watching her, waiting, and she finally looked up.

"I had seen that he was coming to care for you," he went on. "Yet I also saw that his silence was erecting a barrier, allowing you to think the worst of him. In time, I feared it would create even more grief for him, and he has had enough grief for any man, enough for a lifetime. I simply could not watch him continue to wound you—or himself—any longer."

His searching gaze unnerved Susanna. She turned from him and sat staring at the stone front of Bantry Hill. But she heard every word he spoke as he continued.

"Michael is a man of God, not a man of deceit, Susanna. I think somehow you know this. It is true, he is a very complex man, difficult to understand. But more than anything else, he is a *good* man, a godly man who wants nothing more than what is best for the people he loves. Michael is a man who lives for God, for his family, and for his music."

A question occurred to Susanna, and she turned back to him. "You said that Deirdre used Michael to advance her own career, that she took it as a personal betrayal when he left the opera. Was Deirdre the reason he left? Was she responsible for that, too?"

He shook his head. "No. She resented him for it, of course. When he gave up his own career, it took much away from Deirdre as well, for it meant Michael would no longer be in a position to exert influence in her behalf. But, no, that is something apart from Deirdre, something I can't explain."

"More secrets?" The words were out before Susanna could call them back, and she cringed at the bitterness she heard in her own voice.

Paul impaled her with an indicting look of great sadness. "No, Susanna. Michael makes no secret of that part of his life, but it is very complicated. Even now, I am not certain I understand it myself. But I'm sure Michael would tell you about it if you were to ask."

He continued to watch her, his expression gentle but measuring. "I wish you could allow yourself to know Michael as he really is, Susanna. Could you not give him this much grace, to begin again, and at least accept the friendship he would like to offer you?"

Could she? Now that she knew the truth, could she bring herself to start over, this time without the preconceptions, the suspicions that had very nearly poisoned her judgment of Michael, her feelings about him, even her life at Bantry Hill?

Susanna looked at Paul and saw the intensity behind his words, the depth of emotion in his appeal—not for himself, but for Michael, whom he loved. She wished she could answer as he obviously wanted her to. Instead, she could manage only the weakest reassurance.

"I don't know, Paul. I need time. There's so much I need to think about. I feel—"

She broke off. How *did* she feel? Apart from the hurt and the confusion, the anger and shock engendered by Paul's accounting of Deirdre's lies and the immorality that had spilled over to bring pain to everyone who loved her—apart from all that, how did she feel?

The acid of self-pity threatened to eat through her soul. For the moment she could think of nothing except the losses she had suffered in such a brief time. Her sister. Her parents. Her home. Even her *country.*

And as of today, she had lost Deirdre *twice:* once to death, and then again to truth.

While they had never been truly close, they had always been tied by the bonds of blood and memory that made them sisters. Not only had death broken those bonds, it had also destroyed any chance for reconciliation, any hope for developing a real relationship. Even when Deirdre had finally reached out to her, confided in her, it had all been a lie, making the pain of her loss seem doubly bitter.

Suddenly, as if he had sensed her thoughts, Paul touched her hand, saying, "You have lost a great deal, Susanna. It must be a terrible grief, to lose your family as you have, to leave your home for a life among strangers, and now this. I cannot tell you how much I wish I could make things easier for you."

Susanna looked at him, seeing the genuine kindness, the desire to help, even to heal, that brimmed in his eyes. But Paul could *not* help, could not heal, could not make things easier. She was the only one who could begin to move beyond the loss and the lies, the hurt and the disillusionment, and eventually forge her way toward something better.

At that instant, Susanna knew that she stood at a cross-roads. She could choose to hold on to *yesterday*, to what might have been, with all its heartache. She could barricade herself behind a past that could never be restored, allowing that past to overshadow the present and consume any hope for the future. Or she could move forward, slowly but deliberately, committing one step at a time to God and whatever plan he might hold for her life.

In short, she could retreat or she could go forward. And she recognized with piercing clarity the sacrifices, the responsibili-ties, inherent to either choice.

"We have been gone a long time," Paul said. "Michael will be worried by now."

Susanna turned to see the massive front doors of the house swing open to reveal Michael, standing there, tall and dark and solemn, his face lifted slightly as if he was listening for some-thing. She watched him for another moment, then shifted her attention back to Paul.

"He needn't know you've told me," she said.

Paul had been about to step out of the buggy, but now swung around to look at her. "What?"

"You're worried that Michael will be upset when he learns you told me about Deirdre." She put a hand to his arm. "But it's all right. Michael doesn't need to know just yet."

"Susanna, he will have to know—"

"But not today," she said firmly. "And you needn't be the one to tell him. I'll tell him myself. When the time is right, I'll explain."

Paul's face creased in a smile of unmistakable relief. "*Grazie!* Thank you, Susanna."

She closed her eyes for a second or two, then opened them and drew in a deep, bracing breath of the cool air coming up off the river. Again she turned toward the house and saw that Caterina had come to the door and was now at Michael's side, waving and bouncing from one foot to the other. Michael, too, lifted a hand in greeting.

Susanna sat staring for a long time at the man and the little girl framed in the doorway, waiting.

Waiting for Paul.

Waiting for her.

And in that moment, though her heart was still heavy, her spirit still wounded, she stepped away from the crossroads. She made a decision.

Summoning all her courage, Susanna lifted her face and prepared to take the first step on the road that pointed to the future. The road that led to Bantry Hill, and whatever waited beyond.

A Time for Singing

BUT SHOULD THE SURGES RISE,

AND REST DELAY TO COME,

BLEST BE THE TEMPEST, KIND THE STORM,

WHICH DRIVES US NEARER HOME.

AUGUSTUS M. TOPLADY

November

Thanksgiving was still two days away, but for over a week now Caterina had been urging Susanna to help her learn some "new piano pieces for Christmas." The suggestion that they might at least wait until the calendar was turned to December was invariably met with such a patent look of disappointment that Susanna could hardly refuse.

So on this snowy November evening they were ensconced in the music room, Caterina at the piano keyboard with

Susanna on a chair beside her. The girl had not as yet progressed beyond a basic treble melody line, but with the confidence of youth she had assured Susanna that by Christmas she would be playing "parts."

Given her niece's stubborn bent and obvious musical aptitude, Susanna had no reason to doubt that declaration. Nor was she surprised when Caterina showed no particular preference for the simpler music of the season. She had already detected in her somewhat precocious niece a distinct taste for challenge, so when the child insisted on adding "Angels from the Realms of Glory" to her limited repertoire—in part because its composer, Henry Smart, had been "blind like Papa"—Susanna had merely resigned herself to the task at hand.

Near the end of their practice time, her pupil turned to Susanna, her piquant features set in a decisive expression. "On Christmas Eve," she announced, "I'm going to play my new hymn for Papa and tell him all about it. Or do you think he already knows its—'history'?" she asked, imitating Susanna's earlier use of the word.

"Well, your papa does know a great deal about music, *alannah*. But I'm quite certain he would be pleased to learn more about whatever you choose to play for him."

At that moment Michael walked into the room, the wolfhound at his side. "What is this about Papa being pleased?"

Caterina put a finger to her lips as if to warn Susanna to silence. "We can't tell you, Papa. It's a surprise!"

"Ah—a surprise!" Michael said, smiling as he came to stand by the piano. "And when shall I find out what this surprise is, hmm? Tomorrow?"

"Not tomorrow," Caterina said, cupping her chin in her hands, clearly prepared to play out this exchange as long as possible.

"The next day then?"

"No, not the next day either!"

Michael feigned a frown. "Why do you tease your papa so? You know I am impatient when it comes to surprises."

Caterina giggled. "You will have to wait a *long time* for *this* surprise, Papa! Maybe as long as Christmas!"

"Christmas?" Michael reared back a little and drew a hand over his forehead with great dramatic flair. *"Impossibile!* I think you must tell me now! This very minute! Else, I will have to squeeze it out of you!"

With that, he made a lunge for her. She squealed, but went willingly. Susanna, by now accustomed to these evening rough-house matches, quickly got out of their way and went to sit by the fire. The wolfhound, never one to be left out, charged directly into the middle of the fracas, and for the next ten minutes pandemonium reigned, with much shrieking and barking and laughter.

Michael was the first to give over. Lumbering to his feet, he lifted both hands in a mock plea for mercy. "Enough! I am too old for this!"

"Then let's sing," Caterina said agreeably.

"How can I sing when you have exhausted me?" But even as he teased, Michael felt for the piano stool and lowered himself onto it.

"Play carols, Papa," Caterina instructed.

"Christmas carols? Cati, it is not yet Thanksgiving!"

"That doesn't matter," she said firmly. "It's snowing, so it *looks* like Christmas. I don't see why we can't sing Christmas carols all the time. Christmas doesn't last long enough to hold all the songs I like."

Michael turned in Susanna's direction and smiled. "A good point, no?" He then launched into a rousing version of "O

Come, All Ye Faithful," and Caterina immediately piped in. Soon they were both singing, though Michael obviously kept his voice restrained so he wouldn't overwhelm Caterina's childish efforts.

As if to make sure Susanna wasn't left out, Gus, the wolf-hound, ambled over and plopped down beside her chair to share the fire. On cue, Susanna rubbed his great head as she sat watching Michael and Caterina.

She had grown fond of their evenings in the music room. These days Michael seldom stayed in the city. Clearly, he enjoyed being at home with his daughter, and just as clearly, Caterina delighted in his presence.

Susanna didn't always join them, intent on giving the two of them as much time alone together as possible. But of late it seemed that one or the other would come looking for her if she didn't make an appearance. By now she had to admit she'd be disappointed if they happened to forget her.

There were times of contentment for Susanna. Indeed, it surprised her to realize just how contented she *was*. Gradually, a subtle peace had settled over her relationship with Michael. As yet, she hadn't told him of Paul's disclosure. If he ever questioned what accounted for the fact that she no longer tried to quiz him about Deirdre, he gave no indication. Perhaps he was simply relieved to have an end to her incessant questions. Whatever the case, he clearly welcomed this unexpected truce and meant to leave well enough alone.

In truth, it seemed that they were, at the least, becoming friends. If Susanna occasionally felt a vague, disturbing longing for something more—or sensed that Michael did—she deliberately refused to attach anything other than a fleeting thought to it.

For now, she wanted only what she had: the joy of loving

Caterina and being loved in return; the opportunity to live a quiet, fulfilling life in a place where she felt cared for and safe and even *needed*; and the dignity of knowing she was earning her livelihood rather than depending on Michael's largess.

At first she had questioned whether she would ever be able to put aside Paul's shattering revelations about Deirdre. She wondered if the awful things she had learned would be engraved upon her mind forever, like a searing, indelible brand. The reality of all she had lost threatened to mire her in a fog of despair.

Like Job in the Scriptures, she had attempted to counter desolation with faith: *"The Lord gave, and the Lord has taken away."* It had been more difficult to add the final *"Blessed be the name of the Lord."*

But as the days passed, she became more and more caught up in Caterina's—and Michael's—busy world. The continuous flow of responsibilities and new experiences gave her no time for brooding, no opportunity for dwelling on the past. And so, almost without her realizing it, a quiet restoration had begun.

In a way she had never before experienced, she began to feel the assurance of God's love for her. Like a dawning sun, the healing warmth spread over her days. As she went about taking care of Caterina, she became increasingly aware that she, too, was being cared for—attended by a love that urged her past the gloom of disappointment and hurt into a better place, a brighter place.

Sometimes she could even think of Deirdre without the accompanying stab of pain or the sick sense of shame and betrayal. She lived, after all, caught up in the swift current of a child's needs, engulfed by a little girl's love and laughter and affection.

And always, there was the music. That same healing love that moved through other parts of her life was also present in the music, coloring and enriching her world, nourishing her spirit and feeding her soul.

Absently she stroked the wolfhound's crisp coat, her gaze returning to Michael and Caterina. Michael kept drifting in and out of Italian as he attempted to teach Caterina the melody line of what sounded like a child's cradle song. It was a sweet, charming little piece, a simple tune.

Caterina's black curls fell about her face. Michael now stood behind her, his hand covering the little girl's on the keyboard. As Susanna watched them, the ancient words of Job, at the beginning of his story, again echoed in her mind: *"The Lord gave, and the Lord has taken away. Blessed be the name of the Lord."* But this time she also heard, even more clearly, the words that came near the *end* of Job's trial: *"And the Lord gave Job twice as much as he had before . . ."*

With her eyes still locked on Michael and his child, Susanna felt an awareness rise up in her soul—an awareness infused by the same indescribable, divine love that had carried her through the past weeks. And in that moment she realized that although she had lost much, she had been given more.

Michael turned just then, smiling. "Come join us, Susanna."

"Yes, Aunt Susanna! Please! Come sing with us!"

Susanna hesitated. Ordinarily, she limited her participation to simply watching from across the room or occasionally accompanying them as they sang. But they insisted, so she rose and went to join them.

When she would have taken the piano stool, however, Caterina stopped her. "No, Aunt Susanna. I want to play 'Joy to the World'! You sing with Papa."

Always too inhibited to add her voice to Michael's, Susanna simply hummed along as he began to sing. Caterina also chimed in, continuing to play the melody with great deliberation.

At some point Michael had placed one hand on his daughter's shoulder, and now extended the other hand to Susanna. She hesitated only a moment before clasping it.

She had stopped humming and was only half listening when, unexpectedly, her thoughts went back to the day she had stood on the deck of the ship bringing her to America. She remembered the chill of excitement—and fear—that had seized her as she glimpsed New York Harbor for the first time. All the intervening months fell away, and she recalled with startling clarity the question that had been in her mind that day, the question that had nagged at her all the way across the Atlantic:

Was this an ending or a beginning?

For one shining instant Susanna heard the answer to that question ring out above the words and the music of the familiar carol. She had finally begun to move beyond the past, to accept and even exult in the present, to look forward to the future.

Suddenly, eagerly, Susanna began to sing. Michael turned and smiled at her, tightening his grasp on her hand. In that moment, all her old apprehensions vanished, and she lifted her voice in harmony with the voices of her new family.

She had her answer.

Bantry Hill was both an ending *and* a beginning.

It was also home.

Excerpt from

CADENCE

BOOK TWO
of the

AMERICAN ANTHEM
SERIES

COMING MAY 2003

Susanna stopped to listen just outside the music room, marveling at the tones that seemed to flow with such ease, such perfection. He was singing what sounded like an Italian folk song, a tune infused with sunlight and rolling hills and peaceful pastures.

She paused for a moment in the doorway, studying him. He was sitting on the window seat, the late afternoon sun casting a dappled glow on his features. With his eyes closed, his strong profile haloed by the light streaming through the window, he appeared younger. Less formidable, perhaps even vulnerable. Viewed in this informal pose, he was undeniably handsome, with an appeal Susanna managed to ignore only with deliberate effort.

At almost the exact moment she walked into the room, he stopped playing, unfolded himself from the window seat and stood, smiling. "Ah, Susanna, you are here," he said, laying the mandolin on the window seat. "*Buono.*"

There seemed to be no such thing as "sneaking up" on Michael, despite his blindness. And yet it both pleased Susanna and unsettled her that he always seemed to know the instant she entered a room.

"I'm sorry it took me so long. Caterina wanted a story."

He waved off her apology. As he reached for the dark glasses in his shirt pocket and slipped them on, Susanna felt a familiar sting of irritation. Why was it he never seemed compelled to wear the glasses in the presence of others, only with her? It was almost as if he felt a need to *shield* himself from her.

He had changed to a scarlet-colored shirt of soft wool, which only intensified his dark good looks. After smoothing his hair, he gave his sleeves a roll as if he meant to get right to work.

Susanna suddenly felt awkward and uncertain. "Michael—I don't know how much help I can be—"

Before she could finish, he motioned her to the piano stool. Susanna eyed the Bosendorfer's keyboard with a mixture of anxiety and anticipation. She loved to play the magnificent instrument, yet so tense was she that for a moment she could only sit and stare at the smooth ivory keys before her.

Michael, who of course could not see her agitation, leaned over her shoulder to place a pad of manuscript against the music rack, and Susanna gave an involuntary shiver. "If you would play this for me and then make notation, please? Paul will render the Braille later."

The section he directed her to was several pages into the score. Susanna did the best she could, disconcerted as she was by his voice.

And his nearness.

Several minutes later, after she'd finished the notation in a shaky hand, he asked her to go back and play from the beginning. Susanna looked at him, then turned back to the manuscript, flipping through the first few pages to get a feel of the notation. The first part had already been roughly scored for orchestra, but soon melded into a primary melody line with just some harmony and miscellaneous notes.

She eased her shoulders, then flexed her fingers and willed herself to relax. She reminded herself that this was no concert hall, and she was not a performer. She was merely helping Michael through some initial stages of his own music.

Even so, she felt the need to caution him as to her limitations. "Remember, Michael, I'm no virtuoso—"

"I know, I know," he said, smiling at her disclaimer. "So you have said. Just . . . ah . . . play it as you like for now. In parts or with accompaniment. However you like."

At first Susanna had no conception of what she was playing, no real awareness of anything except the cool smoothness of the ivory under her fingertips, the absolute purity of sound as she pressed each key. She did exactly as she was told, initially playing one part at a time while Michael, still standing directly behind her, hummed a little and occasionally uttered a quiet, "No, that's not it," or, "Ah, yes! That's exactly what I want there."

It took Susanna a few minutes to realize he wasn't commenting on her playing, but rather on his own composition. The first time she brought together all the parts she both felt and heard the stiffness in her technique, the utter lack of color and emotion in her playing, and she cringed.

But Michael didn't seem to notice. He merely went on humming, occasionally murmuring to himself. Then he moved around and began to lightly tap the side of the piano to spur her on to a brisker, more strident rhythm as she continued, playing through one page, then another.

The more she played, the more the music began to reach out to her like the hands of a friend, beckoning her, drawing her out of herself. She started, caught off guard when Michael moved behind her again and began to tap her shoulders with both hands, urging her forward, driving her on. After a moment, however, she lost her self-consciousness and simply followed his lead, falling into the tempo and rhythm he was setting for her. Her mind began to resonate with the sounds of dozens of instruments, and she no longer heard singular melodies and disjointed passages, but instead a mighty organ and the voices of many instruments—a full orchestra.

The farther she went, the more her fingers seemed to fly over the keyboard, improvising, adding, drawing forth an extensive accompaniment to the notes on the pages. It was almost as if the force of the music somehow infused her own soul, raising her to the level of performance such glorious music demanded.

Indeed, such was the power of the music that the room itself seemed to become a concert hall, the Bosendorfer an entire orchestra that marched and danced, flinging out sounds the likes of which Susanna had never heard, even as it engulfed her and made her an integral part of the work.

This was Michael's newest work, the *American Anthem*. He rarely spoke of it to her, but she had heard him and Paul working on it together, knew he often worked long hours into the night on it. Twice he had incorporated excerpts from it into the orchestra's concert program. There was a distinct nationalistic flavor that ran through it, as if the work itself was being woven by the people of many nations, striving to form a whole. It was an *earthy*, folk music, yet at the same time symphonic in its structure and complexity.

But more than anything else, it was a music of the spirit. Triumphant and rejoicing, it proclaimed a mighty faith, yet in places it was imbued with such plaintive melodies and sweetness it brought a kind of yearning to the soul.

Too quickly, it ended.

Susanna reached the end of the pages in front of her, her hands clinging to the last chord as she sat in stunned disbelief. She sensed that at most the work was not even half complete; obviously, it was destined to be a huge, expansive score. But even in its unfinished and preliminary state, it had left her both exhausted and exhilarated, her pulse thundering, her mind racing.

Without understanding how such a thing could be, there had been times in Susanna's experience when she'd caught such a strong sense of a composer through his music that it was as if she *knew* him, or had at least caught a glimpse of his heart. So it was at this moment. She was convinced that she had heard Michael's very *spirit* in his music. What she had heard was something of genius, yes, but even more, she knew she had heard something of God.

She felt acutely disappointed, even stricken, by the music's *incompleteness*. It was like being held captive by the power of a thundering, monumental story—only to find that it was a story without end.

Unable to contain herself, she whipped around, an exclamation of praise on her lips. Only then did she realize that Michael's hands had again come to rest on her shoulders.

Her sudden movement caused him to tighten his grasp.

Something in his expression, and in the strength and warmth of his hands, stole the breath from her. She tensed, and immediately he dropped his hands away, leaving Susanna to wonder at the sharp and inexplicable feeling of abandonment that followed.

Acknowledgments

With heartfelt thanks to

Janet Kobobel Grant—
agent, friend, and gift of God.

Ami McConnell—
who knows all about fiction and its writers . . .
and loves us anyway.

Penelope J. Stokes—
relentless editor and faithful friend.

"Blessed are the merciful."